the *Walker*
Collection

Stories by
David Spangler

The Walker Collection

Edited by Aidan Spangler

The Walker Collection Cover & *Walker*
Interior Illustrations by Joshua McDonald & Kaitlin Spangler
Contact Illustration by Kaitlin Spangler
N.E.W. & *The House Christmas* Illustrations by Joshua McDonald
The Spirit of Christmas & *The World Tree* Illustrations by Jeremy Berg

ISBN 13: 978-1-939790-12-5

Spangler, David
The Walker Collection/David Spangler

First Edition: November 2015

Starseed Books
4440 190th Ave SE
Issaquah, WA 98027

Printed in the United States of America

0 9 8 7 6 5 4 3 2 1

www.StarseedBooks.com

Contents

Acknowledgement:

As always, I acknowledge my beloved family who are the immediate inspiration for these stories. But I also acknowledge with appreciation all those lovers of tales of wonder, magic, and the human spirit who have given me encouragement and support over the years to continue doing what I love to do anyway: writing stories.

Foreword

This is my third anthology of stories. Because each of them was written as a Christmas present for family and friends, all six stories have a Christmas theme. But Christmas to me is a time of wonderment, so I think of these really as stories of wonder. They all have an element of magic to them, but then so do our lives. So really these stories are about who we are when we look beneath the surface of our lives and of our everyday world. They each arise from my sense of who we are as human beings and as spiritual beings. At Christmastime, we may come closest to touching the wonder of our deeper selves, but this experience is available to us any time, not just once a year.

So I think of these stories as more than just Christmas tales. My hope is that whenever you read them, they will brighten your heart and bring delight to your day. May you experience in reading them all the joy I felt in writing them.

David Spangler
November, 2015

Editor's note: The other two Anthologies of stories by David Spangler are published by Lorian press. They are:

The Story Tree
Starheart And Other Stories

These can be found at www.lorian.org and other bookstores

Walker

David Spangler

"All right, class," Deborah Little Mouse said, "what is the first rule?"

"Stay on the path," the class chanted in unison.

"And what is the second rule?"

"Stay on the path!"

"And the third rule?"

Amanda Gray sighed as she joined the others in repeating the refrain. "Stay on the path." She'd been traveling in the subtle worlds without paths for thirteen of her twenty years, ever since she first discovered when she was seven that she could step free of her body. She understood why Deborah was insisting, but something in her chafed at the restrictions. Getting a license was not turning out to be nearly as much fun as she'd anticipated.

"That's right," Deborah Little Mouse said, satisfied. "Stay on the path. Ever since the Quickening, these paths have been forged by dedicated Walkers working with partners on The Other Side." Amanda could hear the capital letters in her teacher's voice. "They are there for your protection and ease of travel while in the Murk. Don't go wandering."

Amanda looked around at the other six people in her class. They were all paying close attention to everything their teacher had to say, and their faces reflected their concentration. Of course, none of them had anywhere near the experience that she had. With the exception of Gregory, and even he had not opened up until he was fifty-six, only five years ago, all of them had gained the ability to Journey as a result of the Quickening two years earlier. The subtle worlds were comparatively new to them and as a consequence, still a bit daunting.

Deborah Little Mouse looked at her watch. "All right. Adrian will be here in five minutes, and then your test will begin. While we're waiting, can anyone tell me another important rule?"

Amanda looked around at the other students, wondering who might volunteer next. She knew it wouldn't be her. *Never volunteer*, her military father had said, and it was the only good piece of advice he had ever given her. They were all seated in a circle in comfortable easy chairs. The walls of the room were paneled in wood, two of which were covered with book shelves, creating the atmosphere of being in a library or a study. A door leading out into the hallway was on the third wall, and next to it was a state-of-the-art flatscreen where videos could be shown and a whiteboard where Deborah Little Mouse could draw diagrams, something she did a lot of.

The fourth wall was different. It was one large picture window facing east and framing a panorama of the Cascade Mountain range. When they'd first started meeting in this room, Amanda had had a hard time tearing her attention away from the vista. Which, she learned later, was the point. The room was like the physical world where her body lived, closed in with very specific boundaries whereas the spacious view out the window was like the subtle worlds they were learning to engage, vast and compelling. They were here to learn to live with both and blend them into a wholeness. Being able to love both the room and the view and hold her attention to both was a key part of the training she was receiving.

A hand went up. It was attached to a chubby arm that was in turn part of an even chubbier body. Malcolm had been a successful chef at the Four Seasons restaurant in Seattle prior to the Quickening. He reminded Amanda of a Polynesian shaman she had once met, a large, fat man for whom extra body mass meant extra mana with which to work in the subtle realms. She knew this wasn't Malcolm's reason for his weight. He simply enjoyed eating and cheerfully celebrated that fact. She wondered just how hard it was for his soul to free itself from all that flesh to go Walking.

Deborah Little Mouse, who in spite of her name, was a large woman herself, said, "Malcolm, what do you have for us?"

"BIPS, Deborah."

"Very good, Malcolm! Yes, BIPS! Body in Place Situation." She paused, looking around the circle. "Amanda, you've been quiet. Before Adrian gets here, tell us what this means, please."

I knew she was going to pick on me, Amanda thought wryly. Out loud, she said, "It's a mnemonic reminding us that before we Journey, we attune to and bless our bodies, the place we're in, and the situation around us."

"Very good. And why do we do this?"

"Because it provides an anchor for our consciousness..."

"And because the place itself can be an ally for us," Malcolm said, interrupting. Amanda knew he'd been hoping to explain what BIPS meant himself.

"Quite right, Malcolm, though you should have let Amanda finish."

Malcolm made a waving motion with his hand towards Amanda. For a moment, she had an impression of large sausage links waving in the air and had to stifle a laugh. "Sorry, Amanda," he said. "Sorry, Deborah. I…I just got excited!"

Amanda smiled back at him and nodded. Malcolm craved attention and approval, she knew, but beneath all the flesh was a kindly heart.

Before Deborah could respond, there was a knock at the door. "Oh," she said, "that's Adrian! Come in! Come in!" she said, raising her voice. She pushed herself up out of her chair.

The door opened, and Dr. Adrian Hart walked in. As always, Amanda felt as if a sun had come into the room. The man radiated warmth and power. She opened her Sight for a moment and saw the blaze of Light that was his subtle energy field. It never failed to amaze her. She had seen similar auras around beings she had met while traveling in the subtle worlds but rarely around an embodied human being. Next to him, Deborah's own bright aura seemed like a small candle. She didn't want to think about what *her's* would look like in comparison.

She shut her Sight down as Adrian, indicating with his hands that everyone should stay seated, greeted them. "Good morning," he said. His voice was soft but resonant in a way that made every word stand out. He pulled a chair forward into their circle and sat down as Deborah sank back into her own seat.

"Well," he said, "are you ready?" A chorus of yes's answered him.

"Good," he replied, smiling at them all. "Let me ask this a different way. Anybody nervous?"

This time, three or four people nodded their heads. He grinned. "Well, there's nothing to worry about. You all know how to find and walk the Paths that our inner allies have created for you. You've spent the past two months working on your base camp in the post-mortem realms, again with help from our allies."

"You've all done very well at this," Deborah added. *Actually, it's been a struggle for most of us,* Amanda thought, *but there's nothing like positive reinforcement.*

"Well, compared to what you've been doing, today's test is simple. You will go to this base camp and make contact with a representative from the higher realms where the Path you'll use is anchored. Together, you will link your base camp to these higher realms. This will attach your base camp firmly to the Path, like threading a bead onto the string of a necklace. Then you will return. If you are successful, Deborah or I or one of the other clairvoyants who will be working with us will see the evidence of this link in your aura. At that point, you will be ready for the next stage of your training, which is using your base camp to build a Path of your own."

"What if we fail?" The question came from Gregory, who was the oldest of the students, though he looked ten years younger than his age of sixty-one. He was, Amanda knew, a dedicated Yoga practitioner and trainer, to which he attributed his youthful vigor. Unlike Malcolm, he was lean and sinewy. The two of them could not be more opposite—Malcolm regarded exercise with the same distaste he regarded a badly cooked meal whereas Gregory would rather run ten miles than eat—but the two had become close friends.

"Then you'll try again later," Adrian replied. "There's no pressure here, Gregory. Each person develops at a different rate, and each person's relationship with the inner worlds is wholly unique. The only way you won't become a licensed Walker is if your allies tell us—tell you—that it would be unwise or dangerous for you to continue. But unless this happens, if you don't succeed this time, there will be further opportunities. This school is here to serve you and the timing of your unfoldment, not the other way around."

"Thank you, Adrian," Gregory said.

There came another knock at the door. "Ah," said Adrian, "that will be our other monitors. Come in," he said, raising his voice.

The door opened, and a man and two women, all in their early thirties, entered. Amanda recognized two of them as Jenny Longforth and her husband Will. Jenny was Adrian's daughter. She and Will had only recently married. The third was a striking black woman whom Amanda didn't recognize at all. She was about to open her Sight again to catch a peek at her aura when another knock came at the door and two men entered. One was Adrian's younger brother, Jonathan. The other was an older man who looked to be in his mid-fifties whom she also had not seen before. She was struck by his alertness and how his eyes took in everything in the room. There was little, she thought, that this man wouldn't see. She bet herself that he was a cop. He just had that vibe.

"Welcome, everyone," Adrian said. "Let me introduce you." He turned to the class. "I think you all know my brother Jonathan, my daughter Jenny and my son-in-law Will Longforth." There were nods around the room. "The other two are Ebony Coutré and John MacKenzie. Ebony works as a political consultant and John is a Seattle police detective, at least he was until recently." Amanda grinned inwardly. Got it in one, she thought.

"As you know, when it comes to Walking the subtle worlds, I teach a buddy system, just as if you were swimming or hiking in the wilderness. While you're Journeying, your partner will see that no harm comes to your physical body as well as clairvoyantly monitoring the local subtle environment and the beginnings of the Murk." He indicated the group of newcomers that had clustered around his chair. "Along with Deborah and myself, these folks will act as your clairvoyant monitors today. As you take this test, one of us will pair with each of you and act as your partner. Rest assured that each of us is a skilled clairvoyant. When you come back having made the link with allies on the higher realms," he smiled confidently at the class, "your monitor *will* be able to see the evidence of it in your aura."

"Should we expect any trouble?" This question came from Wilma, a small, shy woman who hardly ever spoke in class. Of all of them, she had had the most difficulty with the Murk.

"Given the state of the subtle realms these past two years, it would be rash to make any categorical statement. But you've all faced the Murk and worked hard to tame or eliminate your own fears that could take form within it. And you've all been Journeying successfully for several weeks now with no problem. Further, as you know, this house is extensively protected and aligned with the highest of spiritual energies. So, no, I don't expect any trouble."

Wilma nodded and sank back in her chair, looking relieved. *Personally*, thought Amanda, looking down at her hands. *I'd welcome the excitement of a little trouble. Well, maybe not trouble! But something exciting. I'm starting to feel bored.* She looked up to see Adrian looking at her, and she blushed, wondering if he'd read her thoughts. She wouldn't put it past him. As if on cue, he said, "I'm going to pair up with our youngest student, Amanda. Deborah, you go ahead and assign the rest of the monitors. Let's get this show on the road!"

The entire class stood up and began arranging the chairs so that each student sat next to his or her monitor. Amanda sat so she could look out the window at the mountains beyond. Far from being a distraction, she knew that the vista would call her soul out and make the transition into the inner realms easier. Adrian settled in next to her. "They never fail to inspire me, too," he said, indicating the mountains, obviously aware of what she'd been feeling. "So, Amanda, a quick word. I know this will seem easy to you given your experience, but don't be overconfident. Since the Quickening, the subtle realms can be unpredictable."

"Don't worry, Adrian. I'll be all right. Besides, I have Pants to protect me." Pants was the affectionate name she gave to her primary spirit ally, a being who appeared most of the time as a large, black panther. He had been her inner companion on her out-of-body Journeys since she'd been seven years old. The night she had discovered herself awake and floating above her body still lying in the bed below her, he'd been there waiting for her, along with her grandmother who had died some years before Amanda had been born.

"And I'm sure he will. But let's not give him cause to have to, OK?"

"OK. I'll be a good girl," she grinned.

Not that I've been anything else, she thought. Her mother often said she was headstrong; "You've got your father in you," she'd said. But Amanda preferred to think of herself as *adventurous.* Still, Adrian had a point, just as Deborah had earlier with her insistence on staying on the Path. She had no plans to take any chances. *It'll be a straight run,* she thought, *in and out, and then I'll be one step closer to my license as a Walker.*

She leaned back into the soft embrace of the chair and began to relax, allowing her breathing to deepen and slow down. Have to do my BIPS, she thought. She turned her attention to her body, thinking of how it served her, thinking of all the trillions of cells that made it up, thinking of how grateful she was to have it. She sent her blessings into her body and felt its energy respond.

Then she turned her attention to the chair she was sitting in and sent love and appreciation through her fingers into it. She felt its deep energy, the sentient energy that was in all things, flare up in response. She widened her attention to take in the whole room and all the people in it, sending blessing to the space she was in and all it contained. She felt herself deepening into this space, deepening into harmony with the world around her. The way out of the body was by going deeply into the life of the world.

As the final step, she held the purpose of what they were doing in her mind, feeling it part of the larger purpose of the school which in turn was nested in a broad desire to serve humanity in a time of transition and transformation. She greeted the spirit of this purpose, the spirit of the situation in which she now was embedded, and blessed it. In return, she felt held and protected by this spirit, anchored deeply into its intent.

Her BIPS protocol complete, she turned her attention to the view outside the window. She felt the pull of the mountains on the horizon, felt their spaciousness opening her mind and heart. She focused her intention and attention on a space about three feet in front of her, letting the mountains pull her, setting her soul free....

And then she was out, floating in the etheric environment closest to the earth. Looking back, she could see her body in the chair, its own energy field radiant around it. *Not too shabby*, she thought. But then she looked at the miniature sun that was Adrian sitting in his own chair next to her and realized with a sigh that she had a ways to go yet to be at his level.

At that moment, Adrian raised his hand and waved, and she realized he was seeing her clairvoyantly. *Good Journey*, he said, his words forming in her mind telepathically. *Blessings*.

She waved back. *Thank you*, she sent to him in return. Then she looked around for Pants. Surprisingly, he was nowhere to be seen. *I wonder what old Whiskerface is up to*, she thought. *Well, no matter. He'll show up. He always does.*

She turned her mind inward, looking for the vibrational signature of the Path she'd been using. As she found it, a ribbon of Light appeared before her that widened into a literal path. *Except that's not what it really looks like*, she thought. *That's just how my mind interprets it.*

Journeying in the subtle worlds wasn't a matter of crossing space the way she might walk somewhere in the physical world. Rather it was moving across energy differentials. She never really left the room where her body was. She just shifted vibrational levels, tuning into different frequencies that co-existed with each other the way radio waves and x-rays could co-exist in the same place on earth. The process had more in common with tuning a radio than it did with going for a walk. The Path in reality was a linked sequence of "notes" which, as they vibrated within her, progressively shifted her away from the energy patterns of the physical plane to those of her destination. However, the human mind was so attached to the experience of moving through space that it transformed this shifting of frequencies into the appearance of actually walking a path.

This is what the astral is, she reminded herself, *illusion masking the reality of what's happening.*

Nevertheless, being more literal minded than not, she appreciated the illusion. Seeing the shining Path before her, she stepped onto it, and the room around her disappeared. At first she was surrounded with a grey light, like moving into a sunlit cloud or an illuminated fog bank, but as she moved onward, the surroundings grew darker as if she were moving into the dense, pea soup fog that used to plague Nineteenth Century London.

The Murk, she thought. *Ugh!* It was the psychic pollution of the lowest astral levels stirred up by the Quickening, the successive waves of cosmic subtle energies now impacting and flowing through the aura of the planet, bringing so many changes in their wake. To her subtle senses, it was unpleasant and smelly, like walking beside an open sewer. *No wonder that beings from higher levels have a hard time moving through all this!*

Her Path continually cut a swath through the Murk as she moved, a clear space of Light always a few feet in front of her and behind her as if she traveled within a moving bubble as she went forward, automatically attuning to the next higher vibrational frequency. This was different from how she used to Journey when she was on her own. The Path, a line of subtle energy anchored within the precincts of the school at one end and within the higher realms at the other, added its power to her own inner Light, as well as providing direction. The Murk was a constant pull upon any one moving within it. How much of a pull depended on many factors and was not a constant, but the effect could be like moving through mud that clung to your legs and slowed you down. Being "on the Path," that is, in alignment with this stream of energy and light, was like walking on higher ground through a swamp. There was still a pull, but it was much, much less.

I should be there by now, she realized. *It's never taken me this long before. It seems like I've been walking quite awhile.* Time flowed differently in the subtle realms where subjectively it could seem like days or even weeks went by when only minutes passed in the physical realm. Normally, though, this was not a long or difficult Journey for her.

It's the Murk, she thought. *It seems harder to push through for some reason. It seems denser and more clingy than the last time I Walked this Path.* She wished that her ally Pants were with her and wondered where old

Whiskerface had gotten off to. Not for the first time, she wondered just what Pants did—or for that matter, what he was--when he wasn't with her. For years she had assumed he was just what he appeared to be, the ghost of a black panther. But she had come to realize he was much more, an elemental spirit that took on the panther form and qualities for reasons of his own. When she'd asked him about this, he'd switched his tail and said, "I'm not sure you would understand. For now, just accept me as I appear to you."

Ahead the Murk seemed to be lightening up. *At last! It's about time I was getting somewhere.* Just as she thought this, she sensed movement in the surrounding clouds of astral substance. "Pants? Is that you?"

"Help me!"

The mental cry was faint, so much so that at first she wasn't sure she'd actually sensed anything. But then it came again. "Help me!"

Amanda stopped and looked around. Unlike hearing a sound with her physical ears, this cry appeared in her mind with no sense of the direction from which it was coming. It could be from anywhere, and, telepathic communication being what it was, it could be from any distance. She focused in on the inner sensations accompanying the cry. She felt fear and desperation. *It's someone lost in the Murk*, she thought. "I'm here," she thought back. "Where are you?"

"Help me!" This time the cry was stronger, and Amanda realized that by giving it her attention, she was drawing the communication in to her like fine tuning the reception on a radio. "Please!"

Amanda focused her full attention on the presence behind this cry, mentally drawing it closer to her. All at once, a figure appeared in the shadows next to her Path. It was a little girl of seven or eight. *About the age I was when I started Journeying*, she thought.

"Help me!" the figure said again, looking directly at her and holding her arms out in a way that told Amanda that the girl could see her, too.

"Of course, I'll help you," Amanda said, kneeling down in front of her. The Light from the Path shone on the girl, revealing delicate features that were currently drawn tight with fear. "Don't be afraid. Are you lost?"

The girl seemed puzzled by this. She looked around, and Amanda wondered what she was seeing. The astral plane had a way of taking on the appearance of a person's thoughts and feelings so that two people could be standing side by side and yet to each other seem to be in different places. "No....not lost. I don't think so. But I can't....I can't..."

"You can't what?"

"I want to wake up, but I can't..."

So, Amanda thought, *this isn't a lost spirit but someone wandering in her dream body.* "Just think of your body very strongly and you'll go back to it."

"I try, but she won't let me...."

"She?"

"I...I'm in her house...." the figure looked around fearfully, her hands rising up to her mouth as if to stifle any sound. Whatever the little girl was seeing, it was invisible to Amanda. Then she turned to Amanda, her eyes wide. "She's coming for me..."

"Who? Who's coming for you? What's your name?"

"Help me! Help me!"

"How?"

The little girl suddenly jerked as if someone had grabbed her arm and was pulling. Amanda still couldn't see who or what it was, but she could feel a dark, sad presence. The girl began to merge back into the Murk.

"Oh no, you don't!" Amanda muttered. Impulsively, she reached out and grabbed the girl's free arm, pulling her back towards the Light of her Path. But even as she did so, she could feel the force on the other side redoubling its efforts. Whatever it was, it was stronger than she was or at least had a stronger hold on the girl.

Damn! She thought. *Where's Pants when I need him?*

She could feel the tension building and feared that the girl would be injured. She had to either let her go, surrendering her to whatever was pulling on her in the Murk or follow her into the depths of the astral plane in the hopes of discovering what or who this adversary was and how to free the girl.

For a moment she remembered her own wish back in the classroom for something exciting. *Maybe I'm creating this encounter out of my own desire. Reflecting back one's fears or desires is exactly what the Murk can do,* she thought. But then she felt again the desperation in the girl as the tug on her became stronger. *No, this isn't my projection. This is real!*

She didn't think more about it. As the pull increased and the fear and tension in the girl's face became more acute, Amanda stepped away from the Path and into the foggy darkness of the Murk.

Immediately, the Path disappeared as she broke her connection with her base camp. Instead, the Light collapsed around her, becoming the glow of her innate Self-Light. While bright enough under most circumstances, her aura wasn't in a league with the sun-like brilliance of Adrian Hart, and her Light struggled to pierce the increasing gloom about her which was growing steadily denser.

As she allowed her adversary to pull them deeper into the lower astral, Amanda didn't fear for her own safety; she'd been in the Murk before and knew how to handle it. She feared for the little girl who seemed helpless in the grip of this unknown force. And rather than gaining more knowledge about just what this force was, it was getting darker all the time. In fact it was getting harder and harder to actually see the girl, though she still had a firm grip on her arm.

Amanda knew this couldn't continue. She could feel her own aura contracting under the pressure of the Murk. If she were going to act, it would have to be right away or she would have to let go, leaving the girl to her fate. But what could she do?

Then she remembered that this girl wasn't a spirit, a denizen of the subtle worlds. She was a dreamwalker, and somewhere she had a body asleep in a bed. That meant there was an umbilicus, a silver cord, connecting the two together. Why it hadn't pulled the girl back into her body in reaction to the obvious fear she was feeling, Amanda didn't know, but there was something she could do. It was risky, but it could do the trick.

She gripped the girl's arm with her other hand and held on. Knowing it had to be there, Amanda looked and finally saw through the astral fog the thin silver cord that connected this wandering soul to her body. Then, very carefully, she sent a surge of energy gently into the silver cord itself. A mistake here could rupture the cord, severing it from the body and resulting in the girl's death.

The little girl looked at her in surprise and then disappeared as the energy Amanda sent caused the cord to retract, pulling her back into her body.

There, she thought. *She may wake up screaming from a nightmare, but at least she's back in her body.*

Through the Murk there came a scream of anger and despair, and Amanda reeled back from a wave of hostile energy directed at her. Immediately she put her shields up, surrounding herself in Light. She felt the dark energy battering at her in rage, and then it disappeared.

She was alone.

Whew! That was something else! She thought. *I wonder what that was all about.* But she knew she wasn't about to go exploring further to find out. The little girl, whoever she was, was safe for now, and Amanda could only hope she would stay close to her body and not go roaming into dangerous places.

She could feel the girl's energy signature still tingling in her fingers. This feels familiar, she thought in surprise. *Do I know this child?* But searching her memory, she could find no recollection of the girl she'd seen. *Interesting. Was this just a random occurrence or was this girl attracted to me specifically?*

She had no answers.

She knew she had to get on to her base camp. She had broken the rules by leaving her Path. Even though she felt it had been for a good purpose, she knew that stay-on-the-path Deborah would not be happy. She hoped Adrian would be more understanding.

She refocused her attention on the vibrational pattern of the stream of energy she'd been following to her base camp. It took her a moment to find it, but suddenly she did and her Path flared up in Light before her. Putting all her attention on her destination, she moved quickly up her Path. As she did so, she noticed that the atmosphere was getting steadily lighter and brighter.

Abruptly her surroundings changed. The Murk was gone and with it, her Path to her base camp disappeared as well, no longer needed. She had arrived.

The signature quality of the astral realm was its malleability. Thought and emotion could shape astral substance into anything, a process that went on all the time. Most shapes, though, had little staying power. Thoughts changed and emotions dissipated, and when this happened, the astral shape usually disappeared as well. But focused and dedicated thought could produce something with substance, and they had been learning techniques that allowed an astral shape or "thought-form" to be long-lasting. This is what her base camp was: a thought-form that she had created over time with the help of her allies. It was infused with a quality of presence and duration that would only grow and become more established the more she used it.

She had visited some of the base camps created by others in her class. Most were very elaborate as her classmates indulged their fantasies and creative abilities. She preferred something simple. As a consequence, she now found herself in an open meadow dominated by a single large oak tree which exuded an inviting presence of peace and calm. Around it, the meadow itself was filled with various kinds of wildflowers whose colors and fragrance were healing and invigorating. On the horizon in all directions were majestic snow-capped mountains lending a sense of spaciousness and inspiration to the scene.

Near the oak tree was a pond about sixty feet across filled with clear, sparkling water. A small wooden walkway led to a wooden platform floating on the pond. This platform was the contact point with higher realms of life and consciousness.

The oak tree, the meadow and the pond were all modeled after a farm that had belonged to her father's mother. She had loved to go there before her grandmother had died and her parents had finally divorced, driven apart by her father's alcoholism and his long absences while on duty in faraway countries. It was a safe, stable place in her memory, and she had recreated it here to be an equally safe and peaceful place for those whom she would bring when, as a licensed Walker, she qualified to be a pyschopomp, an escort for the newly dead.

For that's what this base camp was, a place to bring the newly deceased through the Murk to where they could meet loved ones and allies who could not approach the physical realm but who would then take them on into the true post-mortem realms.

As she stood in the meadow taking it all in, a black figure emerged from around the back of the oak tree. "Pants!" she exclaimed. "There you are! Where were you?"

The black panther walked over and rubbed affectionately against her leg. "I was waiting for you here, Amanda."

"But why didn't you join me as you usually do?"

"You needed the practice to get her on your own."

"On my own? Oh...that was part of the test?"

"So I was told."

She looked around. "But where is everyone? Where's Tim? Shouldn't he be here to meet me?" Tim Guthrie was the soul that had been helping Amanda create this base camp. He'd been an English aviator who'd been killed during the Battle of Britain in the Second World War. Sometimes he was joined by Kaspar Grunewald, the German pilot who had shot him down and who had himself been killed later in the war. Since then, the two souls had become fast friends.

"I don't know. I've not seen anyone else here." He raised his head and seemed to sniff the air in a pantherish manner. "I do detect the traces of his energy, though. Apparently he came and then left."

"Left? But why? I need him to complete my test."

"I sent him away, Amanda," said a melodic voice from behind her. Amanda whirled around and saw a slim Chinese woman standing on the platform on the pond. She was dressed in a simple light-blue robe with a golden sash around her waist. Her jet-black hair was piled high on her head in an intricate hairdo. One moment she was on the platform, the next she was standing next to her. "I felt you and I should have a talk."

"Who are you?"

"My name is Taliana."

"Taliana!" Amanda was stunned. She'd heard rumors about this being around the school, and Adrian had spoken of her once or twice. She was a mysterious figure who was allegedly Adrian's teacher. If the rumors were true, this being came from the highest soul levels, one who had long ago mastered the intricacies and lessons of earthly life and had no further need for physical incarnation.

"I'm...I'm honored," Amanda stuttered. "I didn't expect...." She wondered if she should bow or curtsy or something. But this thought no sooner entered her mind than a wave of peace flowed through her, calming her down and making her feel held in a comforting love.

The woman lowered herself gracefully onto the grass and patted the ground beside her. "Sit beside me, child," she said. Amanda did so, feeling clumsy as she did. Beside her, Pants lay down as well, his golden eyes unwaveringly fixed on Taliana. He even began to purr, something Amanda had never heard him do before.

"You have a wonderful and powerful ally here," Taliana said, reaching out to stroke the panther's head and tickle him behind the ears. The purring grew louder.

"Thank you. I know it," Amanda said, still wondering what this was about. "But where is Tim Guthrie? Isn't he the one I'm to link with for my test?"

"Yes, he was."

"Was?" Amanda felt thoroughly confused.

Taliana smiled and put her hand on Amanda's knee. "I'm afraid, Amanda," she said, "you failed the test."

"What? But...but...how? I made it here OK." Still, she had a sinking feeling that she knew why. It looked like Deborah had been right when she'd told them that rule number one was to stay on the Path. *But dammit, that little girl needed help!* she thought stubbornly.

Her feeling was confirmed when Taliana said, "You stepped off the Path, Amanda. You broke a rule that was an important part of the test."

In spite of the Chinese woman's loving and calming presence, irritation began to rise up within her. "But I had to. There was a girl in trouble. I couldn't just ignore or abandon her. She was lost in the Murk and something was trying to harm her. I had to try to do something!"

"No, Amanda, in this case, you didn't. You jeopardized yourself, and if you had been escorting a soul, you would have jeopardized that person as well. The rules are there for a reason."

"But she needed my help. She was asking for it! How could I refuse her?"

Taliana sighed. "Amanda, your heart is in the right place. But are you sure of what you saw? Remember, the Murk is part of the Plane of Illusion. It is filled with thought-forms of many kinds. Some are there to lure Walkers such as you deeper into the astral where you could be harmed, even lost for a time. You cannot always be sure of what you see or hear. You know this."

"Wait a minute." A suspicion was blossoming in her mind. "Are you telling me she was an illusion? Was she part of the test, something that you or the teachers, or someone, dreamed up to tempt us?" If this were true, then Amanda knew she'd royally screwed up.

"No, Amanda," Taliana said. "I have checked. This was a real encounter."

"But if it was real, then I had an obligation to help. She needed me!"

"You don't know that. You acted impulsively without fully assessing the situation. Engaging in a contest of wills with an unknown force in the Murk could have endangered both the girl and yourself."

"But I had to act fast. And I was careful…"

"Amanda. Listen to me. I do not doubt the motivations of your heart, and I understand fully why you acted as you did. But consider. You are being trained to be a psychopomp, one who uses her talents as a Walker to escort those newly born to our realm to where they need to be. Your responsibility lies to the soul who is in your care at a time when he or she is most vulnerable. In fulfilling this responsibility, you may face many temptations and obstacles from the lower astral. There are others who are charged with providing aid and rescue within the Murk. You may be one of them on occasion, but not when you are acting as psychopomp and escorting a soul and not when you are using one of the Paths. If you cannot be trusted to follow this requirement, then we cannot use you for this task."

"But...but Taliana. This isn't fair! There was no soul with me. IF I'd actually been escorting a newly deceased soul, then of course I wouldn't have gone after the girl."

"Are you sure? Can you trust yourself not to be carried away on impulse in the moment?"

She wanted to say yes, but in the presence of this high being, she could only be truthful even when it hurt. "I...I don't know. I want to say I can, but...."

"But you're not sure?"

Amanda had to shake her head. She looked down, feeling ashamed and confused. *I just tried to help*, she thought. *Surely that can't be wrong?*

The Chinese woman put her hand under Amanda's chin and raised her face up so that she had eye contact once more. "Amanda, you have failed the requirements of this test, but you are not a failure. Look at this place you have created. It's beautiful and filled with healing energy. You have a real talent for this work. You have experience that others in your class do not have, and you have a caring heart. But you are impulsive. Learn from this experience. Understand the impulses that can control you and master them. You need to know yourself. You have gained valuable knowledge in this direction today."

"So, what happens now?"

"Why, you return to your body and try again at a later date. I have no doubt you will succeed." She reached out and touched Amanda on her head. She felt a thrill of energy move through her. "You have my blessings, Amanda. I honor your compassion and courage. I would only have you add wisdom to them."

"I'll try." Then she amended her statement. "No, that's not right. I'll do it."

"Excellent!" Taliana said, smiling. "I have no doubt you'll succeed and be able to serve not only the souls in your care but the Paths as well."

A memory surfaced. "Wait a minute. What does this mean, 'serving the Path'? A moment ago, you said I could not step off a Path if I were using it. Why?"

Taliana was silent for a moment, then she said, "I told Adrian he should have given your class this information at the beginning, but he felt he wanted to wait until you all had more experience."

"What information?"

Taliana laid her hand on Amanda's head again. "Let me show you something."

Abruptly, the landscape changed. Her base camp disappeared, and Amanda found herself sitting on a ledge jutting out from the side of a mountain. Behind her was the entrance to a cave, and all around her, other mountains, tall, majestic and snow-clad, surrounded them. Below was a valley, but it was obscured by thick fog.

"The Murk, Amanda," Taliana said from beside her. She sighed. "It has taken us by surprise. It's proving more troublesome than we anticipated."

Amanda looked at her with astonishment. "It took *you* by surprise? But you're one of the High Ones. I thought you knew everything,"

Taliana laughed. "Only the One knows everything, and even It gets surprised. After all, it created a universe that is constantly coming up with new things."

"But you're..."

"What? A Master?" She laughed again. "You mustn't believe everything you read. I'm a soul just like you, evolving just like you, facing challenges just like you. Think of me as an older sister. I have more experience, but I'm certainly not infallible. And neither is any other being I know, no matter how highly advanced it may be. Not even the World Soul knew exactly what was going to happen when the cosmic influences arrived."

"So...you didn't know the Murk was going to happen?" The thought that all this had caught even the most advanced human souls on the planet, not to mention Gaia herself, by surprise was proving a difficult concept for her to take in. She began to understand why Adrian might have wanted to wait awhile before sharing this with the class.

"Oh, we knew it was going to happen." She gestured at the fog below. "This is the residue of thousands of years of unregenerated, unintegrated thoughts and feelings arising from humanity's darker impulses. Much of this negative human emanation was transmuted and cleared away by a combination of both divine and human healing work, but not all of it. Some of it settled into the lowest parts of the astral plane, where it was compacted by continuing human experiences of inflicting and suffering pain and fear."

"It couldn't be healed with the other?"

"No, because people held on to it in one way or another. Have you never had an angry thought, maybe even one of hatred that you cherished in your heart and refused to release?"

Amanda thought immediately of her father and the anger she had felt over the years towards him. Even though he had left them when she was still a child, he had been a distant, fearful presence who, for many years until he died in an automobile accident, would call when he was drunk and scream at whoever picked up the phone. It had taken her a long time to forgive him. "I'm afraid so," she admitted, "but I'm working to let all that go."

"Of course you are, Amanda, for that is who you are as a soul. You know the danger of holding on to negative thought and emotion. But humanity as a whole doesn't know this yet, and what it clings to, we cannot pry loose."

"So the Murk is all that negative energy set free?"

"Yes, essentially. It's psychic sediment, Amanda, and for millennia it's been buried so deeply that we've been unable to get to it. But imagine someone walking in a river and kicking up the mud and debris on the bottom. It rises like a cloud and turns the water murky. This is exactly what the cosmic energies of the Quickening are doing."

"Couldn't it have been prevented?"

"But we didn't want to prevent it. We want it stirred up and loosened, for now all that ancient hurt that has been a toxic presence in the life of humanity can be reached and healed. Amanda, this is a good thing overall." She waved her hand over the fog below. "We knew it was going to happen, and we were prepared. What we didn't know was how much there was or how active it would become. The Murk grew faster and stronger than we had anticipated. In many instances, it has sealed off the lower realms of the astral plane to our influence."

"But how? How could it stop the Light?" This was something that had bothered Amanda ever since the Murk had appeared soon after the Quickening had begun.

"It can't, Amanda, that's not the issue. But Light is a form of energy.

If we try to force our Light through the Murk…"

"It only stirs it up more, making the astral even more cloudy."

"Yes, Amanda. And there are soul's trapped in the Murk, accustomed to its shadows. When someone's eyes are only used to darkness, the Light can blind rather than help. We have to be careful."

"So that's why you're depending on us to form these Paths with you. In a way, our eyes are adjusted to darkness so we can see where you cannot."

Taliana laughed. "You're quick, my child. And your assumptions are correct enough, though there is more to the picture. But look, this is what I wanted to show you."

She gestured at the fog roiling in the valley below, and Amanda could see sparks of Light moving through it. They brightened and dimmed, always changing, never constant. "Those points of Light are individual souls moving through the Murk, seeking to help. They carry Light with them, but its range and effect is restricted. And conditions can affect how much a soul can radiate. But this…."

Now Amanda saw lines and trails of Light reaching down into the fog from the surrounding mountain tops. These lines were thin at first but their Light was consistent and steady. As she watched, they slowly began to expand, pushing the Murk back around them and creating clear lines of energy and Light.

"The Paths," Amanda whispered.

"Yes. Lines of safe passage through the Murk that those who are trained, as you are being trained, can use to escort those who have newly died in the physical realm to where they need to go in their afterlife. But that is not their most important function. They are Paths, yes, but the term is misleading. They are much more."

As Amanda watched she saw Light circulating up and down the Paths and as they did so, the Paths widened and deepened, their influence upon the surrounding Murk becoming greater.

"They are lines of living energy, Amanda," Taliana continued. "They are arteries, veins, part of the circulation of Light within the earth. And as the Light moves in a consistent and regular way between our realm and yours, it imprints itself in ways that allow the Light to expand into the Murk."

As suddenly as they had left it, they were now back in the meadow that Amanda and Tim had created. "Imagine, Amanda, that you walked the same trail through this meadow every day. What would happen?"

She knew, for she had seen exactly such beaten trails through the land around her grandmother's farm. "The trail becomes pressed into the earth."

"Yes. The challenge with the astral is that it is fluid, as you know. A single passage between your realm and ours will create a line of Light, but it will not last. It will dissipate, just as the grass will spring up and cover any trail you walk through it only once. But if you walk the same trail over and over..."

"It becomes permanent."

"Yes. And from such stability, the Light can spread."

She stood up, and Amanda did likewise, sensing that this remarkable and unexpected interview was over. "The Murk is the problem, and the Paths are one way to begin to dissolve it. But they work only when used consistently and with faithful deliberation."

"When we stay on the Path."

"Yes."

"Even when we see something in the Murk that needs our help."

"I know you felt a responsibility to the soul who was in trouble. There is more at stake here, however, than the fate of one soul, who, under the Law, will eventually find the help it needs. That is inevitable. Not even the Murk can prevent this. But when you are on a Path, your dedication must be to the integrity and energy of the Path. To leave it impulsively may weaken it"

"But how? I don't understand."

"What you call a Path is a living presence, built up out of the energies of all the beings who use it, as well as those who first brought it into being. You don't 'walk" a Path, Amanda. You become it while you are attuned to it. If you break that attunement and step away, you carry some of its living energy with you, causing it to dissipate into the Murk. Over time this could weaken its integrity, even cause it to collapse."

"Oh! Did I do that? I'm sorry!" The thought of destroying a Path filled her with horror.

"No, my child. Not this time. The Path you used is well-established and strong. But when the time comes that you create your own Path, and it will come, then you must guard its integrity, for in the beginning it will be tenuous and weak."

She smiled. "Now I must go. I had not intended to stay with you this long. I'm afraid there may be repercussions for you, and if so, please forgive me."

On impulse, Amanda reached out and grabbed her hand. "Wait," she said. "Before you go… there's one thing I don't understand. Why you? Why did someone of your stature come here to tell me I'd failed? Why not Tim? He was the one I was supposed to meet here. For that matter, Pants could have told me, for heaven's sake! It didn't require you, though I'm honored you came. From what I've heard, you're Adrian's teacher. Why didn't my own teacher come?"

Taliana leaned forward and kissed Amanda on the forehead. "Why, Amanda," she said softly, "I *am* your teacher." And with this, she disappeared, leaving Amanda feeling stunned once again.

"You didn't know?" asked Pants, rising from the ground and stretching.

"No! I've never seen her before. How would I have known? You've been my ally all these years…and my grandmother, but she's hardly been a teacher. Even Tim's been more of a buddy than a teacher."

"The ways of the Wise Ones mysterious they are," Pants intoned, doing his best Yoda impression. "Perhaps it was a matter of timing. Whatever you did, it led Taliana to feel this was the time to announce herself."

"I…I only tried to help someone."

"And that is the calling card of all the great ones, Amanda."

She snorted. "I'm far from a 'great one', Pants. And I failed my test. Now I need to go back and face the music."

"Then if it's music you're facing, I wish you well in dancing with it. The next time you Journey, think of me and I shall endeavor to be with you." With that, the panther vanished as well.

Amanda turned her attention inward and focused on the cord connecting her to her body. She imagined herself flowing gracefully down it, back to her body, returning to earth, returning to physical life….

And she was there, feeling the pressure of the chair beneath her, feeling the breath in her body, feeling the solidity of the earth wrapping around her.

She opened her eyes and saw Adrian looking at her with concern. "That was quite a trip," he said. "You've been gone awhile. The others have all returned. I sent them away so as not to disturb you." He smiled. "I felt you were all right. I saw no distress in your aura. But I admit, I was getting worried."

"How long was I gone," she asked.

He looked at his watch. "Nearly two hours. Do you want to tell me about it?"

She felt tears brimming up in her eyes, and she wasn't sure if they came from the joy of meeting Taliana or the shame of having failed her test. "I met Taliana and I failed!" she blurted out.

Adrian's eyebrows rose. "Whoa! Let's take this one step at a time. You met Taliana? Wait…yes, I see her sigil in your aura." He whistled. "I'm…I'm impressed. But…you're right…there's no evidence of linking with the Path. So as you say, you didn't pass the test." He rubbed a hand through his hair. "I think you'd better tell me everything that happened from the beginning, Amanda. But I think something hot to drink and some food would be in order. Come with me."

Together they walked out of the class room and down the hallway to the wing of the house where Adrian had his office and his own private quarters. Amanda knew he had another house somewhere in Seattle as well, but he had bought and remodeled this mansion specifically to be home to his school for Walkers. Located in the hills on the east side of Redmond, overlooking the Carnation Valley and the Cascade Mountain range, it had both the privacy and the views that Adrian had wanted.

He took Amanda into his small apartment which consisted of a sitting room and a tiny bedroom. Both were tastefully but sparsely furnished. There was also a kitchenette. The house had a much larger kitchen and communal dining room where students and staff ate. When he was in residence in the school, Adrian usually joined them, but occasionally, he liked to fix his own meal. Right now, he had Amanda sit down in a comfortable chair while he bustled about preparing food. "I think a salad with a bit of chicken for protein would be perfect right now, and a cup of tea. Something light for your body that won't demand too much of it while you recover from your journey."

"Actually, I feel fine, Adrian."

He chuckled as he chopped up pieces of chicken he'd taken from the small fridge. "You do now, but trust me. When dealing with Taliana, there's often a backlash. In a little while you're going to feel like a truck hit you."

"She did say something about repercussions and apologized in advance. But I don't understand. She seemed so loving…"

"Oh, she is. Never doubt it. But the energy differential between ourselves and where she exists is huge. Your subtle fields have to expand to take in the extra force that accompanies her, even when she steps it down for our benefit, as I'm sure she did for you. It's like stretching your physical muscles when you do heavy work or lift weights. In time, you get used to it, but at first, your muscles will be sore. Your inner muscles, in this case." He placed a plate of chicken salad in front of her. "This should help, though. Earl Grey?"

"Yes, please." Now that the food was in front of her, she realized she felt famished, exactly as if she'd been working hard for several hours. She took a bite. "Oh. This is delicious. And you're right, I feel like I'm starving. But I've never felt this way after a Journey before."

He chuckled again. "I daresay you've never encountered someone like Taliana before. And I suspect other things were going on, am I right?"

She thought about the tug of war she'd had with the unknown force in the Murk. She nodded, her mouth full.

"Well, eat first, then I want you to tell me everything and leave nothing out."

She finished her meal and drank two cups of tea. Then, as he'd asked, she told Adrian everything that had happened from the time she left her body to when she returned. He listened intently, occasionally asking a question for clarification. His very presence seemed to draw information out of her, and she understood why he had been such a successful psychiatrist.

When she'd finished, he sat back in his chair, steepling his fingers before him. "That, young lady," he said, "is quite a story. You say you knew the girl who appeared?"

"No, not exactly. She was a stranger, but still, there was something about her, something I felt afterward, that was familiar. But I can't place it."

"Well, if it's important, I'm sure it will come to you." He leaned forward as if to emphasize his next words. "Amanda, Taliana was right. I should have shared the larger picture about the Paths with all of you before this."

She grinned wryly. "As I had to admit to Taliana, I don't think it would have made a difference in what I did."

"Well, we don't know that. It's just that this situation has never come up before."

"You mean, no one has ever failed this test before?" Amanda's heart sank. This was a distinction she was not happy claiming.

To her relief, Adrian replied, "Oh no. Students have certainly failed before. In fact, you're not the only one who failed this time. It's your reason for doing so that's unique." He got up and went into the kitchenette. "I'm going to have another cup of tea. Would you like one?"

She shook her head. "No, thank you."

He busied himself preparing his tea, then returned to his seat. "I make it a policy of never saying who failed a test. I find student's take it the wrong way. The work we're doing isn't an academic subject, so there are no grades, but students are often trained by previous educational experiences to think of it in those terms. I prefer to think that a certain part of the training is incomplete and will be finished on a second or third try. No one has ever been unable to do this, and I certainly know you won't be the first. So after the Holidays, we'll reschedule this test."

"Holidays?"

He looked at her strangely. "Good heavens, Amanda. Have you forgotten? Christmas is only two weeks away."

She was startled to realize that she had forgotten this, or simply hadn't paid any attention to what was going on in the world. Ever since her mother had died just before the Quickening, she'd stopped celebrating Christmas. She had no family to celebrate it with, and Christmas memories for her tended to be painful.

"If you noticed the Murk may have seemed particularly tough to get through, this is why. The Holidays always stir up emotions in people, and a lot of these emotions aren't particularly nice. There's a lot of depression and anger this time of year, unfortunately."

She nodded. "I can sympathize, Adrian," she said, "but then you'd know. You know my family history and I know you've evaluated me up, down and sideways."

He laughed. "Well, maybe not the sideways." A soft look came over his face. "Amanda, have you ever met your parents on the inner since they died. I'm particularly thinking of your father. I know you had a rough time with him."

She shook her head. "No, I haven't. And I've not wanted to. Grandma was always there for me when I started Journeying, but she's the only family....and she's gone on in her development, so I don't see her much anymore." She yawned.

"Ah, forgive me!" Adrian said. "I forget how tired you must be after this experience. We can talk more later. Now just go to bed and sleep. I bet you'll be out as soon as you hit the pillow. And if you want to stay in bed tomorrow, do so. You may need it."

She yawned again and got up. "Thank you. And thank you for dinner and everything. I appreciate it."

"Well, young lady, it seems we are linked, if Taliana is teacher for both of us." He walked her to the door of his apartment. "There's one other thing I want to say."

"Oh?"

"You may not have come back with the evidence of having passed the test, but you've come back from your Journey with something far more precious and significant."

"What's that?"

"Why, Taliana's blessing, of course. She's a remarkable being, a true high initiate, one of the highest. Her mark—her energy signature—it's there in your aura now. This is worth far more than I can say. It's something you'll discover for yourself over the rest of your life. You may have failed a school test but you succeeded at gaining something far more important. Well done, Amanda!"

And with that he sent her on her way to her room where, as Adrian had predicted, she fell into a deep, dreamless sleep as soon as she crawled into bed.

She slept late. When she awoke mid-morning, she did indeed feel as if a truck had run over her or as if she'd spent the whole previous day working out in a gym. A cup of coffee and an aspirin helped, but part of her wanted to crawl back under the covers and sleep the rest of the day.

Unfortunately, she had errands to run. It was Saturday, and she needed to go home to her apartment in north Seattle. She had laundry to do, bills to pay, and other tasks to make sure her mundane life stayed on track while she was cavorting on the inner realms during the week. *At least, I wish I were cavorting*, she thought. *That would be more fun than the drills we do every day.* And thinking this, she then studiously ignored the little voice in her mind that said, *do you think the trouble you got into yesterday could be due to this attitude?*

Half of the students lived here at the school, but she and a few others had local homes or apartments. A couple of people lived close enough that they even went home every evening and returned in the morning. With traffic, it could be close to an hour for Amanda to make the trip home, so she opted to rent a room here during the week. Now, though, she had to make the trek.

She put all her dirty laundry in a bag, grabbed her iPad, a book she was reading, and her journal to take with her, and headed down the stairs to her front door. There she found Wilma standing, staring at a small booklet in her hand, a distraught look on her face. She was obviously dressed for going out as she wore a long brown overcoat whose color was as faded as her personality, and an equally nondescript scarf covered her graying hair. The clincher was that an overnight bag and a large suitcase sat on the floor next to her.

"Hi, Wilma," she said. "Going on a trip?" The other woman turned to face her. Five inches shorter than Amanda's five ten, she had to look up, which she did briefly before she looked back down again. In Amanda's experience, Wilma was not someone who easily made eye contact.

"Oh, Amanda," she said, "Are you going out? Could you give me a lift?" She fluttered the little booklet which Amanda now saw was a bus schedule. "I seem to have missed the bus."

"Sure, no problem. I'm just headed home. Where are you off to?"

Wilma looked around furtively. "Can I tell you when we're in the car?"

"Absolutely. Here, let me help you with that suitcase..."

"Oh, there's no need," said Wilma. "See, it's on wheels." She pulled up a handle and gave the suitcase a little push back and forth to prove that it rolled.

"All right. Well, follow me, then, and we'll see if I remember where I parked last Sunday."

This was a joke since the parking lot of the school was small and only had room for eight cars. However, Wilma responded seriously with, "Oh, I hope so," as they went out the door.

It did not take long to load everything into the back seat of Amanda's Prius. Then they were coasting down the long drive way to the road below that would take them into Redmond and from there to one of the bridges leading to Seattle.

Once on the road, Amanda asked Wilma again, "So, where to, Wilma? I'm off to Greenwood where I live when I'm not here, but I can take you anywhere. I'm in no hurry."

"Can you take me to my sister's house? She lives in Madison Park just over the bridge. I'll be glad to pay the toll."

"Don't be silly! Besides, I have one of those." She pointed to a green and white sticker on the driver side window near the rear view mirror. It said Good to Go! "Pays the tolls automatically." She jerked a thumb at the suitcase on the back seat. "Spending the weekend with your sister?"

Wilma was silent for a moment, then she said quietly, "I'm leaving the school. I'm getting a bus down to San Francisco on Monday."

Amanda looked over at her. As usual, Wilma had her head turned away and was looking out the passenger window at the passing buildings as they made their way through Redmond toward the 520 freeway. "What! Why, Wilma? You're one of the best!"

"No, Amanda. I'm not, though it's nice of you to say so. The fact is I failed the test yesterday."

"So what?" Amanda said. "I failed, too. We'll just take it again."

This time Wilma looked right at her, her eyes wide. "*You* failed, too? But...but that's not possible!"

Amanda snorted. "Why? I made a mistake and the Powers That Be ruled against me. This time, at least."

"But Amanda, you really are one of the best in the class. You're not scared of the Murk like some of us, and you've had way more experience Journeying than the rest of us."

"Well, I've been doing it longer, if that's what you mean. But I've never done some of the things Adrian and Deborah are having us do. For me, it was just a lark, visiting cool places that people had created in their imaginations. I never tried to help anyone."

"Still, you feel comfortable out of your body. I don't. Besides, I can see that you didn't fail."

"What? What do you mean, Wilma?" Amanda pulled onto the freeway and headed towards the toll bridge.

"Why, I can see it in your aura. Adrian said there'd be a sign, and I can see it above your head. You must have made it."

Amanda wondered for a moment just what Wilma was seeing. Then she remembered the mark that Taliana's blessing had made in her aura. "You can see it?"

"Yes." A note of pride came into her voice. "I may not be much at Journeying, but I know I'm a good clairvoyant. And I know what I'm seeing wasn't in your aura before we took the test. And I know from its color and light that it comes from a very high realm. You *must* have succeeded!"

"But I didn't!" Amanda insisted. She wasn't sure whether she should tell Wilma about Taliana or not. What was the protocol here? "I stepped off the Path. Something...something came up in the Murk and I thought I could help. I did, too, but I broke the rules of the test. So I was told I failed."

"I don't understand.... I know what I'm seeing..."

Amanda slowed down as she passed through the toll booth on the bridge. There were no human toll-takers, only electronic eyes reading the code on her Good to Go! Pass. Had she not had one, they would have read her license plate instead and she would have received a bill in the mail. "I...I got a blessing, Wilma. I tried to help someone in the Murk. It cost me the test, but I got a blessing from an inner teacher."

"I see. Well, it must have been a high being judging from what I see, so you're fortunate, Amanda. You say you stepped off the path into the Murk? I can't even imagine doing that. Remember when we had to face the Murk? I had such a hard time doing that. I almost left the school then."

Amanda did remember. The first lesson for all of them had been to step into the Murk and face whatever it threw up at them. This was the nature of the astral plane. It reflected back to you what was in your unconscious and mirrored your thoughts and emotions. This could be pretty terrifying, and Amanda had had to face her anger towards her father and her fear of him as well when he would fall into a drunken rage. He had appeared to her in the Murk as something close to a demon. What had saved her was knowing that she was facing her own creation based on her own emotions and not her father himself. She could tame what she created.

"But you made it, Wilma. Whatever it was, you saw it through, otherwise you couldn't have continued with the program."

"Yes, I made it...or I thought so. But yesterday it all came up again and I couldn't face it. It...it was just too much. So I came back. I never made it to base camp."

"But why now, Wilma? You've made it so far. You created a base camp, didn't you?" Out of the corner of her eye she saw Wilma nod.

"Yes. But it was hard, very hard." She sighed. "I'm just tired, Amanda, tired of the struggle. Yesterday it just seemed too much. If I have to face…what I face….well, I can do it now and again. But if it's every time I Journey, it's just not worth it. I can't do it."

Amanda thought about this in silence as they crossed the bridge and took the turn off for Madison Park, a neighborhood along the shore of Lake Washington, the lake they had just crossed. "Have you told Adrian?" She asked finally after Wilma had given her directions to her sister's house.

"No. I…I couldn't bring myself to do it. He'd just try to fix things if he could, and I don't want that. I'll…I'll write him a letter from California."

Amanda had nothing to say to this. They wound around a bit through the Madison Park neighborhood until she found the address where Wilma's sister lived. As Wilma started to get out, Amanda put her hand on her arm. "Wilma, I'd really like you to reconsider. Maybe being a Walker isn't for you, but you're obviously a fine clairvoyant. You can still give an important service. Won't you stay?"

Wilma hesitated. "I don't know, Amanda. I'll think about it. But please, don't mention this to anyone else."

"You have my word."

Leaving Wilma at her sister's house, Amanda got back onto I-5 and headed north on the freeway to the exit that would take her home. The thought of Wilma's leaving bothered her. She didn't know the older woman that well and had no idea what devils she had inside her that could have taken form within the Murk. Wilma made a habit of keeping to herself. There was about her at times the feeling of a dog that had been whipped and now saw danger in every movement. She had wondered at times why Adrian had her in the program.

But Wilma had made it through the initial trials that each candidate for licensing had to pass which involved facing up to one's fears as they might manifest in the Murk. If a person couldn't handle the Murk, he or she had no business trying to Walk between the worlds. And Wilma had passed, which said something about her core strength and determination. It was a mystery.

One mystery too many for me right now, she thought, as she neared her apartment building. She parked in her space under the building. Getting out and going up to the door to the lobby, she keyed in the code on the door lock, determined to put Wilma out of her mind. Holly wreaths and a decorated Christmas tree in the lobby reminded her again of the Holidays. *One more thing to think about,* she muttered to herself, waiting for the elevator to come and take her up to the fourth floor where she had her one-bedroom apartment.

Once she was inside, she collapsed on the sofa with a sigh of relief. She enjoyed being at the school, but there was nothing as comforting as being in her own place. She lay there for a moment, feeling again the aching in her muscles. *Well, this isn't the first time I've run into a high-energy presence and felt the consequences later,* she thought, *though never quite as intense as this. But I know just what to do about it.* Though part of her wanted to sleep, she knew the best remedy was to be active, allowing her body and its subtle counterparts to ground themselves through physical action. So she started doing her laundry and cleaning her apartment, which didn't need much as she hadn't been there for a week. But it still gave her something to do.

Two hours later, she sat back down on the couch, feeling much better. She looked over at her drawing table set against one wall of the living room. She earned her bread and butter as a graphic artist and illustrator. She'd started her own business while she was still in high school, and now she was well enough known and sought-after, particularly for her fantasy illustrations, that she always had contracts to fulfill. Most of the tools of her trade she kept at the school where she could do her work in-between classes, but there were special projects she liked to work on over weekends here at home.

But she was still sleepy. So instead of working, she decided she'd catnap on the sofa for a couple hours then go out for dinner at a little Thai restaurant a block away. She kicked off her shoes, lay back and pulled a blanket over her that she kept nearby for just such occasions. A minute later, she was sound asleep.

She dreamt that she was traveling. When she awoke, she discovered she was no longer in her apartment, and no longer in her body for that matter. Instead, she was sitting on a snowy hillside. Although she was dressed in the slacks and blouse she'd had on when she'd gone to sleep, she felt no cold. *Of course not,* she thought. *I look like what I think I should look like and feel what I want to feel.*

She looked around and saw her black panther sitting nearby, its golden eyes steady upon her. "Hello, Pants," she said. "Where am I, and what am I doing here?"

"I don't know, Amanda. You were Journeying in your sleep. I simply followed you to make sure all was well."

Amanda had Walked in her sleep before, but usually she knew when she was doing it and where she was going. It was rare for her to wake up in the subtle worlds with no idea where she was or how she had gotten there.

"Well, I don't know either. But there must be some reason I'm here, wherever here is. Some part of me must know what it's doing."

"Presumably. Why don't you look over the top of the hill. You may find a clue."

She grinned. "You old whiskerface, you do know where we are."

"I did some scouting while you slept. And yes, I do know *where* we are, but I don't know why. Maybe you'll know."

She stood up. "So, where am I?"

"Take a look and tell me if you know."

She looked askance at her spirit ally. "This isn't some further test, is it? Something Adrian thought up? Maybe Taliana?"

"No, not that I know of. All I know is that I felt a need to be with you, and when I came to your side, you were separating from your body on the couch. It was evident you were still asleep, but you began to move purposefully, so I followed. That's all I know. This may well be the doing of one of the Higher Powers, but if so, I'm unaware of it."

"OK. Well, let me climb this hill and we'll see what's so mysterious."

She started to climb and immediately found herself at the top of the hill as if she had teleported there. *So*, she thought, *that's how it's going to be, eh?* She was confident she was in some part of the astral plane (*but if so, where's the Murk*, she wondered), a place ruled by thought and desire. You had but to think of moving and you were already at your destination.

She looked down. It took her a moment to make sense of what she was seeing. The hill she was on was part of a circle of hills, forming a bowl in the landscape. Down below in the bowl itself, she saw a number of small figures throwing snowballs at a larger figure dressed in a red suit trimmed with white fur, a wide black belt around his middle and black boots on his feet. He had no hat, but his thick white hair and trimmed white beard shone in the light.

"Is that....?"

"Yes," said Pants. "Santa Claus."

"Santa Claus," she repeated. "And who are the little people with him, elves?"

"No. Those are children. His elves are over there watching the snowball fight." Sure enough, arrayed on one of the hillsides off to the right from where she stood was a group of small figures clad in red and green.

She looked at Pants, a spill of black ink against the white snow. "What is this place?"

"The North Pole, I expect. Isn't that where Santa lives? I can't always keep up with your human myths. There's a huge house over behind the hill where the elves are sitting, by the way. It's beautiful!"

She glared at him. "Pants! Where is this really?"

If a panther could grin, he did so. "It's a dream world, of course. I thought you'd have figured it out. And before you ask again, no, I don't know why you're here. But maybe he does..."

Turning in the direction the panther was indicating, she saw that a man looking a bit like Santa himself, except that his suit was green instead of red, had appeared a few feet away. "Hello," the figure said. "Are you here to watch the children?"

"Um...no," Amanda replied. "Are you?"

The man came up to her, chuckling. "Every chance I get. I created this place for them." He reached up and adjusted the Santa hat on his head. "I can tell you're one of the sleeping ones. Most people who come here are. Are you one of the moms?" He gestured to the gaggle of laughing children down below.

"Heavens, no!" Amanda said. "I...well, I don't really know why I'm here. Frankly, a Santa dream world is the last place I'd expect to end up on a Journey. Santa and I were never on very good terms when I was growing up. Not many merry Christmases in my family, I'm afraid."

"Oh, I'm sorry to hear that!" And indeed the man looked pained at the idea. "My name's Fred, by the way. Back on earth, I used to be a department store Santa. I even rode in a couple of large Christmas parades. When I died and came over here, I thought I'd continue the tradition."

"So you're Santa now?"

He laughed. "No, *he's* Santa," he said, pointing to the figure down below. "I'm just the custodian of the place. It takes a lot of work to keep one of these dream worlds together." He walked over to where Pants was lying. "Say, I've never seen a spirit like you before. I saw you prowling around earlier, and it got me to wondering. I don't see many panthers here in Santa's world!" He laughed again. "When I saw you two appear here, I had to come over to say hello and appease my curiosity."

"I'm pleased to meet you," said Pants. "I am Panther, but she calls me 'Pants' or sometimes Old Whiskerface. If you get to know her, you'll find she has very little respect. But I'm fond of her anyway."

Fred laughed again. "I'm sure you are! So," he said, spreading his arms wide to take in the whole landscape around them, "if you're not one of the mothers and you're not here to watch the children, why are you here? Just exploring the astral?" He lowered his voice. "Not as pleasant a thing to do these days, not since everything got all stirred up."

"Frankly," Amanda said, "I'm not sure why we're here. My body's asleep on my couch back in my apartment, and I'm positive I had no intention of dreaming about Santa Claus when I started my nap. But something drew me here...." She looked around again. "So, you created all this?"

"Yes," Fred said proudly. "With help, of course."

Amanda had encountered such dream worlds before, places where the astral substance, so malleable and responsive to thought and imagination, had been shaped to form specific locations. Sometimes they were even created by dreamers themselves, though such creations vanished quickly once the dreamer awoke unless he or she continued to put thought and energy into them. She had once visited a world created by a famous writer and sustained by her continued imaginative input. It was an elaborate and rich place where the soul of the writer herself came at night to get inspiration while her body slept.

But most of these worlds were created by spirits like Fred as specific environments designed to help embodied people, often to provide places of rest and healing or instruction.

"You made this for sleeping children?" Pants asked.

"Yes. Children love to dream of Santa Claus. I give them a place to come to where they can experience their dreams. Here they can play with Santa and his elves, visit his home and toy factory, pet the reindeer..."

"And is Santa a spirit like you?"

"Sometimes. Sometimes, I take the role as I did on earth. Usually, he's a dream figure, a thought-form who responds to the children's needs and wishes. I never cease to be amazed at what you can create and animate here in this dimension."

"Yes," said Amanda. "It is amazing, and sometimes scary," she added, thinking of the Murk.

"But not here. This is a protected area. But come, would you like a tour? I'd be happy to show you around."

Amanda felt puzzled. She frankly had no interest in a Santa Claus dream world. Her mother had done her best for as long as she could to keep the dream of a magical Santa alive, but her father's alcoholism and repeated depression during the Holidays worked against her. Christmas Day was usually the scene of fights between her parents, when her father was home and not deployed somewhere in the world.

Yet something in herself or coming from some higher Power had drawn her here for reasons she couldn't fathom. Could it be for her own healing? But she doubted any of her spiritual allies particularly cared whether she believed in Santa or not, and she had long ago come to terms with her childhood which could have been much worse than it was. Belligerent and mean as he could get, her father had never laid a hand on her which was something in his favor.

"Amanda?" asked Pants. "Would you like a tour?"

"Huh? Oh, sorry, I got lost in my thoughts there."

"Bad Christmas memories?" asked Fred. "Me, too. Grew up in the Depression. We were never sure we would have food on the table, never mind presents or visits from Santa. I never was a believer."

"Then how....?" Amanda indicated the scene below them.

Fred laughed again. "Funny thing, that. The night before my first child was born I had a dream. Now I know I probably came to a dream world much like this one, but I didn't know it then. In my dream, Santa Claus appeared to me and said, 'I *am* real, you know. I don't have to look like this and often don't, but I am a real spirit here to bring people joy. Will you help me?' I was so impressed by that dream that from then on I did everything I could to help people experience Santa as a real presence."

"So when you died, you decided to build this?"

"Well, not right away, of course. I had to find my sea legs in this new world, so to speak. But yes, when I could, I decided to carry on the tradition. I'm not the only one, you know. There are thousands of these Santa dream worlds, all built on behalf of children but sometimes to help their parents, too, the way I was. There are enough images of meanness and cruelty in the world. Anything we can do to promote the image of someone who inspires the joy of giving and merriment, well…we should do it, don't you think?"

Amanda nodded. "I'd never thought of it that way, but you're right…"

Fred beamed at her. "Of course I am! So, come, let me show you around. Wait until you see Santa's workshop. I'm particularly proud of what I created there."

He took her arm and led her down the slope of the hill to where Santa and the children were still having a jolly time having a snowball fight. They could have teleported, she knew, but Fred obviously wanted to walk to give her the full flavor of the tiny pocket world he had created.

As they came closer to the children, some of them stopped making snowballs and looked up at them. One or two waved. One young girl, though, stepped forward, looking intently at Amanda.

Amanda stopped and gripped Fred's arm. "That girl….I know her!"

"A relative?"

"No…no…she's someone I just met here in these realms…I was on a Journey and she appeared out of the Murk and asked for my help."

"The Murk? Ah, you mean all the dark stuff that's been stirred up. Good name for it! But you say she asked for help?"

"Yes. She was terrified. Something was after her, and I ended up fighting it before I was able to send her back into her body."

"Really? Whew! Are you sure it's the same girl?"

"Positive! Do you know who she is?"

"No, I don't know any of these children. But I do know they're all children who have needs back on earth. When I was embodied, I often visited children in hospitals and orphanages. It was my specialty, what I most loved doing. So when I created this world, I set it up so it would attract the dream-selves of children who were having a hard time in their bodies." Fred pointed down the slope. "But look, she seems to know you. She's coming towards us."

"She must recognize me from our encounter yesterday. How strange. I have to talk to her and find out who she is."

Amanda started down the slope to meet the little girl who was walking slowly towards them. Suddenly, the girl stopped and turned her head, looking behind her. On the top of the hill on the far side of the bowl, a figure had appeared. It was a woman, but Amanda couldn't make out the details. She seemed hazy, as if standing surrounded with a gray smoke or fog. The little girl threw her hands up to cover her mouth, and her body began to shake.

"Who is that?" said Amanda, pointing to the figure.

"I don't know," Fred said. "That's usually where parents of the children stand if they've joined their child's dream."

"I sense darkness with her," said Pants. "She brings the Murk to this place."

All at once the figure on the hill made a pulling gesture. The little girl jerked and let out a small cry, then disappeared. She immediately reappeared beside the shadowy woman who reached out and grabbed her around the waist.

"Pants! She's kidnapping her! That's what happened yesterday when the girl asked me for help! We have to stop them!"

As quick as thought, the panther disappeared and reappeared on the distant hilltop where it crouched, growling, as if ready to pounce. "Come on, Fred!" Amanda shouted, and she willed herself to join her spirit ally in confronting the invading spirit. She immediately appeared next to Pants, in time to hear the shadowy spirit say, "You can't have her. She's mine!"

"Stop!" Amanda said, but it was too late. The child and the woman disappeared, leaving only a smudge of dark smoke where they had been standing, remnants of a negative energy.

"She held me off," Pants said. "Something stopped me from helping."

"The same thing that fought me yesterday, I imagine." Impulsively, Amanda stepped into the dissipating cloud of subtle energy and breathed it in. She immediately felt loneliness, despair, anger, and fear. And something else, something darker...

"Amanda!" cried Pants. "What are you doing?"

"It can't harm me, Pants. I want to get the feel of this energy. Maybe I can track it."

The panther snorted. "In that case, you'll need my help!" And he stepped into the cloud with her just before its last traces disappeared.

"Hmmn," he said. "There are two energy signatures here." Amanda was impressed. She'd only felt one, and it had been very faint. "One is definitely human. The other is....something else." He shook himself all over. "Nasty!"

"Can you track it?"

He looked up at Amanda. "Maybe. There's not much to go on. Do I want to? You remember about fools rushing in or about leaping without looking...."

She sighed, remembering Taliana's admonishing about adding wisdom to courage and impulsiveness. "You're right. But I hate to think of that girl in trouble."

"You have to trust she has her own allies, Amanda. No soul is ever entirely abandoned unless it chooses to cut itself off."

"But she knew me somehow! She reached out to me. Maybe I'm one of her allies! That's why I was brought here. We were supposed to meet so I could help her."

"You don't know that."

"No, but why else would I come here? I have no ties with Santa Claus. But apparently I *do* have a tie with this child."

The panther switched his tail in what Amanda knew was the equivalent of a human shrug. "Then a way will be shown to help her. In the meantime, you must be patient."

Amanda looked at Fred who was wringing his hands in despair, his face a picture of anguish. "I'm sorry," he said. "I don't know how this could have happened. This place is under protection—divine protection, at that. I don't see how something like this could have happened. The only way...."

"Yes?" said Amanda, grasping at straws. "the only way...what?"

"Well, if the figure we saw was related to the girl...if they were tied together in some way...it's possible. Parents who are asleep often come here to visit their child's dream and watch them play with Santa."

"You're saying that woman was the girl's *mother*?"

His face fell even more. "I don't know! I'm just saying that's one way she could have gotten here." He moaned. "Children should be safe here! I need to see about increasing the protections."

"Not a bad idea, these days," she said. Down in the valley, she could see Santa and the other children continuing their play, oblivious to the drama that had taken place around them. "I can't stay here, Pants," she said. "I need to go home and wake up."

"I understand, Amanda. Go. I'll be available."

She closed her eyes and focused inward on her body and the silver cord connecting her to it. The next she knew, she was opening her eyes on a darkened living room. She had apparently slept past sunset.

She went into her bedroom, undressed and then stepped into the shower where she let hot water run over her body until she felt fully back from her latest excursion into the subtle realms. She deliberately avoided thinking about what had happened. There was a mystery here, obviously, but she didn't have enough information to resolve it. Better to let her subconscious work on it, trusting that, as Pants had said, something would emerge and a way would be shown.

She dressed and went out, walking down the block to the Thai restaurant where she had a leisurely dinner of phad thai noodles and panang curry and rice. Then she came back home and turned on the television, seeking the mindlessness of some sitcom to occupy the little gray cells of her frontal lobes.

What came on the screen, though, was Adrian's television program *Hart to Heart*. A video of him talking on the nature of the Quickening was being shown. It was a show she'd seen before, and she realized she'd left her television tuned to the local television station when she'd returned to school the week before. There was talk, she knew, of syndicating his program nationally. There was still a great deal of unrest as the effects of the Quickening spread throughout the population—some people were still claiming it was all a terrorist attack using psychedelic drugs in the nation's water supply—and Adrian's show was one of the few places where people could find solid information and practical advice about what was happening.

This show was a way of trying to instill a sense of normalcy and calm into what was a volatile situation at best. The world hadn't collapsed yet, but it was still touch and go as centuries of assumptions about the nature of reality, scientific theories, religious teachings, and social structures all crumbled as more and more people experienced the non-physical dimensions whether they were ready and willing to do so or not. Adrian led a consortium of individuals and groups who were doing their best to keep things stable, giving the country, and the world, time to adjust and work things out.

His school was part of this strategy and hopefully a model for similar schools elsewhere. As more and more people opened up to subtle phenomena, in the resulting confusion and fear, it was easy for charlatans, or even genuine but unscrupulous psychics and clairvoyants, to prey upon a confused and ignorant public. To combat this, Adrian had used his friendship with the Governor and his standing in the medical community to set up a State-sponsored licensing program with professional standards for anyone offering counseling services or help in dealing with the subtle worlds. His school was the first to offer training for getting this license. But it was still just a drop in a very large ocean.

The good thing, Amanda knew, was that the effects of the Quickening were not uniform around the world. Many places were still untouched and others only lightly affected, though she knew this would change. Adrian had likened the effect to that of a wave hitting along a coast. The contours of the land would be uneven, with promontories that stuck out into the water being hit first and inlets and bays being hit later.

As it turned out, Seattle and the Pacific Northwest where she lived was a promontory and was one of the places in the country most affected by the waves of subtle energies that were altering human consciousness and awakening long-dormant sensitivities to the invisible ecologies that made up the world's non-physical half.

Seeing Adrian on the television, Amanda made a decision. She reached out to her cell phone lying on a table next to the sofa and dialed Adrian's number. It rang three times, and then he answered. "Hart here," he said.

"Adrian, it's Amanda."

"Amanda! You went home for the weekend, right? Is everything OK?"

"I'm fine, but it's happened again."

"What's happened?"

"I saw the child again, the same one whom I tried to help yesterday."

"Where? Where you live?"

"No, on a Journey." Then she explained to him how she'd laid down for a nap and found herself in a Santa Clause dreamworld with Pants. She told him all that had occurred, ending with the apparent abduction of the little girl.

There was silence on the other end of the line for a time, then Adrian said, "There's obviously a connection here between you and this girl, if we could just determine what it is."

"Adrian, I don't have a clue where to start. But having met her twice and felt her energy, I think I could track the girl on the inner. With Pant's help, I know I'm good enough to do that."

"But then what, Amanda? It sounds like there are other forces involved. If the woman you saw was the girl's mother, is she alive? Is she on the other side? How would you deal with the bond between them? And what about that darker energy you felt?" He paused. "There are some very nasty things in the Murk these days, the remnants of ancient evils long buried in humanity's unconscious but liberated now by the Quickening. You don't know what you might run into that's behind this."

"I know, Adrian. That's why I'm calling for your advice. I don't think I can let this go. This girl is asking me for help, and I'm not sure how to respond. Is there something Taliana could do?"

"I doubt it. Oh, she's powerful enough, but as the comic book says, with great power comes great responsibility. Her energy can be painful to beings on the lower level of the astral, like bringing bright sunlight to someone's who been living underground in the dark. And she has to be careful not to stir up more psychic sediment, making the Murk worse. That's why for the time at least, we're needed to do the leg work in these lower frequencies."

"Well, I could be one of her feet in this matter, or at least a toe."

Adrian laughed. "Amanda, with your passion, you could be a whole leg! But no, not this time."

"But I feel I need to do something."

"I know. Let me look into it. But in the meantime, don't go wandering out of your body. Remember, you can control what happens when you sleep. Just give your unconscious the necessary instructions when you go to sleep. No more Journeying until you get back to the school where the protections are greater."

"All right, Adrian. But something seems to be orchestrating all this beyond my control."

"Amanda, remember, you're in charge of what your spirit does. Just let it be known you don't Journey anywhere without your conscious knowledge and willingness. This is important. Can you do this?"

"Yes, of course. I had to learn that lesson long ago, Adrian. I'm pretty good at putting my foot down when I need to."

"Well, until we know more, I think this is one of the times when you need to."

"All right. Thank you, Adrian." She thought momentarily of telling him that Wilma was leaving the school, then realized this wasn't her news to deliver. Wilma would have to take care of it herself. "See you on Monday."

"Yes," he replied. "And don't worry. We'll figure this out." Then he hung up.

She put her phone down, still feeling unsettled and uncertain. She knew Adrian's counsel was correct. It was the wise course for her to take. Still....

"Please, Powers That Be," she whispered. "If there's anything I need to know or anything I can do, please bring it to my attention."

Then she switched channels on the TV and tried to watch a sitcom she normally enjoyed, one that invariably made her laugh. But tonight the jokes seemed flat, and she knew her energy was dropping. Finally, she turned off the television and went to bed, making sure she let all her inner allies know that she was not available for Journeying and telling her body, "Don't let me out tonight!"

She woke early the next morning. Her sleep had been happily uneventful, and she had no memories of any dreams or any other interactions with the subtle realms. She arose, stretched, and padded into her kitchen to make some coffee. Then she went out for a run around Greenlake, returning an hour later feeling happily winded but better in her body than she'd felt for the past two days. She showered, put on fresh clothes, and made herself a light breakfast.

She had just finished eating when someone began knocking at her front door. Opening it, she saw a woman only a little older than herself standing in the hallway. Black hair falling around her face didn't hide the fact that she'd been crying.

"Maria! What's the matter?"

Maria Hernandez lived in an apartment one floor above her. She had only recently moved in, and Amanda didn't know her well. But they had met in the laundry room more than once, and Amanda knew she was a mother with a daughter. She had never met Maria's daughter, though.

"Oh, Amanda, please," she said, a frantic note in her voice. "I need your help."

"Of course. Come in." She stood aside so the other woman could enter, but she made no move to do so.

"No, I have no time. My daughter is in the hospital. I need to go to her, but my car won't start!" All this came out in a breathless rush.

"You want me to drive you there?"

The other woman nodded. "Please. I...I didn't know who else to ask. I don't know many people here, you know. I thought maybe you...."

"Of course I'll drive you. Let me get my coat and car keys and we'll go right away."

The look of gratitude on Maria Hernandez's face was all the thanks Amanda needed, but all the way down in the elevator to the parking garage under the building, the other woman kept thanking her. Finally, as they got to her car, Amanda said, "Maria, you don't need to keep thanking me. I'm happy to help. If you want, you can tell me what happened while we're driving to the hospital. I'm sure it will be OK."

"Yes, thank you," Maria said, getting in.

Amanda pulled the car out of the garage. "Which hospital is it, Maria?"

"Oh, I'm sorry! I should have told you that first. She's in the Children's Hospital. Do you know where that is?"

"Yes. And it's not far. We'll be there in fifteen minutes if the traffic is kind, which it should be on Sunday morning. So tell me. What happened?"

Maria sighed. "I don't really know. Gabriela—that's my daughter— she lay down to take a nap yesterday afternoon and I couldn't get her to wake up for dinner. She was like someone....vacant...do you know.... here but not here, awake but not awake. I took her to the hospital and they took her in right away. She...she slipped into a coma. They couldn't tell me why." A sob surfaced, and Maria wiped tears from her cheeks. "I stayed with her all night, but this morning I had to come home and get some things. Then my car wouldn't start...."

Amanda reached over and patted Maria's hand which was resting on her lap. As she did, she felt a tingle of familiar energy. Surprised, she jerked her hand back. She knew that energy. "Maria, how old is your daughter?"

"She is eight years old. She's a wonderful child, very beautiful, very kind."

"Has she been troubled lately?"

"Troubled? No, not that I know. She's been looking forward to Christmas. She dreams of Santa Claus." A frown briefly crossed Maria's face. "She had a nightmare two nights ago....but that's all."

"A nightmare?" Now Amanda's antennae were fully alert. "What kind of nightmare?"

"She...she couldn't tell me. Something was after her, she said, but a nice woman saved her."

Thank you, Powers That Be, Amanda thought silently. *This can't be a coincidence. Gabriela must be the child in my Journey. The link was that her mother and I knew each other. But surely, the woman I saw yesterday can't be Maria. Who else would have a tie to the child?*

"Maria," Amanda asked, excited now and pressing for more information, "tell me about the rest of your family. Where's your husband? And what about your mother or his mother, Gabriela's grandmothers?"

"My husband is dead. He was a soldier and died in Afghanistan three years ago."

"Oh. I'm sorry."

Maria shrugged. "It is what it is. Gabriela and I miss him, of course, but we've been building a new life. We've had to."

"And her grandmothers?"

Maria looked at her strangely. "How funny you should ask. My mother is in San Diego, but my husband's mother..." she sighed. "That is a sad story."

"Oh? How?"

"She was a strong woman. Very loving. She loved Gabriela. But when her son died, it was hard for her. She grieved a long time. Then... then..." she fluttered her hands in the air..."you know, all this strangeness happened....what did that man on the television call it...?"

"The Quickening?"

"Yes. The Quickening happened. I don't understand it, but something changed with Emilia. She became a *bruja*. Do you know this word?"

"A witch?"

"Yes. She began having visions, going places in her dreams. She tried to find her son in the World Beyond. She was driven with grief."

Amanda could picture it. The waves of subtle energies that made up the Quickening directly affected the subtle energy fields that surrounded and permeated every individual. In nearly every case, it heightened their energy, "quickening" them, and the result was often the awakening of dormant capacities for clairvoyance and other psychic sensitivities, as well as giving some people the ability to Journey out of their bodies. For most people, this was confusing and disorienting. The incidences of mental illness had skyrocketed since the Quickening. But others tapped hidden memories in their souls and quickly came to realize what was happening.

It sounded like this might have been the case for Gabriela's grandmother, though Amanda knew that if she had tried to find her son in the post-mortem worlds, she would likely have been blocked. There were powerful veils and boundaries in place to protect both the newly dead and the grieving on earth since the emotional ties and the sorrow could form bonds that tied a soul to the earth plane, preventing it from moving on into its new life. Even the Quickening did not weaken these veils.

"What happened to her?"

"She was unsuccessful, but this only added to her grief. She turned her attention on Gabriela. At first I welcomed this, especially at Christmastime which she loved to spend with her granddaughter. But then I saw that it was becoming unhealthy. She was making Gabriela a... what's the word...a substitute for her son. She became obsessive. She began making demands about Gabriela. Emilia...she had a strong will. She was very proud. She told me once she had great ancestors in Mexico who had been powerful wizards." Maria rubbed her hands over her arms. "I became afraid of her and her new powers, afraid for my daughter."

"What did you do?"

Maria looked at her. "We moved."

"You came up here?"

"Not right away. We went to my mother's. But then I found a good job up here, so we moved again."

"And your mother-in-law? What did she do?"

Maria was quiet for a time. Then she said, "She died."

"She died?"

"She had a heart attack." Maria paused. "I can't help but feel I killed her by moving away." She began crying softly.

"Listen, Maria. You had nothing to do with your mother-in-law's death. And you had to protect your daughter. You did the right thing."

"Did I? Lately I've been feeling...feeling like we're being haunted. I haven't said anything to Gabriela, but sometimes I feel Emilia around, and it's not a good feeling. They say a *bruja* still has powers after death."

Amanda would have said something about this, but she saw they had just arrived at the parking lot to Children's Hospital, so instead she concentrated on finding a parking place. When she turned the car off, she turned to Maria and said, "Maria, may I come up with you to see Gabriela?" Amanda was nearly one hundred percent sure that Maria's daughter was the little girl whom she had met in the subtle worlds and that her grandmother Emilia was the woman who had taken her from the Santa dreamworld, but she wanted to confirm this.

"Of course. I would like this. But you must have other things you need to do. I didn't mean to take up your day."

"Nonsense! I said I wanted to help and perhaps there's more I can do. I have nothing else to do today anyway."

Maria acquiesced, and Amanda could see she was pleased and thankful to have someone else with her. Being a single mother was hard at the best of times, but especially so when your child was ill and you felt alone in an unfamiliar town.

Together the two women made their way into the hospital and up to the room where Gabriela lay, a small bundle seemingly asleep in a large hospital bed, surrounded by beeping and twinkling machines that constantly monitored her vital signs. There was only one chair in the room, but with a nurse's permission, Amanda brought another chair in from an empty room. Then she sat by the girl and held the tiny hand that rested on top of the covers. An IV drip was connected to the other hand.

There was no doubt now for Amanda. This was the girl who had asked her for help. The connection had been made through her mother, Maria. But now that Amanda knew who she was, she was no closer to knowing just what to do.

As she sat there pondering the situation, a doctor came in and talked quietly with Maria. Amanda knew it wasn't good news when the mother's hands flew up to her mouth and she began weeping. Amanda got up and came over. "What is it, Maria? What's happening?"

She looked at Amanda. "Amanda. The doctor says Gabriela is slipping deeper into the coma. Her vitals are diminishing, and they don't know why. They can't seem to stop whatever's happening. " Amanda looked at the doctor, who face reflected her sadness and frustration. "There's nothing wrong organically with her body that we can find. It's like her mind is shutting down, as if she's simply lost the will to live. I'd almost say something is leeching the life from her."

"Maybe it is. Do you have a clairvoyant attached to the hospital, someone who could *see* what's happening on the subtle plane?"

The doctor looked at her askance. "Clairvoyant? I'm sorry. We haven't given in to that mumbo-jumbo here yet."

Amanda bit back a retort. This was still an all-too-familiar response to the phenomena of the Quickening, even here in Seattle where such experiences were becoming more and more common. She could understand the reluctance on the part of many, particularly those trained in pre-Quickening science, to accept the reality of the subtle worlds. So all she said was, "I understand." She had no intention of making waves for Maria here in the hospital. But when the doctor left, she turned to her and said, "Maria, I think I can help. You see, I *am* a clairvoyant..."

"You? You are a *bruja*?" A flash of fear crossed her face.

"No, no. I'm not a witch. I can just *see* into the next world. And in spite of what the doctor said, it's not mumbo-jumbo. It's an ordinary talent that more and more people are going to be developing as time goes by."

"I...I see." The doubt in her face went away, replaced with resolve. "If you can help Gabriela, then that is what's important. I trust you, Amanda. Do what you must do."

Amanda sighed with relief. Having Maria's support was important. "It's very simple. All I'm going to do is sit in this chair and close my eyes. Then I shift my attention to the eyes of my spirit. And then...well, then we'll see." She smiled reassuringly at the young mother. "I may be able to find Gabriela's soul and bring it her back."

Maria gripped her arm hard. "Do it!" she said, fiercely. "What one *bruja* has done, another can undo!"

"Um..yes...but I'm not a...oh, never mind. It's not important." Amanda sat down in a chair next to the hospital bed. "Maria, it will help if we can be undisturbed."

"I'll see to it," she said.

Amanda settled herself in the chair, then closed her eyes and opened her inner Sight. As she suspected, Gabriela's aura was grey and dim, a sign that her body's vitality was diminishing. But the silver cord was still there. She could see it rising up into the air above the bed and then disappearing as it crossed the threshold into the subtle realm. She could see the energy pulsing along it, the life-force keeping, as they saying went, body and soul together. But she could also see that the pulse was slow as if something were interfering with it.

And that was all she could see. Wherever Gabriela's soul was and whatever was happening to it was outside the range of her inner Sight.

Damn, she thought. Clairvoyance really wasn't her strong suit. She could see perfectly well if she stepped out of her body, but she didn't want to do that here without support. In her body, the best she could do was see the energy fields or auras around people and things. She needed someone here who truly had the gift of inner Sight.

She opened her eyes and reached for her phone. Maria started to ask her what was happening, but she held up her hand to stop her. She then dialed a number.

The phone rang twice, then a soft woman's voice answered. "Yes?"

"Wilma? This is Amanda. Are you busy?"

"Amanda? Why, no. My sister and I are just chatting over coffee."

"Wilma, I need your talents. " She then explained the situation. "Can you come to the hospital?"

There was silence at the other end. Then Wilma asked, "Are you planning to do a Journey? I don't think that would be wise, Amanda. I don't think I could help you if you got into trouble."

"No. No Journeys, Wilma. I just need someone who can *see* into the subtle worlds better than I can. Once I know what's happening, I can get help from Adrian."

"Why not call Adrian now?"

"Assuming he's available, he's out on the far side of Redmond. Frankly, I think timing is critical here. You're only ten minutes away, fifteen at the most." She paused. "I really need your help, Wilma."

Another silence. Then Wilma said. "I'll be there in twenty minutes. I have to get dressed. What's the number of the hospital room?"

"Thank you! Thank you! This means a lot!" She gave Wilma the information she needed and then hung up.

"Another *bruja*?" asked Maria.

"Maria, we're not *brujas*. Just ordinary folks like you."

"No, not like me. I don't see the Other World like you do."

Well, not yet, at least, Amanda thought, but she said, "Well, it doesn't make us special."

Maria shook her head skeptically, then said, "But you need help, you said. So, it's bad for my daughter?"

"I don't know. Wherever she is, I don't have the power to see that far. But I'm hoping my friend, Wilma, can. Once we can see Gabriela, we can take steps to bring her back."

There was nothing more to say after that. It was now a matter of waiting for Wilma to come and hoping that her ability would enable them to help Gabriela. A nurse came in while they were waiting, checked the vital signs, then went out again.

After ten minutes had passed, Amanda thought, *It wouldn't hurt to check on her again.* So she sat back in the chair, closed her eyes, and opened her Sight. What she saw shocked her. Gabriela's aura had darkened even more and the silver cord had thinned, looking very tenuous and vulnerable as if it might tear apart at any moment. The pulse of life energy up and down it was noticeably slower, even feeble.

Amanda had seen this only once before. That had been when she had sat at her mother's bedside when she was dying. She had seen the silver cord thin just like this until it simply dissipated and was no more, the spirit that was her mother rising free to enter the afterlife. *Gabriela's dying,* she thought, *and it's going to happen very soon. There may not be time for Wilma to get here.*

Amanda knew what she had to do. If there were any chance to save this little girl, it wouldn't happen in the physical world with her sitting in this chair. She would have to Journey after all. She would have to find Gabriela's soul and retrieve it, sending it back to its body if she could.

She knew this had risks. She would be Journeying alone without backup, and she knew instinctively that she was going to have to enter the Murk. Her body would be vulnerable here in this hospital room. She knew Adrian wouldn't approve. It went against everything he was teaching them. But she couldn't help it. It was either break the rules or let Gabriela die.

She opened her eyes and looked at Maria who was watching her anxiously. She decided not to mince words. "Maria, it's bad. Things have gotten worse. I'm afraid your daughter will die if I don't go to her and bring her back."

"Go to her? You mean, die yourself?"

"No, no! But I can step out of my body…I can project my soul into the Other World and when I do, I will find Gabriela. But…"

"There is a problem, yes?"

"While I'm away, my body will be vulnerable. When Wilma gets here, she'll know what to do to protect me, but in the meantime, it'll be up to you. You mustn't let anyone disturb us. Especially you mustn't let them touch my body. It will look like I'm asleep, maybe even like I've gone into a coma myself. A nurse or doctor may want to wake me up. Don't let them. If my body is jostled while I'm out of it, it will draw me back suddenly, and that can hurt me. Plus it will prevent me from rescuing Gabriela if I can."

"I told you, Amanda, you can count on me. I'll guard the door."

"You won't have to, Honey," said a voice from the door. The two women standing by the bed turned around. There in the doorway stood a large nurse, her black skin even blacker against the white of her uniform. "I'll be the dragon around here." She looked at Amanda. "You're the one with the panther, right?"

Amanda gaped at her. "What?"

"Come'on, Honey, you know what I mean. I'm getting off shift when suddenly this bad ass black panther shows up in front of me and tells me to get myself up here, that his human needs to take a walk on the wild side, and that I'm needed to guard the door." She chuckled, a low throaty laugh. "I see lots of these spirit animals—mine's a buffalo, would you believe it? First time I've seen a black panther, though."

"You're clairvoyant?"

"What is this, twenty questions? You got trouble hearing, honey? Your panther said you needed me right away, time was critical. I'm here, so get your ass out of your body and do what you gotta do."

"The doctor said the hospital didn't have any clairvoyants."

"What, you think I go advertising what I do? Maybe one day, sister. Not yet. Now, are you going to move it or what? That panther's getting antsy." She grinned.

"*Brujas* everywhere," Maria said in wonderment.

"I guess so," Amanda replied. "I've got a friend coming," she told the nurse. "Her name's Wilma. She's clairvoyant, too. She's coming to help."

"I'll be here when she arrives," the nurse said. "No one else getting by me."

Amanda settled back in the chair and closed her eyes. She went through her BIPS protocol, and a minute or so later, she was standing in her etheric body by the side of the bed. Pants was waiting for her.

"How do you like our new ally?" he said, grooming his fur and obviously looking pleased with himself.

Amanda looked at the nurse who, from this side of things, was a bright light. "She's great. How did you find her? And how did you know I was going to Journey?"

"Well, we animal spirits have a network. I talk to Eagle, he talks to Rat, Rat tells me to talk to Buffalo who tells me about his human....you know how these things go. And as for knowing...well, honey," he said, imitating the nurse's drawl, "you were broadcasting your intent pretty strongly. I came right away and could see you'd need help."

"Thanks, Whiskerface. So, can you follow Gabriela's silver cord?"

"Of course. Can you? Remember, there are no Paths this time. You're on your own."

"Try me!"

With that, the two of them began to Walk, shifting in vibration as they followed the tenuous, thinning trail of Gabriela's silver cord. It wasn't long before they were in the Murk and going deeper into its darkness.

"Not a good place!" Pants said.

"Certainly not for a little girl," Amanda replied.

As it got darker, their own inner Light got stronger. But they had to be careful. If they put out too much Light, it would only stir up the sediment of the Murk, making their progress even more difficult. *It's like driving through fog*, Amanda thought. *If you put on your high beams, you just end up blinding yourself.*

Without warning, they found themselves in a clear area. Looking around, Amanda saw that they were in a neighborhood cul-de-sac. Around them, the small houses were dark and empty, all save one. In that one, dim light shone through the windows. As she looked closer, she could see through the large picture window that fronted the street a Christmas tree, its lights on but dim.

"I think we've arrived," she said.

The panther growled in response. "I really do not like the feel of this place, Amanda."

"Nevertheless, I think it's where we must go. Look...see? Gabriela's silver cord...it disappears into the house."

"Then enter we must....but cautiously."

They went up to the front door. Rather than knocking, Amanda turned the knob and found the door was unlocked. She pushed it open, and they went in.

They found themselves entering a living room. It was furnished with a sofa and two chairs all surrounding a low coffee table. There were two small tables at either end of the sofa, and each contained several framed photographs of a young man in an army uniform. A much larger painting of the same man in the same uniform hung on one wall.

In a corner of the room between a fireplace in the far wall and the front window stood the Christmas tree. It was decorated with lights and ornaments, but as Amanda had seen from outside, the whole effect was muted and sad rather than colorful and joyful. It was as if the lights had barely enough power to glow at all, much less glow brightly.

Under the tree were a number of wrapped packages, but the wrapping was sloppily done and the colors in the wrapping paper, bows and ribbons looked as washed out and dingy as the tree under which they sat.

The fireplace was filled with a pile of cold ashes while above it two stockings hung limply from the mantle.

Amanda walked over to touch the tree. As she did so, dead pine needles fell onto the floor at her feet.

"Ah, look, Gabriela! We have Christmas visitors! Isn't this nice?"

Amanda whirled around to see the tall woman whom she'd glimpsed in the Santa dreamworld the day before. Knowing what she knew now, she knew this was Maria's mother-in-law and Gabriela's grandmother, Emilia. She was standing in the entrance to a hallway that led into the interior of the house, and she had her arm possessively around the shoulder of a little girl standing next to her.

"You see," the woman continued, looking down at the girl while pointing to Amanda and Pants, "I told you we wouldn't be alone for Christmas. Grandma is always right." Looking up at Amanda, she said, "Won't you join us for Christmas tea and cookies?" She gestured towards the coffee table. Knowing the manner in which astral substance could be molded by thought and intention, Amanda was not surprised to see that the table was now covered with a white tablecloth on which lay a plate of decorated cookies and a tea service. The speed and precision with which they had appeared, however, told Amanda that this woman had a skilled and powerful mind.

Not sure of what to do next and wanting time to feel her way, Amanda nodded and, leaving the tree, sat down in one of the chairs by the table. "Thank you," she said. "Christmas tea would be lovely."

"Excellent!" said Emilia, and she walked over and sat on the sofa, making sure that Gabriela stayed close beside her. She began pouring tea. Behind Amanda, Pants started to prowl back and forth through the living room.

"That is a big cat you have there," the woman said. "Milk? Sugar?"

"Both, please," Amanda said. "Yes, he is. He's my spirit ally." She saw no reason to pretend Pants was anything else, certainly not a pet.

"A spirit ally? Well, well. Is that what they're calling them this year? What will they think of next?" She handed Amanda a cup of tea. She sipped it cautiously. It was tasteless, as she had suspected.

"I saw you admiring our tree. I've been telling Gabriela how beautiful it is. Wouldn't you agree?"

Amanda looked at the little girl who had been sitting very still on the sofa, watching her. "Do you think it's beautiful, Gabriela."

Gabriela shook her head. Without looking up at her grandmother, she said to Amanda. "I think it's dead."

"Nonsense, Gabriela," said her grandmother. "How can you say such a thing about such a beautiful tree? I admit we're having some trouble with the electricity, so the lights aren't as bright as they should be, and they're not making ornaments as colorful these days as I'm used to, but it's the thought that counts, granddaughter. We have our Christmas tree and we're together. What could be better?" At this last comment, Emilia looked challengingly at Amanda.

"Where is Mama? Is she with you?" Gabriela asked, looking at Amanda.

Before Emilia could say anything, Amanda said, "No, but I'm here to take you to her. She's waiting for you at home and wants you to come to her more than anything."

"No," said Emilia, setting down the teapot with which she had been about to pour her own cup of tea. "Gabriela just got here, and she's going to spend Christmas with her grandmother. Her mother has her every other day of the year. It's only right I have her on Christmas."

Ignoring her, Amanda focused her attention on Gabriela. "Do you want to come with me to your mother?"

"Yes!" said the girl.

"Then I think we should go. Right now."

"No!" said Emilia again, only louder this time. She stood up, her arm going possessively around her granddaughter and holding her down on the sofa. "She's here to stay with me for Christmas. You can't take her away. Her mother doesn't need her. I do! Besides, she needs to be with my son, her father."

"And where is her father?" Amanda asked.

The woman look momentarily confused. "He's....he's fighting a war somewhere...but he'll be home any day now, and when he is, he'll want to be with Gabriela. So she has to stay here."

"Gabriela," Amanda asked gently, "do you know where your father is?"

"Mama says he's in heaven. He was killed in a war."

"What?" said her grandmother. "Hush, Gabriela. That's nonsense! I don't know why your mother fills your mind with such stories. Your father's on his way here right now. We'll all be together for Christmas."

"Emilia," Amanda said, turning to the older woman, "do you know where you are?"

The older woman looked puzzled. "What a silly question! I'm in my own house...and frankly, I'd like you to leave."

"No, Emilia. This isn't your house. It's just something you've created out of your loneliness and grief for your son's death."

"What are you saying? My son isn't dead. Please leave!"

"Emilia, you're dead. Gabriela is alive. That's why she can't stay. That's why she can't be here."

"Why, I've never heard such nonsense! Me, dead? I'm as alive as you are, as alive as Gabriela here."

"Yes, but not in the same way, Emilia. Gabriela has a body and must return to it or else she will die. But you left your body. And your grief and longing brought you here. This isn't your house. It's a shrine to your grief." Amanda knew she was being brutal, but she had to break through to Emilia's soul and awaken it to its true condition if she were to free her from this shadowy realm crafted from her own sorrow and loneliness.

"How dare you!" Rage contorted Emilia's features. "*She* sent you, didn't she? That wicked woman! Trying to keep a granddaughter away from her grandmother! Taking her away! Never again! I won't let her go!" She wrapped her arms around the girl.

"Emilia," said Amanda. "If you try to keep Gabriela, she will die, as you died. But her soul will not stay here. She will go to where she needs to go, and I know that is not here in the midst of your own little world. You will be more alone than ever."

"Lies!"

"Even you shouldn't be here, Emilia. Let your granddaughter go, let go of your grief for your son, and you can leave this place. I know this isn't your soul's true home."

For a moment Amanda thought she'd gotten through to her, for Emilia's face suddenly went blank. Amanda could see confusion in her eyes. "Think, Emilia," she said, pressing the point. "This isn't your home. This isn't what your soul wants."

"Amanda," said Pants behind her. "Something is happening. I feel a force...."

Suddenly Emilia fell back onto the sofa as if she were a puppet and someone had cut her strings. With a cry, Gabriela darted forward, and Amanda grabbed her and drew her into a protective embrace. Pants growled.

Behind them there was a crash, and when Amanda turned, she saw that boards criss-crossed over the glass, boarding it up. Similarly boards appeared across the front door, and the entrance to the hallway disappeared, replaced with a solid wall.

"It seems someone doesn't want us to leave," growled Pants.

Everything around them grew darker. The Christmas tree, the furniture, the painting on the wall all disappeared , and they were in a blank empty room. Emilia lay prone on the floor, seemingly unconscious. Amanda held Gabriela more tightly and sought for the Light. There was no way, she thought, that this woman could keep them trapped here.

"Well, we're leaving anyway." She wrapped her arms more tightly around Gabriela. "We need to get you back to your body."

But try as she might, she could not make the energy shift that would allow the two of them to return to their bodies. It was as if something very heavy was weighing her down, making it hard for her to think.

"Pants, what's happening?"

Pants growled more loudly. "I think Emilia was just a stalking horse for something else."

"What something else?" Amanda cried, looking around. The

window and door had now disappeared, and the four of them were in a featureless box.

"I think we're about to find out!"

The room around them now vanished, leaving them seemingly adrift in the dark fog of the Murk. The presence of something evil grew around them, and she felt that she was sinking into the ocean where the pressure continued to grow the deeper they went. Amanda redoubled her efforts to draw forth her own Light in response.

The fog lifted. They were in a chamber built from large stone blocks. The room was filled with a blood-red light which seemed to come from no single source but which nonetheless cast shadows in the corners and about the room. In the center of the room was a long slab of stone, grooved and stained. It seemed to pulse as if it were breathing slowly but steadily. Amanda could feel the pain and fear embedded in it. She had no doubt that in some time and some place, people had been sacrificed on this stone, and now its astral duplicate was here in this foul place, wherever this was.

"She was weak, my descendent." The voice was deep and powerful yet curiously grating, like broken chalk across a blackboard. Amanda winced. From out of the shadows stepped a figure, a short man dressed in a loin cloth but with a feathered cloak about his shoulders and wearing an intricate headpiece. A pendant obviously made of gold hung around his neck and lay upon his chest. "She drew me out, seeking my power. But when I gave it to her, she died, unable to contain the presence of the god."

"God?" Amanda asked. "What god?"

"The one whose priest I am. The brother to Quetzalcoatl. Huitzilopochtli, the god of war, the sun, and human sacrifice."

Good lord, thought Amanda, *Aztec gods? What have we gotten ourselves into?* "I hate to disappoint you, but there are no human sacrifices here. Release us in the name of the Light!"

The priest laughed. "You wish the Light? It will be with you soon, the Light of the one I serve."

"That is no Light," Amanda declared. "Let us go!"

The priest pointed to the figure of Emilia lying on the stone floor. She was regaining consciousness and softly moaning. "She gave herself to me willingly, and that one as well." He pointed to Gabriela. "They are mine! And now you are here as well. My lord will be pleased."

"Your lord will be pissed off when we leave." But try as she might, she couldn't summon the energy to break free of this place.

Emilia sat up. "You promised she would be with me for Christmas," she said, petulantly. "You promised! She's mine!"

"You are both mine," the priest said with contempt. "What is this 'Christmas'? It is a pale reflection of the true festival at this time when the blood of sacrifices runs from the altars and my lord, Huitzilopochtli, god of the sun, grows strong enough from his feasting to return and wage war on the dark. Now you will all feed his strength and become part of his victory! Prepare yourselves as he comes."

The priest turned and vanished into the shadows.

"Hoo, boy," said Amanda. "Pants, what is going on here? Are we still on the astral? Nothing is responding to my will."

"Amanda, we are deep in the ancient sediment of human terror and evil. We are deeper even than the Murk, though the Murk arises from places such as this. Here are the souls so lost in their hungers and their hatreds that they have become living darkness, like the one we just met."

"And this god, this Hui...Hui...whatever?"

"Huitzilopochtli. Now it is itself no more than an embodiment of all the fears, all the suffering, all the rage that went into its creation. It is no god, but what it is, is rightly to be feared. On this level, it is a Power."

"That's so...comforting, Pants. How do we get out of here?"

"I've been trying, but these walls are compacted of hatred and fear so dense that even I cannot find a path out."

"Then...what? You're saying we're trapped here?"

"No," said Pants. "I fear we're going to be eaten here..."

A wave of noxious energy passed over them, and Amanda turned to its source. The altar at the center of the room was transforming, turning into a dense blackness shot through with red streaks the color of fresh blood. It felt obscenely alive, and Amanda felt the hunger from this thing as its attention turned towards them. She instinctively turned Gabriela's face into her side, trying to shield her from whatever was coming. "Pants," she said. "If you're going to do something...."

At that moment, a small mouse ran across the room between them and the pulsing mass that had been the altar, and in its wake came a line of pure, white Light. It was dim in this place, but it was Light nonetheless, a stream of sacred energy. It formed a shield between them and the thing that was Huitzilopochtli, which jerked back from it.

"Tilea!" Pants shouted.

"Who? What?" said Amanda, bewildered by the sudden turn of events.

"It's Wilma's partner, her spirit ally. Tilea is her counterpart to me!"

Of course, Amanda thought. *Wilma's spirit ally would be a mouse!* "But how did she get here?"

The mouse appeared in front of her, a tiny figure standing up at her feet. "There's no place a mouse can't go," it said. "Aren't you glad?"

"I'm ecstatic!" exclaimed Amanda. "Thank you!" She remembered one of the principles that Adrian had taught them about subtle world phenomena, that you couldn't judge anything by its size. "Often the smallest entity is the most powerful," he had said. "Remember, a mighty warrior can be felled by a tiny bacterium."

Amanda could feel the thing that called itself Huitzilopochtli raging behind the shield of Light. "I cannot hold this long," the mouse said. "We must leave."

"NO!" the power of the voice struck them even through the shield Tilea had created. It was the priest returned. He had a stick in his hand woven round with colored threads in which stones were embedded. He pointed it at them. The shield of Light began to waver.

"Quickly," said the mouse. "I've weakened the barriers holding you here. Leave now."

Amanda looked around and saw Emilia lying prostrate on the stone floor, trying to rise up. Her face was contorted in fear. "Help me..." she said.

Amanda decided. "Pants, you and Tilea take Gabriela and leave now. I'm going to rescue Emilia. She doesn't deserve this fate. She's just a lonely grandmother!"

"If I go, the shield will collapse," Tilea protested.

"I'll be fine. I eat Aztec gods for breakfast!"

Pants looked at the mouse. "Go, Tilea. My human is being her impulsive self, so I must impulse with her. Take the child and go."

The mouse didn't question. She turned and ran up Gabriela's leg, and a moment later, both of them had disappeared. Amanda wasted no time. She ran over to where Emilia lay on the floor and pulled her up. The woman weighed nothing at all. "We're getting out of here, too," she said.

A force slammed into her and knocked her back on the floor. The shield of Light vanished. The priest, his stick pointing at her, cackled. "You're mine, remember! You're my gift to my lord on his festival! Eat, my lord, feast and let their life swell your strength!"

The dark mass swept forward towards them while at the same time drawing back as if a giant mouth were opening revealing an abyss of endless emptiness and hunger inside. Amanda threw up her hand. "Light!" she yelled.

There was no Light.

However, there was the dark form of a black panther that interposed itself between her and Emilia and the descending form of Huitzilopochtli. Pants seemed to swell, and his growling filled the room like thunder. The mass paused in its descent. The panther crouched, then leapt into the maw of darkness which immediately closed around him. Both Pants and Huitzilopochtli disappeared in a blast of force.

"No!" cried Amanda, still lying on the stone floor. "Pants!"

"No!" cried the priest, from where he had been knocked down. "My lord!"

The two of them stood and faced each other.

"Your god is dead, priest," said Amanda.

The priest sneered. "You think the God of War hasn't eaten jungle cats before? Look!"

To Amanda's dismay, she saw a small black mass beginning to form again where the altar stone had been. The priest was right. Huitzilopochtli was coming back. *And probably more pissed off than ever*, she thought.

But she knew she couldn't give in to fear. Whatever happened, her fate and that of Emilia now depended on her ability to withstand the darkness with whatever strength she could muster.

"You fight your fear," the priest said. "This is good. You are a warrior. Unlike my weak ancestor, you will be a worthy sacrifice for my lord. You will bring him much strength!"

"She will bring him nothing, you bastard!"

The burst of Light and energy from behind her and the angry voice that went with it caught her completely by surprise. She saw the shocked look on the priest's face as he stumbled and fell down, then standing next to her was a woman radiant with fiery Light.

"Wilma?" Amanda said, incredulously.

"I've got your back, Amanda."

"Wha...how...Wilma, how did you get here?"

"Tilea showed me the way. I followed her trail through the Murk. I could feel you were in trouble."

"But you hate the Murk! You fear it..."

"Yes, and I decided it's time I stopped being afraid. Not just of the Murk. Of everything." She pointed at the priest who was picking himself up, his face contorted with rage. "Especially of men like him, the bastards. They think they can do anything they want to you, use you anyway they want...Well, by God, no more! I'm mad as hell, and I'm not going to take it anymore."

After decades of suppressing her power, even her identity, her anger had obviously shattered her fear and liberated her inner Light. Now, blazing with that Light, she pointed at the priest, and a line of power struck him in the chest and bowled him over. She then turned her energy on the mass curling up from the center of the room, and it, too, retreated before her flame. "God, but this feels good!" she crowed.

"I bet it does," said Amanda. "But I think we'd better take the opportunity to get out of here!" She went over and picked up Emilia, who was at this point thoroughly dazed.

"You're right, but...."

"NO!" cried the priest. "You cannot escape!" Before Wilma could blast him again, the little figure leapt forward toward the black mass that was his god. "Take me, my lord, and let my strength give you the power to kill our enemies." He plunged into the swirling darkness and disappeared. The blackness surged forward in response, quickly growing larger and more menacing.

"Wilma..."

"I've got this, Amanda. I've wanted to do this all my life. My father thought he was a god, too, and could do anything he wanted to me. Well, no more! This woman's fighting back! You get out of here and take her with you. Like I said, I've got your back!"

With that, Wilma ran forward toward the growing cloud that was Huitzilopochtli, her aura blazing with the fire of her anger. There was a burst of Light, and Amanda found herself flung free of the dark, stone room, her arms still wrapped around Emilia.

Dazed, she looked around her. All was darkness. *Where am I now,* she wondered, clutching Emilia to her.

Without the pressure of the thing that claimed to be Huitzilopochtli pressing in on her, she could feel her own inner Light returning from where it had retreated deep within her core, preserving her essence in the face of an onslaught of evil. She drew the Light out and into her aura. It was not as bright as she would have liked, and she realized that her own energy reserves were low. *I'd best be getting back to my body soon,* she thought, *or Emilia won't be the only spirit trying to find a new place in the post-mortem worlds.*

As if she had become a dim lantern, the glow of her Light illuminated the terrain about her. Once she had seen pictures of the blasted landscape of No Man's Land in Europe during World War I. The place she found herself in now was if possible even more deformed and lifeless. She felt a dull apathy coming over her, and knew it was the emanation of the feelings of depression and worse that made up the actual substance of the land around her. While there was no temperature in the way that her body would feel it, the psychic environment here was frozen and cold with abandoned hope.

Whoa, girl, she thought. *Enough of this. If I give in to the nature of this place, I'll never get out. Time for happy thoughts!* She steeled herself and tried to think of something happy that would boost her spirits. *Christmas,* she thought. *Christmas is a happy time!* But for her it wasn't, and thinking about it made the gloom creeping into her from the land about her even worse. So she gave up and thought instead about finding her way out. *Getting home is the happiest thought!*

Like a diver trying to determine where the surface was, she extended her senses gingerly into the darkness around her. Emilia was no help in this regard, for she was unconscious. The break from her ancestor had been traumatic. *She's going to need a lot of healing,* Amanda thought.

Using her will, she pushed her Light out further. At the edge of her vision, something dark and deformed scuttled away and disappeared into the shadows of a crater. *Good Lord,* she thought, *was that a person? But what kind of soul would exist in this place?* But she knew. Though she had never encountered anything like this, she had heard Adrian speak of it once. In the deep sediment of ancient human suffering and hatred were found souls so pathological and debased as to become bottom-feeders, living in the darkness and drawing a faint semblance of life from the debased energies around them. Occasionally, circumstances permitting, some of these blighted beings would become aware enough and active enough to try to expand their dark, psychically-polluted environment by using their hungers, their angers, and their hatreds to influence incarnate individuals to behave in ways that added to it. Such dysfunctional souls were the source of all the demonic legends within humanity. But most individuals lost here were too apathetic even for that amount of activity. Of all the hells people could create for themselves, depression, she knew, could be the worst.

It's way past time to get home, but how? The longer she stayed here, the more the depression and cold of this place sapped her energy and sought to penetrate the very core of her soul. In some ways, this was more threatening and dangerous to her than had been the active evil of the ancient Aztec priest and his sacrifice-hungry god. It was getting harder and harder for her to think or even to care. She felt so weary she just wanted to drop Emilia, collapse and sleep forever. *And in this place,* she thought, *it really could be forever.*

She knew that the simplest way out was just to surrender to the ache and pull of her silver cord. It would pull her instantly back into her body. She would be safe. But there was no such cord for Emilia. She would remain behind in this place, and Amanda knew that, given the emotional state of Gabriela's grandmother, she would easily be trapped her.

No way in this hell I'm letting that happen!

"I really have a bad feeling about this place," said a familiar voice, as something warm and soft pressed against her leg.

She looked down to find a familiar feline form looking up at her.

"Pants! I...I thought you were..."

"Eaten?" The panther chuckled. "I was! But I'm a hard cat to kill. You'd have to destroy the World Soul first. I admit it wasn't a pleasant experience, and it took me awhile to find my way out of where I ended up, but..." He held up a paw and looked admiringly at his claws. "I think Huitzilopochtli got the worst of it. There's certainly a lot less of him now than before he tried to swallow me!"

She kneeled down, laying Emilia on the ground, and then gave the panther a long hug. "Oh Pants! You old Whiskerface! I'm going to call you Godkiller from now on!"

The panther purred. "Well, I wouldn't go that far, Amanda. Huitzilopochtli still exists. Ultimately, he can only be dispersed and removed by humans, for humans created him in the first place. Until then, he's a very nasty thought-form. "Pants lifted his head and looked about as if trying to detect a smell. "And speaking of him, I suggest we get out of here, because what is left of him is on your trail."

"What?"

Pants indicated Emilia lying beside them. "Her ancestor is most persistent. Having claimed her, he wants her. If she reaches the realms of Light, he can never reach her, but here he still has power. And he can track her by the link she created with him."

"But I saw him give himself to his god..."

"Who in this place is a thought-form as dependent on the priest as the priest is dependent on it. They feed each other all the time anyway."

"Wilma...?"

"I don't know. I knew she had come...but I was pulling myself back together, so to speak." The panther paused and closed his eyes. When he opened them again a moment later, he said, "Tilea says she's back in her body and all right."

"You can talk with her, even here? I can't get through to anyone."

"Why do you think Walkers like you have animal allies like Tilea and me? We feel the Murk's impact upon us, but it's humanity's creation. It binds humans in ways that do not affect us. So we can move in it more easily than you. Also, we are part of the World Soul, always in contact with each other. That's how Tilea could find us when we were in the priest's domain. And it's why Huitzilopochtli couldn't destroy me. He would have to destroy the World Soul first. No mere thought-form is ever going to do that!"

Amanda hugged the panther again. "So, oh Great Piece Of Gaia, can you get us out of here? I really, really, really want to go home."

"I can help, Amanda. But if you want to save this woman, you will have to carry her out. I cannot do this for her. And we really do need to hurry. I wasn't kidding when I said that Huitzilopochtli and his priest are coming for her...and you, too, if they can get you."

"All right. Then what we need is to find one of the Paths. Can you do that, Pants? Can you find us a Path to follow?" Amanda knew that if she could get onto one of the Paths through the Murk such as the one she'd been on during her recent test, it would give her the energy she'd need to get Emilia to her base camp or at least somewhere safe out of the Murk. *Not to mention the energy to keep me alive, too,* she thought.

"Amanda, there are no Paths here."

"What do you mean...there are no Paths here? Adrian said there are

Paths all through the Murk."

"Yes, but we're not in the Murk."

"What? But where else can we be?"

The panther switched its tail in what Amanda knew was agitation. "We're deeper than the Murk, Amanda. This place is lower in vibration even than the physical plane where your body resides. We are in the lowest and most densely compacted of the many layers of the astral. It's being broken up by the Quickening and its ancient evil's being liberated to where the forces of Light can finally deal with it, but as yet there are no Paths this deep."

"But...but what can we do, then? Deeper than the Murk? I...I don't have the strength to lift us out of this, Pants! Can't you get help?"

"Maybe....but we are so deep it would take any of the Higher Ones time to get here. And I'm afraid time has run out for us!"

Amanda felt it even as Pants spoke, a wave of hunger, lust, and anger so potent that if she hadn't been kneeling already holding onto her spirit ally, she knew her knees would have buckled. In the gloom of the landscape around her, she couldn't see it, but she knew Huitzilopochtli had found them and was advancing rapidly.

She could feel the panther's frustration. Amanda could easily save herself, even this deep in the bowels of the hells humanity had fashioned for itself, but she could not save Emilia in the same way. But she didn't have the strength to run, to lift them both into the Light....not before the wrath of the thought-form of an Aztec god enveloped them.

Pants shook himself. "I..I am not back at my full strength. I can't do what I did before to disperse the thought-form. Neither of us can be destroyed, but if Huitzilopochtli devours you, it will strip your life force. Your body will die and your soul...well, your soul will be trapped here in this place."

When Amanda didn't reply, he continued. "You must let her go, Amanda. She will eventually find the Light again. Even the wretched beings caught in this place are not forgotten by the One. The Murk will be dispersed and healed in time and this dark place redeemed as well."

"But how long, Pants? How many hundreds, maybe thousands of years will it take, even with the Quickening?"

"I don't know. But time is different here. You can't think of time the way a human does on earth."

"No, Pants. I'm a Walker. My task is to Walk with people like Emilia to make sure they reach the Light. It's what I'm being trained for. It's what my soul wants. If I abandon her, I abandon myself and all I stand for. I can't do it, Pants! I can't!" She could hear the desperation in her voice.

"You haven't been trained to deal with this, Amanda. Even Adrian would be challenged to function in this place. There's no shame in recognizing your limits."

Out at the edge of the feeble illumination cast by the Light in her aura Amanda saw something move. It was too small to be Huitzilopochtli, but she could feel that entity growing and getting closer. She stood up. Better to face it standing up. "No, Pants," she said. She could feel tears forming in her eyes, so strong was the passion she was feeling in this moment. "I'm a Walker Between the Worlds. If I fall, it will be as a Walker, not as someone who fled to safety when she was needed."

The panther was silent for a moment. Then he said, "This is what I admire about you humans and why it is a privilege to be your ally. I stand with you, partner."

"Thank you."

Amanda reached down and picked Emilia up, cradling her close to her so she was held in the Light of her aura, such as it was. The older woman was light as a feather, so it was no burden, and she didn't want to take the chance that either Huitzilopochtli or the priest would grab her while the other distracted Amanda. At her feet, Pants growled.

Huitzilopochtli appeared at the edge of her Light, the little priest stepping out of the seething mass of blood-red darkness.

"There are no mice to save you here, warrior woman, and I see your jungle cat is exhausted," the priest said. "As I said, you will make a tasty feast for my Lord," and Amanda could have sworn he smacked his lips.

She didn't waste energy trying to reply. Instead she turned her attention inward to the core Light of her soul, drawing out as much as she could, bitterly aware that given her state of exhaustion, it was woefully little. *But it will have to do,* she thought.

As she drew the Light into her aura, she momentarily blazed up like a star in the night, and the priest and his hungry god drew back. It gave her satisfaction, but she…and, she was sure, they…knew it wouldn't last long. But as the Light filled her energy field, she saw something there, something new and unfamiliar.

Taliana's sigil, Amanda thought. *It's her mark, her blessing. I forgot it was there!*

In that moment, she knew that while there were no Paths this deep in the lowest reaches of the astral plane, maybe she could make one. A Path in the final analysis was no more than a relationship that became imprinted into the astral substance forming a link that others could use to traverse the dimensions, a "Path" others could walk.

"Hold them back, Pants," she said. "We're not done yet!"

"As you wish." Drawing on his own resources, the panther began to grow in size, bursting into radiance, his growl reverberating through the darkened landscape. Amanda knew that in his weakened state, Pants wouldn't be able to keep it up, but for the moment, it kept Huitzilopochtli and the priest at bay.

Rather than letting her Light fill her aura, she now drew it back, focusing it like a laser on the glowing sigil in her aura. The landscape around them would have plunged back into blackness as she did so had it not been for the Light that Pants was radiating. As she focused all her attention on the sigil, she remembered her time with Taliana and what the woman adept had felt like. She felt her love for this being welling up in her and remembered how she'd felt Taliana's love for her when the woman had given her a blessing. *Taliana,* she thought, projecting her consciousness with as much power as she could, using the sigil as a link with this high soul. Around her, the Light began to dim as Pant's power and strength began to fail. She felt Huitzilopochtli gathering itself to pounce. *Taliana! I form a Path with you!*

I thought you'd never ask, came the reply. Then the now familiar voice intoned, "We are a Path together!"

All at once, it was as if a sun had come into their midst. In the sudden brightness, Amanda could see Huitzilopochtli and its priest fall back, the latter crying in anguish as the Light burned into him. Beside her, a slender Chinese woman appeared. Immediately the Light turned down. "We mustn't burn the inhabitants of this sorry place," Taliana said. "But you…you are something else. We've wanted to get at you for a long, long time!" She stretched out her hand, and a searing lance of Light struck the mass that was Huitzilopochtli. An unearthly howl went up as the thought-form of a god suddenly lost its cohesion and began to break apart in wispy streamers of inky energy. "Let's gather you up, shall we?"

Taliana's aura expanded until it surrounded all the dispersing elements of energy that had been Huitzilopochtli. She drew them into her, and as they entered her luminous form, they turned into sparkles of Light and disappeared. "Well," she said to Amanda. "That's one thought-form that won't bother anyone anymore! You've done very well, my daughter."

Amanda didn't know what to say, so she simply said, "Thank you."

"No, I thank you. You've given us a Path into deep places that we had been unable to reach. It will serve to salvage and redeem many in the time ahead."

A suspicion formed in Amanda's mind. "Taliana, did you set this up so all this would happen?"

The Chinese woman laughed. "No, Amanda. But knowing your impulsiveness, I suspected a time would come when my sigil and blessing in your aura would come in handy. I confess I didn't expect it to happen in quite this way." She looked at Amanda with a love and respect that made the young woman feel weak in her knees. "Had you not called me, I could not have interfered. There would have been no link for me to travel this deep into the Dark. But I had faith in you, Amanda."

Then Taliana became all purpose and briskness. "Come, we must make repairs. This woman must be taken to where she can recover and heal and find her way again. And you, Amanda, must return to your body immediately if you are to avoid permanent harm. And you," she said, putting her hand out and stroking the black panther's head. "As always, you and your kind have my deepest thanks, Child of Gaia."

Pants purred loudly.

Taliana gathered them all into her aura like a mother gathering children to her breast and began to move along the new Path that had formed. The Light enveloped them, and Amanda could feel her consciousness falling away. As she sank into a deep and healing sleep, she had a moment to whisper in Taliana's ear. The adept grinned. "Yes," she said. "I think that would be most appropriate."

Amanda awoke to darkness. For a moment, fear gripped her. Had she somehow fallen back into the Murk...or even lower? She cried out.

Immediately she felt a hand laid on her arm. A solid hand. An earthly hand. It felt wonderful.

"Peace, Amanda. You're safe." The voice was barely a whisper, but she recognized it instantly.

"Adrian?"

A light came on, and she blinked. Leaning over her, she saw Adrian's face, worry lines smoothing out as he saw that she was now awake. "Where am I?" she croaked.

"You're in your room at the school," he said. "I brought you here yesterday when you collapsed at the hospital."

"I collapsed?"

"Well, you didn't fall down, but you seemed to go into a coma sitting in your chair. The doctor wanted to commit you. Fortunately, my own medical credentials allowed me to take you into my custody and bring you here."

"But...but how did you get there?"

"Wilma called me, of course. As soon as she arrived at the hospital room and saw that you were off journeying, she called me. Good thing she did, or you'd be in that same hospital, iv tubes in your arms and medicated up to your eyeballs. Of course, I had to get past that nurse who was guarding the room! Where did she come from? She was a lion!" He frowned at her. "You gave everyone a scare, young lady. Not least of all, me!"

She sighed and closed her eyes. "Wilma?"

"She's fine. She told me everything that happened...at least as much as she knew. And yes, she's staying in the school. I'm sorry she ever felt she had to leave."

"Good. She was magnificent!"

"So I heard. She had many fears to overcome and a deep core of anger that I'd been unable to help her with. But now....now she is a different woman."

Amanda laughed softly, remembering how Wilma's aura had blazed when she'd attacked Huitzilopochtli. "Don't ever get her angry at you, though...."

"I'll remember that." Adrian pulled his chair closer to the bed and took Amanda's hand in his. "Ah, Amanda, what am I going to do with you? No student of mine has ever died while Walking. You came very close to being the first...too close."

"I...I'm sorry. I'll do better next time..."

"I should hope so! You broke every rule I have." He held up his hand. "You went Journeying in an unprotected place, even after I told you not to do so." One finger bent down. "You went on your own without a buddy." Another finger bent. "You not only didn't go on a Path, you went where no Paths had ever been created." His thumb bent in to cover the other two fingers and begin forming a fist. He paused, frowning as if trying to think of more rules she'd broken so he could use the remaining fingers.

Amanda wished she could hide under the covers. As each finger went down, she felt worse and worse.

"And…" Adrian continued, "And…you saved a little girl from death. You salvaged a soul that would have been lost in one of the worst hells humanity's own thinking has created. You created a Path of Light within the deepest parts of the astral. You helped destroy an ancient evil. And you lived through it!" As he enumerated all these points, all his fingers bent back up and out until he had an open hand again. "Taliana is very pleased."

"You…you talked with her?"

"Yes, she made a point of telling me of your exploits."

Amanda's heart lifted. "I guess I didn't so badly after all…"

Adrian frowned again. "Amanda, you broke every damn rule of this school…." Then he grinned, "And you passed with flying colors! "

She sighed with pleasure. "Of course," she said. "I'm a Walker!"

Adrian squeezed her hand. "Indeed you are! Indeed you are!"

A week later, Amanda was cleaning up after a small Christmas Eve dinner party in her apartment with Wilma, Maria, and Gabriela. Gabriela had survived her ordeal with no obvious side effects, though Amanda knew Adrian was keeping an eye on her. Earlier, the girl and her mother had helped Amanda decorate the first Christmas tree she'd had as an adult. Amanda had decided she needed to come to terms with this holiday and build some happy memories around it. So many lines of human longing and aspiration, fears and hopes converged on this time of the year as the days grew shorter and shorter. Most were filled with love and merriment, but some, like Huitzilopochtli's solstice festival with its parade of human sacrifices to feed the god's strength for the coming year, were not so pleasant. After the Spanish conquest, the Catholic Church had replaced this festival with Christmas. While this had created a new and lighter tradition, the ancient darkness remained untouched and festering in the unconsciousness of humanity. *And because of the time of year and Emilia's link with her ancestor,* Amanda thought, *we got caught up in it.*

So now she felt she wanted to do what she could to nourish a thoughtform of happiness and joy, love and giving this time of year. She'd had enough of sacrifices! Bring on Santa!

She finished the tidying up and sat for awhile just enjoying her new tree with its glowing lights and bright decorations, so different from the dim shadow-tree she'd seen in Emilia's own private astral hell.

Finally, yawning, she went off to bed where she read briefly before turning off the lights and falling asleep.

Only to find herself standing on a snowy hillside, her black panther beside her.

"What's this?" she asked. "Am I sleep-Walking again?"

"Only because I wanted to show you something." She turned and saw Taliana standing nearby, her long black hair as much a contrast against the snow as Pant's black fur. Next to her stood Fred, dressed as before in his green Santa suit, his eyes twinkling beneath busy brows.

"Hello, Amanda," he said. "It's nice to see you again."

"Hello, Fred. Taliana, it's always a joy to see you, but why am I here?"

The Chinese woman smiled. "Surely you know. It was your idea, after all."

"You mean…"

Taliana held out her hand, and Amanda took it. "Come with me and see."

They walked over the hill, and on the other side was a large house with towers and gables and gingerbread trim, decorated with holly and ivy, and blazing with lights of all colors.

"Santa's house," said Fred. "Designed it myself….with the help of the children, of course. I try to match it to their dreams."

Around the house were many children talking and playing with Santa's elves. Santa himself was hitching the reindeer to his sleigh which carried a huge, bulging sack of toys. "It's Christmas Eve," Fred said, "and children are dreaming of his coming." Amanda saw that one of the reindeer in the front of the team had a glowing red nose. *Ah, come on,* she thought. *Really? But then, why not? What else should children dream about tonight?*

A door opened, and a woman came out of the house carrying a tray stacked high with cookies while around her a team of elves carried mugs of hot chocolate with steam rising from them.

"Meet the new Mrs. Claus," said Fred, proudly. "She's fit in perfectly, and she's a huge help to me."

The woman looked up in their direction and winked at Amanda, then turned to passing out dream cookies and cocoa to dreaming children. It was Gabriela's grandmother, Emilia.

"It was a risk," said Taliana, "but I took your suggestion and brought her here to Fred. She's found a mission to bring joy to the dreams of children, and it's helped immeasurably with her healing."

"She's a wonderful Mrs. Claus!" said Fred. "She loves the children."

"I wasn't sure it would work," said Taliana. "She's suffered a lot, and I had to be sure the link with her ancestor was broken. But thanks to Fred here, it is turning out well. You were wise to suggest this, Amanda."

If Amanda had been in her body, she would have blushed, but as it was, she glowed a little brighter. "I'm so glad," she said. "Thank you for showing me. This is a wonderful Christmas present!"

"It's not all," said Fred. "We've located her son. He's going to join us here, too, at least part of the time."

"Really? But where's he been? Why hasn't he contacted her before, when she died?"

"He couldn't," said Taliana. "She had forged the link with her ancestor before then, and it had awakened a darker side of her. Her soul felt the power of her lineage but didn't realize just what evil lay at its roots. As long as she had that link to the past, we didn't want her son exposed to it. Without realizing it, when she tapped a power she hoped would bring her son to her, it actually pushed him away."

"But now?"

"Now they will be reunited. Not yet. She has more healing to do. But soon. And when they are together, Gabriela will be able to visit them at night, and perhaps at other times. She's a powerful soul, that little one. I have my eye on her."

"Adrian, too," Amanda said. "He thinks she may well become a Walker."

Fred left to go help with the children. Taliana watched him go, then turned to Amanda. "You may wish to come here at times, as well. I think there is some healing for you, as well."

Amanda smiled. "I'll give old Santa a try," she said. "After all, I did put up a tree today!"

Taliana smiled. "Very good! Now I must go. Blessings, my Path-Partner."

"Blessings, Taliana!"

As Taliana disappeared, Amanda looked at Pants standing beside her. Curiously he had his paw over his nose. "Merry Christmas, Pants….say, what are you doing?"

Pants removed his paw, and Amanda was startled, then amused, to see his nose was now glowing with a bright red light. "That's a heavy sleigh for those horned herbivores to pull. " His golden panther eyes twinkled. "I thought I'd be ready in case Santa needed claws!"

And Amanda woke up in her bed, laughing.

THE END

Contact

David Spangler

Jake stood on a small rise, looking out on a flat, airless plain pockmarked with craters. Above him, the sky was black and filled with stars. Over the horizon, which seemed very close due to the small size of the moonlet on which he stood, he could see twin stars locked in gravity's embrace. Brighter than either was the accretion disk between them, a stream of matter and energy flowing like a curving river of light from one to the other. It was this even more than the two stars that gave faint illumination to the barren moonscape around him.

If he turned around, he knew he would see a ridge of jagged rock that had never known the soft caress of wind or water to smooth away its sharpness. And off to his left about a hundred yards away rose the white tower, jutting up from the desolate expanse around it like a thin, shining blade. *Not again,* he thought.

He had visited this moonlet with its tower several times already. In fact, it seemed lately he went nowhere else. Where this place was in the universe, he had no idea. Sirius, he knew, was a binary star system, but its stellar companions were nowhere near as close to each other as these two. Normally destinations were set by computer, but *esp*-travel was far from being an exact science. *The technician proposes but the psyche disposes,* he thought, acknowledging that the psychic space through which he and his team traveled was filled with mysteries they were still discovering.

Like, why do I keep coming back here? Is there some significance I'm missing?

He stood there in the casual slacks and turtle-neck shirt he'd worn to work that day. As this was pretty much what he wore every day, he wasn't surprised that his subconscious now deemed this his official uniform and replicated it for his journeys. Although he knew intellectually that he was here as an *esp*, he still seemed solid and physical to himself. It was therefore emotionally miraculous to him that he could stand here unprotected in a vacuum, seemingly exposed to the cold touch of the cosmos, and suffer no ill effects.

Miracle or not, it was becoming frustrating for him. All six members of his team, Jenny, Michael, Allison, Michelle, Thomas, and himself, recruited for the Project from various universities and parapsychological research centers, had been on this moonlet at least once at one time or another. All of them had made the trek across the cratered plain to the tower. And all of them had found no entrance in the featureless, slightly glowing opalescent material from which the tower was built.

In his case, though, this seemed to be the only place he could go. Where the others explored planets and moons in the attempt to contact an alien civilization, he came again and again to this tower.

He sighed. Perhaps this time will be different. It had become his mantra. *This time will be different.*

One thing was never different. He always appeared on this moonlet a football field's length away from the tower. How he covered the distance between them, he discovered, depended on him. He could bound carefully towards the tower, reflecting the lower gravity in this place. He could also walk normally as he would if he were walking in the part near his house. Or he could just teleport himself, one moment standing on the rise, the next moment being a few feet away from the tower. All of this was consistent with the characteristics of the *esp* state in which he was essentially a coherent mental field capable of transcending physical conditions.

This time he decided he would walk normally. He wasn't in a hurry. The chances were good the tower would be no different than it had been before, and he didn't have to rush into that disappointment. Instead, he would take some time just to enjoy the view. For truly, the sight of the two stars and the glowing river of light between them was wondrous, possessing an awesome beauty. On the one hand, it could be seen as an act of cosmic violence, for one star was literally eating the other, its greater mass pulling material from the heart of its companion. In fact, that is how Thomas had described it in his report when he first came to this place. But he saw something else. For him, the two stars were locked in an embrace in which one was giving itself to the other. Where others saw feeding, he saw love-making. Thomas had laughed at this and Michelle had called him a romantic, but it didn't matter to him. He felt what he felt, and that was that.

Even stopping now and again to admire the spectacle above him, it did not take him long to reach the tower. As always, it struck him as forlorn, an artifact built by some unknown race and abandoned on this moonlet. Why? Why had they done it? Why was it here?

It was about thirty feet in height and looked as if it had been carved from a giant pearl rather than constructed of separate blocks and pieces like a normal building. Its roof was pointed, which would have made the whole thing look like an obelisk except that eight feet below the point, there was a balcony that went all the way around the circumference. From the ground, this balcony looked as if it were two or three feet wide, and the wall that formed its outer edge was about the same distance in height. The top of this wall was not straight but undulated with curves of uneven length and height. He could imagine someone—or something—standing up there watching the two suns in their cosmic dance. Was that what this place was? An observatory?

If so, whoever built it and used it must have been small. The tower itself was narrow, only about fifteen feet in diameter, giving the impression more of a spike or a spire than that of a tower meant for habitation. Yet lately when he came here, he felt a presence of life. It was as if someone were inside it watching him, though there were no doors or windows anywhere. *Or perhaps, the tower itself is alive,* he thought, not for the first time.

He reached out and touched the side of the tower. The milky substance felt slightly warm to him, reinforcing his thought that this structure might in some way be a living creature. *But here? In this environment? What living being could survive unprotected?* He glanced down at his turtle neck and slacks. *Not that I'm in a pressure suit or anything,* he thought. But then, *I'm not really here, am I?*

He walked around the tower. It was no different from all the other times he had been here. He looked to the ground. There were no footprints in the dust that coated the surface of this moonlet. He didn't expect to see any signs left by him or his colleagues, for *esps* left no physical trace. But there were no signs of those who had erected this building, either. The moon's surface, wherever in the universe it was, looked as if it had been undisturbed for millennia.

Well, he thought, *I might as well head back.*

He stepped back from the tower, already forming in his mind the algorithm that would trigger his return to his body. Before he closed his eyes to complete the process, he looked up and saw the tower silhouetted against the twin suns, a galaxy of stars spreading out around them in an infinite wreath. It was a breath-taking view, and for a moment, he was struck with a sense of kinship with this artifact. It stood alone on this moonlet, just as he did, a sign of life in the universe. No matter how spectacular the view, it paled before the wonder and significance of the intelligence that had build this structure or that enabled him to journey as an incorporeal presence into the vastness of space.

On impulse, he reached out and touched the tower with his fingers, feeling a sudden flow of love and companionship with this strange tower, as if it were not a structure but a fellow being sharing this little moonlet with him. As he did, he thought he saw his fingers sink into the opalescent surface as a wave rippled out from the point of contact and a warmth flowed into his body. Then the feeling was gone as if it had not been there, and the tower was as impersonal and unresponsive as ever.

What the hell? He thought. *Did that just happen, or was I imagining things?*

He walked around the tower again, examining it closely, but he could see no changes in its surface. There was nothing to indicate that it had responded to him at all or even was aware he existed. He pushed against the surface, pressing hard, but aside from feeling slightly warm as it always did, it was solid and firmly resisted his pressure.

Finally he gave up. *One more mystery*, he thought, *if anything even happened at all.* He formed the algorithm in his mind again and closed his eyes. For a moment all was black, then he felt himself back in the warm water of the coffin-like isolation chamber. Groping for the button on the side of the chamber, he pushed it. There was movement, and he knew an alarm was going off outside in the projection room the team all called "the Enterprise" for it was, as Thomas said, the place where they "boldly went where no one had gone before."

The lid of the chamber slid back, letting a soft light spill in. He blinked the water from his eyes and saw the blurry form of the technician bending over to unhook him from the various electrical umbilical wires that plugged him in to the machinery that powered his journey.

"Welcome back, Jake," the woman said, helping him to sit up. "Good flight?"

He grunted. "It was the tower again," and he knew his face showed his frustration.

His debriefing was short. There was, after all, nothing new to report that was different from his previous visits to the tower. He decided to say nothing about the moment when the tower had seemed to ripple. He could not be sure it even happened. Normally, an artist would be present to sketch whatever he had seen while it was still fresh in his mind, but in this case, no artist was called. They already had several pictures of the tower from his past visits and from those of the other team members.

The debriefing officer simply closed the file and said "Sorry you didn't go anyplace new."

"Yeah, me, too," Jake responded.

He went to the changing room next to the "Enterprise." There he took off the special jump suit he wore while in the immersion tank, showered, and retrieved from his locker the same slacks and turtle-neck he'd been wearing while visiting the moonlet. Dressed, he headed down the corridor towards his office, but was stopped by Bill Whitson's deep voice rumbling out through the open door of an office as he walked by. "Jake, would you come in here a moment please?"

Jake stopped and turned into his supervisor's office. It was a Spartan affair with just a desk and two chairs. Unlike other supervisors Jake knew in the Project, there was no ego wall filled with pictures of the office's occupant with various celebrities and higher ups in the Starmind Project. Whitson's walls held two large framed photographs, one of the Grand Canyon and the other of Crater Lake in Oregon, and a series of drawings created by his twelve-year old daughter.

"Sit down, Jake," said Whitson, smiling amiably up at him from behind his desk. An open file folder lay before him holding several sheets of paper. He tapped the one on top. "I just got the report on your journey. You went to the tower again? What does this make it?"

"That's the fourth time this week. And twice the week before."

"Have you talked with the computer techs?"

"Not today. I did a couple of days ago. They swear that there's no glitch in the program. The navigation software should orient me to a different place each time. But you and I both know that *esp* travel is as much art as science. The computers can point me but it doesn't mean I'll go where they point."

"I'm wondering if you're caught in some weird psychic loop. Self-generated maybe?"

Jake shrugged. "It's possible, but I can't imagine why my subconscious would be doing such a thing. It's not as if the tower is *that* interesting. Sure, it's an alien artifact, which proves that someone's out there, and I admit it's a spectacular location with the binary stars. But it's a dead end, Bill. There's nothing there. There's no reason for me to keep going back."

"Well," Whitson said, "maybe you just need some time off to get away from all this, clear your mind. The good news is we're closing down the day after tomorrow for the Holidays. Don't bother coming in tomorrow. You don't have any journeys scheduled anyway. Hell, Christmas is just a week away. Go shopping. Put up a tree. Get into the spirit of the thing and forget about the Starmind Project for awhile. Relax and come back after the New Year with a whole new slate. I bet this tower problem will have gone away by then."

That night he dreamt. In his dream, he was back on the moonlet, standing by the tower while overhead a river of blazing light flowed between two stars. The tower was as silent and mysterious as ever, but he kept feeling that someone was watching him. This presence, whatever it was, wasn't in the tower, though. It seemed to always be behind him, just out of sight. He kept turning and looking around, but he never saw anything. In time it all faded away, and he woke up.

"You need to rest," his boss had said. Waking up from the dream, he felt that Bill had been right. This was the first time one of his *esp* journeys had bled over into his dream life. Perhaps he was more tired than he suspected. And perhaps there was something in his subconscious that was tying him to this tower, interfering with his work.

So now that he had time off, what was "resting" going to look like? How should he spend the time? There were a couple of books he been putting off reading and there was a movie he'd recorded the other night that he hadn't seen yet. But the more he thought about it, the more he wanted to get out of his house and mingle with people. It was as if he hadn't quite come back from his dream, as if some part of him had been left behind on that airless moonlet with the mysterious tower. He felt a curious sense of disassociation as if he weren't quite all here.

It was an occupational hazard of the work they were doing. They'd all experienced it at one time or another. Journeying to other worlds, looking to make contact with whoever or whatever was Out There, was draining. You could end up feeling a bit thin, as if you had left more and more of yourself somewhere in the vastness of the interstellar emptiness.

He decided to have breakfast at a new café that had opened and which he'd passed by every day driving to the Project center. Then he would spend the day doing what normal people did this time of year.

He was by nature a solitary person, and his work emphasized this characteristic. He kept his occupation secret from his neighbors. There was glamour around being what the press had labeled a "starshaman" when the project had started out, but unlike some of his team, like Michael, it wasn't something he wanted to capitalize on. He preferred to stay out of the limelight and to go unnoticed.

But right now, he wanted to be with others. He would go to the mall to do some Christmas shopping. He had no doubt there'd be lots of others doing just the same thing. Being jostled in a crowd, something he normally avoided, now felt like just the thing he needed.

As it turned out, he did very little shopping. He didn't have a family of his own, and while he had very close friendships, there weren't that many of them. It didn't take him long to find the presents he wanted to give. But he did lots of window shopping, reveling in the spirit of the season and enjoying just wandering about and looking at all the diverse things that human ingenuity and artistry—not to mention the desire to make money—could come up with.

By the time he came home, he felt caught up in the Christmas spirit, something he hadn't really felt in a long time. In recent years, Christmas had been a kind of throw-away event for him: a few presents, a couple of parties with friends, maybe a movie on Christmas Day. To be honest, he didn't think about it that much.

But now he felt totally into the holiday, so much so that he decided he was going to put up a tree and decorate it. This was something he hadn't done in years. He would have to buy the lights and ornaments as he had nothing like that. He looked forward to it. It would be an adventure.

He spent the next two days on what he called his tree project. He found a tree that would fit in his small living room and visited numerous stores that sold decorations, very deliberately choosing the ornaments he wanted. He played Christmas carols incessantly on his sound system, letting his playlist loop endless around and around. There were times when he wondered just what had gotten into him, but he was having too much fun to worry about it. He thought of the barren, dead landscape of the little moon with its mysterious white tower, and it made him even more desirous to bring the color and warmth of Christmas into his life by contrast.

He had no more dreams.

The day after he got his tree up and decorated, he had a phone call from Allison. "I need to talk with you, Jake," she said. "Can we meet for coffee?" He agreed. He wasn't surprised she had called him. In his late forties, he was the oldest of the team, older by five years than Whitson, his immediate boss. Allison as the youngest of them all had particularly attached herself to him as a father figure and often came to him for advice.

Of all the team, he felt she had the most potential. She was by far the most sensitive, able to tune in on faint mental traces. She was the only one who had managed to discover a whole city. Unfortunately, it had been abandoned, parts of it in ruins. It lay on the coast of what must have been a sea at one time, but the water had long ago disappeared. Like Mars, the planet was now a barren desert, bereft of life. Although all of them had been able to home in on her mental trail and visit the city themselves at different times, it had proved a disappointment. It had held nothing that could help them in their quest. But none of the rest of them had come close to finding anything like it.

An hour later, he was sitting across a table from her at a local café. Ugly Christmas sweaters were all the rage among the twenty-somethings, and she had on one of the ugliest he'd seen. It was red with green Christmas wreaths decorating the arms while on the front, a large brown and white Rudolph grinned at him with an electronic nose that blinked on and off. To complete the ensemble, Christmas tree earrings dangled under Allison's blond curls.

The brightness—one might even say the garishness—of her clothing was in contrast to the solemn look on her face. Allison wore her heart on her sleeve. She did not try hard to hide whatever she was feeling in the moment, something that at times irked the cool and very mental Thomas, the Shanghai-born mathematician on their team. Thomas was never less than polite, but he still had a way of communicating his disapproval when Allison's emotions became too evident.

"Allison," Jake said, "your clothes say Merry Christmas, but your face says something else. What's up?"

She pushed her coffee cup around on the table for a moment, then looked at him with a despairing expression. "Jake, I think I need to leave the Project."

Surprise struck him dumb for a moment. If anyone was gung ho about what they were doing, it was Allison. "Whoa!" he said. "Why?"

"Have you talked with Bill lately?"

"No, not since I left. What's happened?"

"Well, the day after you left, Bill said he'd gotten a memo that morning from the Project head, Dr. Halverston. It seems they're upgrading our computers with a whole new software package. In fact, when we come back after New Year's, it will be all installed."

"New software?" He'd heard nothing about this and wondered why Bill hadn't called him. But then he remembered Bill had wanted him to take a break from the Project. He probably figured he would tell him when Jake returned from the Holidays. "So, what does it do?"

"It's designed to control emotional leakage."

"Emotional leakage? What's that?"

"They feel that our emotions may be getting in our way, keeping us from holding a pure mental projection, one that can be more easily controlled and directed."

Jake laughed. "You're kidding, right?"

"I wish I were. You know the problem with direction, yes? They can boost our *esp* field out into the universe but we have little control over where we end up or what we see."

"Yes." It was, in effect, the problem he was having getting away from the tower.

"Well, they think it's our emotions that are screwing things up."

Jake laughed. "Allison, that's ridiculous!"

"No, it's not funny, Jake. That's exactly what they think. Bill said Halverston's psych team—the one's developing this program--believe we're being distracted by our feelings."

"What did Bill think about this?"

She snorted. "You know Bill. He wants to please management. Besides, Thomas is a hundred percent for this change. He agrees with the memo."

"Well, we all know what Thomas is like!"

Ignoring his comment, she went on. "Bill says it won't affect our normal lives, but when we're on a journey, we'll be able to think faster and more clearly because we'll...we'll... Oh, Jake, it's bad enough they rob us of our bodies by putting us in the isolation tanks. Now they want to take away our feelings. We'll all be robots! I don't want to be a robot! I won't stay in the Project if they try to make me a robot."

He reached across the table and took her hand. "Allison," he said as soothingly as he could, "Allison, no one's going to turn into a robot."

"But Shoi's already done it!"

"Done what? Turned into a robot?" He chuckled. "He wouldn't have far to go."

Allison looked around the café and then leaned towards him as if imparting secrets vital to national security. The movement brought Rudolph's blinking nose closer to his face, and in spite of her seriousness, he suddenly wanted to laugh. "Thomas has tried it out. The new software."

"When? He didn't do it in the Enterprise, did he? We would have known."

"No, remember when he left for a few days a couple of weeks ago? He had volunteered to be a test subject. *The* test subject. You know he's a computer whiz. I guess it made him a perfect candidate since he could understand the math involved in the new program or something. I don't know." She shook her head. "Anyway, he told us at the meeting he'd tried it and…and he said it was amazing. He said he could think faster and more clearly and logically."

"Like Spock," Jake said, then realized when he saw incomprehension on her face that she didn't know who he was talking about. "Never mind. He liked it?"

"He loved it. And that's not all." She leaned forward even closer, her voice dropping to a whisper. "He found a technological artifact on that test run. You can imagine how excited that made the brass feel!"

Jake whistled under his breath. Finding technology was a goal of the Project, but one that was rarely achieved. "What was it?"

"A space station, Jake! A whole space station orbiting a planet."

Hearing this, Jake felt excited himself. A space station was high tech, higher than anything else they'd ever found. Who knew what new insights it could offer? "Inhabited?" he whispered.

"No. A derelict. But apparently filled with stuff. Thomas couldn't stay long enough to investigate. The test program was on a strict timer, but he knows how to find it again. Bill said it will be one of the first targets we'll go for next year."

"But Allison," he said, sitting back and taking a sip of his coffee, now getting cold. "This is wonderful news. This is exactly the kind of thing we've been looking for."

"No, no. You don't understand." She pushed her coffee cup away and reached for his hands. He realized with surprise she was going to link with him, something they almost never did away from the Project. Among themselves, the team members had discovered they could sometimes telepathically share mental images and thoughts if they touched each other, a side effect of the psychic work they were doing. But it was not something they normally did in public. "Thomas linked with us to show us what he'd seen. Here, see?"

He closed his eyes, and images formed in his mind. Below him was a planet, but he could see no details. The whole thing was shrouded in clouds, reminding him of pictures he'd seen of Venus. He looked up, and floating before him was a large sphere with bands running around it. Here and there were what looked like hatches and even windows. The top and bottom of the sphere bristled with antenna and dishes, obviously indicating a sophisticated communications technology. But the whole artifact was dark, lit on one side by a distant sun. And it was dark in another way. Something about it repelled him. He couldn't say what. It was a feeling, a sense of danger. He knew he didn't want to get nearer to it. Yet he was moving toward it, towards the darkness, the image repeating Shoi's actions as he had zeroed in on the station.

Then the image vanished, and he was back in the café, his eyes refocusing on Rudolph's blinking nose. He blinked a couple of times and looked up at Allison's worried expression. He shook his head. "Whew!" he said. "I think I need another cup of coffee!" He stood up. "You?"

She nodded yes, and he went to see the barista. When he returned with their coffees, she took the cup he offered and asked, "Did you feel it? The evil?"

It wasn't a word he'd have used, but then Allison was given to exaggeration. Still, he couldn't deny the foreboding he'd felt. "Well, I don't know about evil," he said, "but I know I didn't want to get near the place."

She nodded. "Everyone else in the team felt the same way. But not Thomas. When we tried to explain to him what we felt, he just didn't get it. He said he never felt anything like that. He accused us of projecting our own feelings onto the image."

"It's possible…"

"But Jake, we didn't. I didn't. The fact is some part of Thomas felt the danger as well but couldn't tell him because the program he was using blocked input from his emotions. We were picking up what he really experienced including the reactions the software kept from him.

I'm sure of it." She took a sip of coffee. "Do you see? He felt he'd been enhanced but in fact, he'd been crippled. And that's what they want to do with all of us! That's why I can't stay!"

They broke up soon after, Allison claiming she had Christmas shopping to do. By then, she'd calmed down, but when they parted, in spite of anything he could say, she was adamant that she was going to quit the Project if the new upgrades came into effect.

The meeting left Jake feeling troubled. He felt the team would be weakened by losing Allison. Her youth was an asset; she brought a fresh energy to their work and often perspectives that none of the rest of them had thought about. Also, though he hadn't wanted to say so and add fuel to Allison's mood, he had to admit he wasn't happy about what the Project was planning to do. He had no desire to have anyone mucking about with his emotions, either. It felt wrong. And then there was the image of the space station and the foreboding he'd felt. His own mood darkening, he felt the joy that he'd been experiencing the past couple of days threatening to dissipate.

He decided what he had to do to keep from losing the Christmas spirit was to decorate his house. So he spent the morning shopping for outdoor lights and interesting displays, all of which he immediately went home and began putting up. When he was finished, a nativity scene graced his small lawn, Santa and his reindeer and sleigh were lit up on his roof, and the house and its windows and front door were outlined in twinkling colored lights. Looking at what he'd done, he realized he'd probably gone overboard, but his happy mood had returned, so he didn't care.

By then it was late afternoon, and it was turning dark. He went inside, fixed himself a cup of coffee and collapsed in his favorite chair in the living room, feeling tired but satisfied. Turning on the television, he saw that a local station was showing Dickens's *A Christmas Carol*, with George C. Scott in the role of Ebenezer Scrooge. This brought back a flood of nostalgia for him, for he remembered this had been his father's favorite Christmas story. Every year, his Dad had watched several versions of the story, each with different actors, including one production that was a musical and another that had been done with singing puppets. He'd gotten sick of it and hadn't watched any movie about Scrooge since he'd left home over twenty years ago. But now, it was just what he wanted, so he spent the evening watching and cheering as an old miser became transformed.

That night he once more dreamt that he was on the airless moonlet with the twin stars overhead. But this time, he could see a dark sphere in orbit above him. It seemed to be moving towards him. In the distance was the white tower, and he knew that if he could reach it, he would be safe from whatever was in the sphere. He began to run, but as happens in dreams, the more he ran, the less distance he seemed to cover. The tower always seemed just out of reach. At the same time, he felt something nearby, running with him, but when he tried to see what or who it was, there was never anything there. And then the dream simply faded away, and he slept deeply, awakening late in the morning.

He awoke to sunlight streaming through his bedroom window. He lay in bed, wondering. It was not like him to sleep late. Was he really so tired? As he lay there, memory of his dream came back to him in bits and pieces. It seemed that try as he might to put the Project out of his mind, it kept coming back in one form or another.

He got up and eventually made his way to his kitchen to fix coffee and breakfast. He thought about the dream and about the meeting with Allison the day before. And he thought about what it meant to be a starshaman.

Starshamans. He chuckled to himself as he cracked an egg open over a skillet. Officially, when they were on a journey into the cosmos, they were known as Enhanced Shamanic Projections, giving a new use for the old initials ESP or Extra-Sensory Perception. However, when the Starmind Project had been announced, a reporter had called them "starshamans" and the name had stuck.

The origin of the Project lay some six years earlier when Dr. John Halverson, a neurobiologist, had done brain scans of three Peruvian shamans while they were in trance and allegedly undergoing a shamanic journey, a projection of their consciousness out of the body into an invisible dimension. He had discovered that their brains showed a distinctive pattern of activation. He developed a software program to replicate this pattern and had himself fitted with a neurological helmet that would transmit the appropriate sequence of electrical signals into his brain. To his astonishment, when he activated the program, he found himself standing outside his body.

Jake had heard the story of what happened next many times. Halverson's mother had apparently been a believer in psychic phenomena such as out-of-the-body-travel. When he found himself standing in his lab and looking back at his body lying on a couch, he had the thought, "What until I tell Mother about this!" He'd no sooner thought this than he found himself standing next to his mother in her kitchen, watching her put a tray of cookies into the oven. He watched her bustling about for a minute or two, and then the program automatically brought him back to his body.

As soon as he opened his eyes, he yelled for his cell phone. When a graduate student handed it to him, he immediately called his mother and asked her what she was doing. "Why, I'm baking cookies," she said. At that point he knew he'd made a breakthrough in the study of consciousness.

Halverson postulated the existence of the *psi-field*, an energy field around and permeating the human body that was the true locus of consciousness and through which a person's consciousness could be projected out into the world beyond his or her body. This discovery burst like an explosion in society, challenging many long-held ideas about the nature of reality and of human identity while supporting others. But Halverson didn't care about the philosophical, religious, or scientific debates. He had a different goal in mind. He wanted information.

While the egg sizzled in the skillet, Jake wrapped two slices of bacon in a paper towel and put them in the microwave. He also put the two halves of an English muffin into the toaster. Two minutes later, the bacon came out perfectly cooked just as his egg was ready and the muffin popped up. He had his routine down.

Carrying his breakfast to the table, he sat down and began to eat, his thoughts continuing along the memory trail. Halverson knew that what he called the psi-field had been known for millennia by psychics, occultists, and shamans, even though a materialist culture had denied it. All he had done was prove its existence in a way that science respected. But he had also developed a technological way of producing and enhancing the effect, which became the *ESP* or Enhanced Shamanic Projection techniques that the Project used. He knew that shamans had always used the projection of consciousness or shamanic "journeys" to gain information that could help their community. He wanted to do the same but on a grander scale.

There was a tradition in shamanic cultures that from time to time shamans had succeeded in contacting and communicating telepathically with intelligences on other worlds in the cosmos. With his new insights, Halverson saw no reason to doubt this and decided this was what he wished to do. He felt that with the enhancing techniques that computers and neurological technology offered, it would be possible to have a program in which trained individuals launched their consciousnesses — their Enhanced Shamanic Projections or *esps* — into the cosmos in an attempt to contact an alien civilization. The technological and cultural rewards if they succeeded, Halverson thought, would be immense, including, he hoped, contact with a civilization that could help humanity minimize or even turn back the effects of accelerating climate change. He was able to convince a number of rich donors of his vision, which led to the birth of the Starmind Project and the starshamans.

Jake got up and carried his dishes to the sink where he washed them, then put them away. Being a starshaman, he thought, had become his life. He couldn't imagine leaving the program the way Allison was contemplating. But he had to admit that so far they'd had many interesting experiences but no luck in actually contacting any extra-terrestrial consciousnesses.

They all could feel that such alien consciousnesses were out there, somewhere; they could feel the traces they left — like footpaths — in the mental dimensions in which they worked. But try as they might to attune to them and follow them to their source, they had not yet succeeded. Instead, they always seemed to get sidetracked somehow. They found themselves going to empty planets and moons and occasionally to places where strange artifacts or structures such as the white tower existed that showed that someone had once been there. It was why Allison's discovery of a whole city had been so exciting, even though little had come from it.

Perhaps it is a problem of emotion, he thought. *Maybe a program that shuts that part of us down and concentrates our mental focus is what is needed to follow the mental trails we can sense.* But it felt wrong to him. Already at times he felt like an extension of the computer software projected into the universe and not like a full human being. Wouldn't this new software only enhance that effect? Unlike Allison, he was willing to try it, but he felt it would not take them where they wished to go.

He went into the living room and plugged in the Christmas tree lights. Then he sat down in his favorite chair. After all his activity of the past three days, he had decided he would relax with a good book today. There were several he wanted to read, all stacked next to his chair waiting for him to have the time to get into them. He picked one up and settled back to read.

"What is the purpose of this?"

The voice was clear in his head. Startled, he dropped the book he was holding and looked around. To his astonishment, he saw a figure sitting on the sofa across the room, and not just any figure. It was Santa Claus... or a ghost of Santa Claus, as he could see right through him. The figure was calmly puffing on an old-fashioned curved pipe, and he could see the smoke rising from the bowl and drifting away into the room. Behind a pair of spectacles, two very blue eyes twinkled at him.

"Oh my God!" he exclaimed, pressing himself back in the chair. The figure immediately disappeared.

His heart beating, he got up and went over to the sofa, passing his hand through the air where the Santa figure had been sitting. He felt nothing. The vision or hallucination or whatever it was, was gone. *Maybe I've gone too far into the Christmas spirit,* he thought. There were critics and nay-sayers that said that sending people out of their bodies would drive them insane. *Could they be right? Is this a sign that I'm cracking up?*

He sat down again. *No, I feel alright,* he thought. *I don't feel crazy.* He bent forward and picked up the book from where he'd dropped it.

"I'm sorry," came the voice again. "I didn't mean to startle you."

He looked back over at the sofa, but it was empty. However, he felt a presence in the room. "Who are you?" he asked. "Is someone really here?"

"Oh, yes," came the reply. "I'm really here. " And slowly, he saw the shape of Santa Claus reappear on the sofa.

"Santa Claus?" He exclaimed, his eyes widening. He felt the book fall out of his fingers again, but he didn't care.

"Is that what you call this figure? Thank you. I didn't know. It seems everywhere present in your world. Is it one of your gods?"

"One of our gods....Omigod!" The intuition hit him like a bolt of lightning. "You're an *esp!*"

The figure smiled at him. "I don't know the reference....ah, I get the meaning from your mind. Yes! This is so. I'm a star traveler like you."

Jake felt chills running up and down his body. *Wait till the team hears about this!* He thought. "A star traveler? Oh my gosh, where are you from? Who are you? How did you get here? Why do you look like Santa Claus?" The questions tumbled out. *Slow down,* he told himself sternly. *This is a First Contact. You don't want to make a fool of yourself.*

The being laughed. "You have a lot of questions. I do, too! Curiosity is a trait of star travelers like us!"

Jake began breathing deeply to calm down. "I don't know who you are or how you came here, but thank you for coming. You have no idea how long we've been looking to contact someone like you." Then he said, pointing at the apparition on the couch. "You don't really look like Santa Claus, do you?"

"No. I draw this shape from your mind and from the surroundings. Taking a form familiar to you helps us to communicate, does it not?"

Jake had to laugh. "Well, yes and no. Yes, since you look like a fellow human. No, because you look like Santa Claus, a magical figure of myth and story. It's as difficult to believe I'm talking to Santa as it is that I'm talking to a visitor from another world."

"Ah. Thank you for explaining. Where I come from, we make no distinction between a 'figure of myth' and a figure of flesh. For us, reality has many layers and takes many forms. Would you prefer if I chose another form?"

"What about showing me your true form?"

"No, we have protocols about that. We have found it better, at first at least, to look like the species we're contacting." He smiled. "I could look like you, if you wish."

"God, no, don't do that! You look just fine. I…I'm enjoying talking to Santa. Please stay the way you are."

"Then I will!" The Santa-figure grinned. "I've been around you for several of your days, observing and learning your language and the pattern of your thinking. But there is always so much more to learn. So let us satisfy a little bit of curiosity. You ask a question, then I'll ask a question!"

Jake thought. There was so much he wanted to know. He had so many questions. But what came out was "What is your world like? Your civilization?"

"Ah, a good question. But how to explain it? It is a civilization of wonder."

"You mean it's wonderful? I can only imagine it would be!"

The Santa-figure thought for a moment. "No, I mean...I mean, our civilization is based in wonder. It connects us to the universe. We pursue wonder, and our pursuit is never exhausted for there is so much wonder in the universe, not least of which is life itself."

Then he gestured with his pipe to the Christmas tree. "Now it's my turn. I was wondering what that is for? Why do you bring one of these plants—a 'tree'?—into your home and cover it with lights and other baubles?"

How to explain Christmas and Christmas trees to an alien visitor, Jake wondered. "You've come at a time of celebration," he said. "A time of joy. We call it Christmas. It has many meanings for many people. One meaning is the renewal of life, of which this tree is a symbol. But you speak of wonder. I think that is at the heart of Christmas, as well. The magic of wonder."

The Santa-figure was silent for a moment. "Yes," he said, finally. "I get the meaning from your mind. Beautiful! Then we are not so different! We have a celebration like this on my world, a time of giving thanks for the gifts of life and the abundance of love in our lives, a time to celebrate wonder."

"Really? Well, then you should know that the shape you carry, that of Santa Claus, personifies the spirit of giving. He is a magical being who embodies wonder."

"I am delighted, then, to wear his form." The figure puffed on the pipe a bit, then he continued. "Your searching for star neighbors is not unknown to us. I am part of a confederation of worlds, and we have become aware of your efforts. In fact, members of your species have contacted us in the past, but your world was not ready then to participate in a cosmic community. Are you ready now? We don't know, but we are hopeful. The fact that you have celebrations like this makes me hopeful."

"I'm glad to hear this. But why have you come now? We've been searching for you for months now."

"You have not been looking in the right places or in the right way. We have been curious about this. When members of your species contacted us before, they came as full people. But you go out into the universe as if blindfolded; you place limits on yourselves, and this restricts the wavelengths you can encounter. You don't see us even when we are near. We don't understand this."

Jake thought about this, but it made no sense to him. "I'm afraid I can't explain it. I don't understand what you're saying. Where should we be looking and how?"

The Santa-figure shrugged. "I can't help you. All I can say is that when I see you now, you are a full person, but when we see you moving through the dimensional layers, it's as if you are half-people, only partly there. We try to contact you, but you are like ghosts to us. You are not full-bodied. You are...." The figure paused, obviously thinking how to put what he was trying to say into words. "You are thinned out."

"I don't understand."

"I'm sorry. Something is not right in what you are doing. Until you correct it, you cannot make contact with us. I cannot explain it better than this."

"But you've been able to make this contact now...with me. Why me?"

"Because you made contact with *us*."

"I? But how? When?"

"You do not remember? It was at the *oral*...the...the white tower, you called it. Where the two suns embrace."

"But nothing ever happened there. I didn't do anything."

"I can't explain it to you. You must have done something. An *oral* is a sensor. They are scattered all over the galaxy. You were attracted to one of them. It registers when it senses a mind-traveling species and draws the traveler to itself. Then if the traveler knows how to interact with it, it sends us a signal that this has happened. Then the *oral* opens the portal to our worlds." He thought for a moment. "Yes, this is curious. The *oral* sent us the signal...this is why my world came to you. But the portal didn't open. Why?"

Jake shrugged. "I have no idea. Nothing ever passed between me and the...the *oral*. It certainly never opened up to me."

"Well, you see, it is a mystery. The universe is filled with them. But until it opens up and the portal is revealed, there is little more I can do."

"You mean, unless the tower...the *oral*...opens up and lets me in, there won't be further contact between us?"

"Brother star traveler, I fear this is true. The oral is a lock, but you must be the key."

There was silence between them, then the Santa-figure spoke again.

"My time is nearly up. It takes energy to engage with you in this way, and I must go to replenish myself."

"That I *do* understand," Jake said. "It's the same with us."

"Before I go, I must give you a word of advice. As I have said, for reasons I don't understand, when you go forth into the mind of the cosmos, you narrow and thin yourselves. This restricts the wavelengths you can encounter to those where life itself is thin."

"This is why we keep finding empty worlds or only ruins?"

"Yes. But there is danger. There are worlds on these wavelengths that have failed and sundered themselves from the galactic whole. You risk contacting them, especially if you become more thin than you are. If you do, the results may not be to your liking. They are dark worlds that know they are dying and are consumed with hatred for all that lives. You do not want them to have access to your world. They are hungry. Their life is contracting, and they can pull you into their contraction."

"Like a black hole of life...."

"Yes."

"But how does a whole world fail? I don't understand..."

"Many ways. One is by cutting itself into little pieces that forget they're part of a larger whole. But mostly they give themselves up to hungers that are never satisfied. Now I must go."

"But wait! How would we recognize such a...a *sundered* world?"

The Santa-figure thought for a moment. "If you travel with a full body and a full heart, you would not encounter such worlds for you would not ride their wavelengths, or if for some reason you did, you would know them instantly and be repelled. But when you are thin or if you become thinner, I don't know. You might not know....until it is too late."

"This is not helpful!"

"I'm sorry." Jake saw that the figure was getting more transparent. "I've enjoyed our talk. Your world is interesting. I hope you can open the *oral* fully and join us. I would love to see you again." The figure disappeared. Jake felt a great disappointment rising up within him. So close, and yet seemingly so far.

Suddenly Santa reappeared, faintly but definitely there. "I almost forgot," he said. "There is one thing that came to me." He pointed his pipe in the direction of the Christmas tree. "Look there. It has what you need. Now, how does this go? Oh yes!" He smiled, and laid a finger on the side of his nose. "Ho Ho Ho! Merry Christmas!"

And with that, he disappeared, and this time Jake knew his stellar visitor had truly gone.

It was late into the evening, and the room had gone dark with the setting of the sun. Only the glow of the lights on the Christmas tree provided illumination. But Jake didn't care. He sat in the shadows in his chair, his mind going over and over what had happened. He had gotten his notebook and had written down everything that his visitor had said as closely as he could remember it. Then he thought about it all.

It had come down to three questions. What did it mean when the alien had said that they traveled thin? And what had he done that had triggered the *oral*, the white tower? And what did his visitor mean when he'd pointed to the Christmas tree and said, *Look there, it has what you need?*

He had gone around and around with these three questions, but nothing had resolved itself. At times he felt close to an answer, the way it feels when a forgotten word sits right on the tip of the tongue. Then he would lose it, and mystery would close in around him. And always in the background was the admonition about the danger of discovering sundered worlds. When he thought of this, he could not help but remember the image Allison had shared with him, the world that Thomas had found on his augmented journey. The world that had repelled him so. *Are we about to open ourselves to one of these worlds? Are we in jeopardy? How will we know?*

He finally got up and fixed himself some dinner, surprised to discover that he was ravenous. When he was done, he tidied up, then got himself a notebook and a pen and went back to his chair. He turned on a table lamp next to the chair so he could see to write, but he left the rest of the room dark, the better to enjoy the lights on the Christmas tree. He wrote down each of his three questions.

The first was this: What did I do to trigger the *oral*, the white tower? He had decided it had to be something he'd done on the last visit. His star visitor had said he'd only been present for a few days. He closed his eyes and tried to visualize everything that had happened, everything that he had done. But it had been no different than before. He'd walked across the plain to the tower. He'd touched it.

He paused. It still amazed him that he could interact with physical objects when he was in *esp*-form, for basically he was no more than his visitor had been, a mental projection. There were a number of theories about this, the main one being that he was actually interacting with a replica of the physical object existing on the mental wavelength his *esp* was on. But no one, at least no scientist, knew for sure.

Anyway, he had touched the tower, and it had been as solid as ever. Had that been it? But he had touched it many times before, as had others in his team. So that couldn't have been it.

After he touched it, he walked around the tower as he often did. Then he had left. He scratched his head with the non-writing end of his pen. *Wait,* he thought. *I was going to leave, but I didn't. I paused. I remember. I felt something…a…a kinship with the tower…no, it was more than that. It was affection. For a moment, I thought of the tower as a fellow being, and I reached out and touched it…and my fingers sank into it. The tower wall rippled as if my fingers had gone into water. But it happened so fast. There was so little to it. I thought I'd imagined it.*

But what if he hadn't imagined it? What if it had really happened? What if that was the moment of contact? He had felt affection for the *oral* and had responded to it as if it were a living being. *Was that what counted? Affection? Love? A sense of life?*

He knew he had to go back. He had to visit the tower again and try it out. Perhaps the key was to see and treat it as a being, not as a thing.

The Starmind Project was housed at the local university about a mile and a half from his house. On good days, he walked there and back each day. If he could get access to the Enterprise room, he could be over there in a matter of minutes. But he would need to clear it with his supervisor. No member of the team used the equipment without permission and logging it in.

He pulled his cell phone out of his pocket and rang Bill Whitson's number. It rang twice, and then Whitson's deep voice answered. "Whitson."

"Bill, this is Jake."

"Jake! How are you doing? Getting some rest?"

"Yes. Absolutely. Doing the Christmas thing. But Bill, listen, I have a favor to ask."

"OK. What is it?"

"I need to take a journey back to the white tower. I've been thinking about it, and I have a theory I'd like to try out. Is it possible for me to come in and plug in? I'd like to test this out as soon as I can." He felt it better not to share with Whitson that he'd had a visitor from the stars. That could come later if his theory proved right.

There was a pause on the other end, then Whitson said, "Jake, I'm sorry. That's not possible. The Enterprise is completely down. All the computers are being upgraded and the chambers, too."

"It's the new software, isn't it? You're already installing it?"

"One of the team told you about it? Yeah, that's it. I didn't want to bother you, but I should have known the gossip tree would let you know."

"Bill, are you sure this is a good idea?"

"Who told you? I bet it was Allison, right? She was very upset with the new protocols. Said we were turning everyone into robots. Was it Allison?"

Jake saw no reason to keep it secret. "Yeah, it was."

"Jake, don't let her color your thinking about this. I think this is a great step forward, just what we've needed. In fact, Thomas had fantastic results with the new software—did Allison tell you that?"

"Yes."

"All it does is sharpen your focus so you're like a thin blade cutting through the ethers, getting right to the point." Whitson's tone of voice showed his excitement.

"Wait," said Jake. "What did you just say?"

"I said, the software focuses and sharpens your mind."

"No, no, you said something about a thin blade..?"

Whitson chuckled. "Just a metaphor, Jake. Yeah, mind like a thin blade, a rapier getting right to the point, no more distractions."

"Bill, thanks. I've got to go."

"But, Jake, wait! What's your new theory? What did you hope to find at the tower?"

"Sorry, Bill, can't tell you now. Need to think about it some more. Talk with you later. And Merry Christmas!"

He hung up, his mind racing with excitement. *A thin blade.* "*You seem so thin to us.*" *Was this what his visitor was talking about? But like Bill said, it's just a metaphor. We're not really thin. Or are we? What was it Allison had said?* "*They took away my body and now they want to take away my emotions!*" *Isn't that getting thin...and thinner?*

He thought again about the origins of the Starmind Project. It had arisen out of the shamanic experience, the power of shamans to project themselves into non-ordinary reality and non-corporeal space. What Halverson had done was to couple that capacity to technology in order to enhance it. But maybe it hadn't enhanced it? Maybe it had lessened it?

Jake remembered a conversation he had with Bill Whitson a week or so after he'd been brought into the program. He'd asked Bill why all the candidates were non-shamans. Why not use actual practicing shamans, individuals who already knew how to project themselves into other dimensions? Bill said none of the traditional shamans that Halverson had approached wanted anything to do with the project when they discovered what he had in mind. "They didn't want to contact alien beings?" he had asked. "No," Bill had replied. "They didn't want to go into the sensory isolation chambers." They'd told Halverson it was exactly the wrong thing to do, that nothing good would come of it. One of them had said, "You can't journey without connection to the world."

But Halverson, Whitson had said, wouldn't accept this. It introduced too many variables. How could one control the outcomes? Too sloppy. So Halverson said, in effect, to hell with the shamans, we'll train people in our own way. A powerful tool in doing so was the isolation tank that allowed the mind to focus without distraction, gaining more power.

And now, thought Jake, *he wants to isolate the mind still further by eliminating the distraction of feelings. Talk about getting thinner! Was this what his visitor meant?*

Or was there more to it than that?

He didn't have enough information. Unfortunately, the only place he could think of where he could get the information he needed was at the white tower, and with the Project closed down, he had no way to get there.

Or did he?

What had his visitor said? "Members of your species have contacted us before." Of course they had. The ancient shamans had contacted other worlds. That's where Halverson got the idea for the Starmind Project in the first place. And those men and women hadn't had isolation tanks or computers. They'd only had themselves. Their full selves.

If they could do it, there was no reason he couldn't do it.

He just had to figure out how.

He decided to sleep on it, half-expecting, half-hoping that he'd have a dream in which all would be revealed. But he woke early in the morning with no memory of anything that might have happened while he was asleep. *I guess I just need to do some experimenting,* he thought, as he climbed out of bed.

During his own training at the Project, he had briefly studied some of the traditions and techniques of shamanism, but it had been a cursory affair. The official word was that they were activating an ancient human capability in an entirely new and better way with the aid of modern technology. Halverson didn't want their minds "cluttered", as he had put it, with shamanic lore and tradition. He wanted his *esps*, his "starshamans," to come to the experience "fresh", free of cultural expectations.

He knew that a natural shamanic journey, one unenhanced with computer-guided neurological boosting, was usually a matter of going into a trance state during which the consciousness-field of the shaman would travel in the non-corporeal dimensions. The trance state could be induced in various ways such as through the use of psychotropic drugs or the hypnotic effect of the drone produced by steady, rhythmic drumming. But he had never experienced this process. Drugs had been frowned on in the Project as interfering with a clear mental state, and drums were an archaic technique that had no place in a modern laboratory. In the Project, he had simply shut off all sensory input through the use of the isolation chamber, the computer had activated the appropriate neural circuitry in his brain, and then he was off and flying. He'd never experienced deliberately inducing a trance state and didn't know how to go about it.

But he had been trained in holding a steady mental state in order to focus his intention. A clear intention was key in his work. In some ways, he was like a tracker, looking for the energetic traces of life and intelligence. The non-corporeal dimensions through which he traveled into the cosmos—Halverson called them noetic fields—were like vast plains and forests through which animals had made innumerable paths. He had to discern the paths to follow based on their mental "smell". If he'd been a bloodhound, intention was his nose, sniffing out the right direction. It got him where he was trying to go.

Except when it didn't, he thought wryly, thinking of the white tower.

So even though he might not have experience inducing a trance state, he knew how to control his mind, which had to be close. And he had another thing in his favor. He knew he could leave his body. He had a knowledge born of experience of what it felt like to project his consciousness out of his physical form. It was not something he did outside of the controlled environment of the Project; it was frowned upon and discouraged. Still, he knew the internal signs that marked the transition, and he was sure he could replicate them at will.

And the pull of the white tower that had been creating a problem for him would work in his favor, for this time it was where he wanted to go, where he intended to go.

No time like the present to try it out, he thought. He sat back in his chair, relaxing his body and composing his mind. He closed his mind and called up an image of the white tower and fixed his intention upon it. *This is where I wish to go.* He focused his thinking upon it. Then he recalled what it was like to soar out of his body, to "go astral" as they sometimes called it. He summoned up the memory of what the transition felt like and focused upon it, seeking to activate the internal forces that would make the shift. He held his breath. He could feel something stirring.

And then, nothing.

Nothing happened.

He sat there for a few minutes more, trying in different ways to make the transition, but without success. This was what the computer and the neurological stimulation was for. Without it, he felt stuck. He felt like an engine with plenty of fuel but no starter, no spark plug to ignite the process.

Finally he got up, stretched and decided the best thing would be to take a walk. Then he'd come back, have something to eat and do some research. Surely he could find the information he needed to make the journey.

After breakfast, he hit the Internet, reading whatever he could find about shamanism and its traditional practices. Much of it, he discovered quickly, was of little use to him. Some information was too academic and anthropological. Other was too filled with fantasy and wish-fulfillment. A number of websites he found were simply trying to sell workshops or were using the word "shaman" as a marketing gimmick. He began to despair of finding anything useful.

Then he came across a passage that described many traditional shamans as "journeying between the Upper and Lower Worlds by ascending or descending a mystical tree." This caught his attention. He looked back in his notes from the day before. He'd written, "What did my visitor mean when he said, *Look there, it has what you need,* and pointed at the Christmas tree?" Was the tree itself the key?

He looked across the room at his Christmas tree. At the moment, the lights were turned off. It was a beautiful tree, and he was pleased with the ornaments he'd chosen, but he couldn't see how it could help him with his problem. *The shamanic tree's just a metaphor anyway,* he thought. *The shamans aren't climbing up and down real trees to go into trance.*

He felt he'd come to a dead end and gave himself permission to take the afternoon off. He went to a movie, then to dinner at a new Greek restaurant that had opened in town which he'd been wanting to try. He deliberately kept his mind away from the problem he was facing, letting his subconscious work on it undisturbed.

It was dark when he got home. A timer had turned on all the Christmas lights and displays. He thought his little house had never looked so magical. He bowed to the figures in the manger on his lawn and waved to the Santa Claus on his roof as he let himself in. Standing in the shadows of the living room, he felt reluctant to turn on the room lights. Instead, he went over and turned on the Christmas tree lights. Their colors filled the room, and he sat down in his chair intending just sit there to enjoy them. But the warm room, the dinner and two glasses of wine had their way with him. He fell asleep.

He woke up to the chime of a clock tolling the midnight hour. He realized with a start that it was now Christmas Day. He thought he should get up and go to bed so he could sleep and greet the new day properly. But he felt too comfortable to move. It was pleasant sitting in the dark and the glow of the Christmas tree lights. *I'll just wait for Santa,* he thought. *Maybe he'll come back and take me to his world. Now* that *would be a Christmas gift!*

Thinking of worlds, he remembered something odd his visitor had said. "The *oral* sent us the signal...this is why my world came to you." Not, "this is why I came to you" but "my *world* came to you." What the hell did that mean? Another mystery. He wished he'd had more time to ask questions of his visitor.

But at the moment, he felt too relaxed to think about it. Instead, he just sat there in the soft light from the tree, letting his thoughts drift. He remembered Christmases as a boy. Doing just what he was doing now, sitting in the dark with the Christmas tree lights aglow, was one of his favorite things to do. Looking at the lights and ornaments, they had seemed to him like so many stars and worlds waiting to be explored. He would imagine stepping into the tree as if it were a living portal to another place, a mysterious world.

A living portal....

He sat up. Of course! The *oral* was a living portal, too. He failed to open it because he hadn't approached it right. He'd thought of it simply as an ancient building, an artifact, a *thing*. Yet, it was alive, though he had no idea how that could be. He realized that when, for just an instance, he had reached out and touched it with affection as if it were a living being, *that* was when it had responded and sent a signal.

Now he knew more than ever he needed to get back to the tower. He needed to return to the portal. But this was the same problem he'd been wrestling with for two days. How was he going to get back there?

"Look there, it has what you need," his visitor had said.

The tree has what I need. But what? The oral *is a portal. Did he mean that the tree was a portal, too? From what he'd read, it certainly was for native shamans. But how? How could a Christmas tree be a portal anywhere? Yes, it looks pretty, but it's just a tree.*

He felt his frustration coming back and knew that wouldn't help. He could feel that he was close to an answer, if he could just get his feelings under control. He had to think clearly. He couldn't afford emotion.

Or maybe that was the problem. Maybe he was over-thinking this, becoming too "thin", in the words of his visitor. Maybe what he needed was more emotion. Maybe he needed to feel more.

And what do I feel when I look at the Christmas tree? My mind says it's just a tree, but is it, really? Is anything "just" anything, or is everything so much more than we can see or the mind can label?

He let go and let himself become a child again. What had he felt when he'd sat with the tree those many Christmases ago? He'd felt wonder. He'd felt that the Christmas tree was a doorway to a world where anything was possible, a world of wonder, a world of magic, no, more than that, a world where he was magical, where life was magical.

He laughed out loud as the knowledge blossomed out from his heart. He wanted to get up and dance around and shout out what he knew, but he was afraid to move. He was afraid he'd break the spell, for that's what it felt like to him. He and the tree were in a spell together. It was a partnership. *Everything is a partnership,* he thought.

He realized his visitor had truly given him all the information he needed. He just hadn't recognized it or had misunderstood. His guest had said, "Then the *oral* opens the portal to our worlds." *I thought he meant the* oral *was the portal and it opened up. But he meant the oral would have opened me up. I'm the portal!*

He knew he was right. He could feel it. He could feel it in the way the Christmas tree had opened him up as a child to a sense of an expanded life of wonder and magic. *It opened me to a larger self, a larger me.*

Jake realized that was what the old shamans knew. The tree wasn't just a tree. It was *connectedness*. It was *life*. Everything in the universe is connected because everything is alive. That was also what the shamans knew. The universe is alive, and when they journeyed, they did so by opening to the living connections between themselves and the worlds they wished to visit. They and the universe became a living portal to where they wished to go.

He knew the magic and the power to get to the white tower wasn't in the Christmas tree as a thing. It was in the magic it could evoke in him if he could partner with all the magic it represents, the magic of Christmas, the magic of love, the magic of life.

He laughed again. *No time like the present!* He could feel the excitement, the power rising in him. *Let's go to the tower!*

He sat back in his chair and composed himself. But he made no effort to control his excitement or his joy. Rather, he let them expand. *Connectedness* is the tree, he told himself, and he let his energy, his love, his sense of life, his excitement reach out to all the things around him as if he were a spider spinning a web. It was the exact opposite of what he'd been trained to do. *Which means,* he thought wryly, *this is the right way to do it.*

In that moment, he understood what his visitor had meant when he'd said "my world came to you." One went out into the universe not as a solitary individual but as part of a community of life, part of a world. Once again, it was the power of connectedness.

As he thought this, he understood as well where Halverson had gotten it wrong, the fundamental error at the heart of the Starmind Project that crippled the starshamans and made them so much *thinner* in presence and power than they could have been. Halverson had recorded brain patterns and used them to stimulate the shamanic journey. But this was like reducing the Mona Lisa to a paint-by-numbers picture. Yes, anyone could follow the pattern and put in the colors that matched the numbers. But that wasn't the experience that Leonardo Da Vinci had had. The resulting picture would not be vibrant with the creative spirit.

It was obvious to him now. The brain patterns were only a reflection of something else, and that something else was what he was experiencing in this moment, what true shamans had experienced for millennia. It was the full vibrant sense of being connected to and part of all life. It was, and he had no better word for it, the fullness of love for the world, for the universe, for life.

And with this realization, he slipped freely and gracefully out of his body, not into the limited dimension of the mind alone but into the full presence of the living cosmos. He stood in a rounded body of Light that bore no comparison to the truly thin structure of the *esp*, the mental field in which he'd learned to travel. *Allison was right,* he thought. *We have been crippled. ESP isn't really Enhanced Shamanic Projection but Enervated Shamanic Projection.*

He looked at the Christmas tree before him, itself glowing not only with its myriad ornaments and lights but with the whole mystery and magic of the Christmas spirit, a spirit that and enfolded him as he stepped into it.

He *opened.*

He stood on a small rise on an airless moonlet, and all around him was an aura of silvery Light. *Now,* he thought, *now for the first time, I am truly a Starshaman!*

Above him two stars held each other in gravity's embrace while between them flowed a blazing river of light. It was a familiar place, but now he saw it in a new way, a fuller way. He could sense that the two stars truly were loving each other, sharing themselves in many more ways than his human consciousness could truly comprehend. But he felt the power of their Light, their love, bathing this moonlet, and he knew this was why the tower was here. It drew on this energy and used it to cast its web to find those like himself who were exploring the non-corporeal dimensions of the cosmos looking for partners, looking for other civilizations.

Now the tower didn't seem forlorn or abandoned at all. It was itself radiant with light and with life. *How could I not have felt it before,* he thought. *Actually, I did feel it, but I didn't know what I was feeling.*

But now he did. He set off walking towards it. He could have teleported himself, he knew, but he wanted to feel the effect as he walked into its field of energy and attuned to its life.

Hello, friend, he thought in its direction, and he thought he saw the surface of the tower ripple in response.

It was a short walk. Then he was standing next to it. *I'm sorry I didn't recognize what and who you were when I was here before. I was too thin to really see you.* He reached out and touched the tower—the *oral*—and opened his heart and mind to it, feeling the connections forming, feeling the love. It was the perfect guardian for a civilization that allowed contact only with those beings who could share its connections and meet it in a communion that honored the life in all things. *Thank you inviting me in,* he thought.

The tower rippled and disappeared. In its place was a sphere of light. The *oral*. Grinning, he stepped into it, felt something shift and expand in himself, and then he was somewhere else.

He was standing on a low dias in what appeared to be the middle of a large, circular hall. Around him, graceful columns held up a domed roof which glowed with its own radiance, casting a soft light throughout the room. As far as he could tell, he was alone.

But then, the space between two of the columns shimmered, creating an oval of blue light. Through it, stepped Santa Claus, looking much more solid and real than when he had appeared in his living room. Jake smiled in appreciation. *Of course it would be Santa.*

The being approached him, and a familiar voice said, "You made it! I'm so glad. I thought you would. Should I say, Ho Ho Ho?"

Jake laughed. "That would be in keeping with the season."

As Santa got closer, though, he began to turn transparent again until he disappeared. In his place was something else that looked at first to Jake like a giant snail. But this snail had a shell that was decorated with symbols and hung with ribbons, while under it were hundreds of little protuberances that were moving to propel the being along. The upper part of its body was covered with a garment. And there was a proper head at the same height as Jake's. It was not exactly human-looking by any means, but it had eyes—three of them--and a nose and a mouth. A mouth that was curved in what Jake thought could only be a smile.

"I haven't shocked you, I hope?" the snail said, the words forming in his mind. "I thought since you made it this far, you needed to see me as I really am. I can become Santa again if you would be more comfortable."

Jake took a deep breath. "No, I want to see you as you are. Friends don't hide themselves from each other."

The snail's mouth curved upward even more. "Ah, excellent! I think you're going to fit in here very well." It lowered its voice to a confidential whisper. "Though wait till you see what some of the others look like..."

Jake laughed. "I'm sure my species will be just as strange to them." And he thought of his team, his fellow starshamans. How would he ever be able to describe all this to them?

As if the snail had read his mind, which, Jake realized, it probably had, the being said, "I think we had better let your friends know where you are and what you've accomplished. We need to become part of your connections. There's a long road ahead of us, I think, to bring your world into our confederacy, but shall we take the first step? Oh, and by the way, my name is Ameron."

"And I'm Jake." He automatically held out his hand, but realized his new friend, like an earthly snail, had no upper appendages on its body. But the side of Ameron's body rippled and a thin tentacle with four smaller fingers extended out to grip his own hand with surprising strength. The being's flesh felt warm and ordinary, just like that of another human.

"Ah, I see. You were extending a greeting, and I was extending my hand to form a transmission link. How wonderful! We have much to learn about each other!"

"A transmission link?" Then Jake understood, for it was the same process he and Allison had used when they had met and that all of them used to share images too complex for words.

"How else shall we talk to your friends except through you? Shall we begin?"

Jake felt a surge of energy flow into him from Ameron's appendage, and suddenly he was standing in the room at the Project they called the Enterprise. There in the room were all the members of his team and Bill Whitson as well. Looking at them, he realized they were meeting in a dream, that in fact, their bodies were asleep in the early hours of Christmas morning. He realized that once they understood what had happened, the Starmind project would come to a halt, for they couldn't proceed in the way it had been going. *Well, they wanted to upgrade everything. This will be more than they were expecting! It's time to throw out the paint-by-numbers and become true artists.*

They looked at him through the eyes of their dream bodies, and their eyes widened when they saw Ameron next to him. "Hello, my friends," Jake said. "Have I got a Christmas present for you!"

THE END

The House Christmas

By David Spangler

"Daddy, tell me another story!" Emily looked up at me from under the covers, her brown eyes sparkling with excitement. She looked no closer to being sleepy than when I'd tucked her into bed a half-hour earlier.

"Emily Rose, look what time it is. If I tell you another story, it will have to be the one about a certain young girl who got no presents on Christmas morning because she never went to sleep and Santa couldn't come."

"But why does Santa need me to be asleep to come? The mailman comes, and I'm not alseep."

I sighed. "Because Santa's shy. If he thinks people are going to see him work his magic, he won't come."

Emily frowned. "If I had magic, I'd want everyone to see it!"

"I'm sure you would, but you're not Santa, so it's time to go to sleep."

"Is Santa going to help you bring the presents in from the garage?" She smiled sweetly up at me. Her eyes looked innocent, but I knew a trap when I heard one.

"What presents?" I responded with, I hoped, equal innocence.

"The ones under the tarp in the corner?"

Damn! I thought. *I thought those were well-hidden.* "Emily Rose, you haven't become a snoop, have you?"

She grinned.

"Sometimes, Santa asks parents to store presents for him ahead of time," Alexandra's voice said from behind me. I hadn't heard my wife come up behind me. "After all, his sleigh can only hold so much at one time. This saves him making extra trips."

"Oh," said Emily, considering this. It was obviously something she hadn't thought of. "OK!" she said.

Alex gave me a squeeze. "Why don't I finish up here and you go do something else? I think as long as the family storyteller is in the bedroom, Emily's not going to go to sleep."

Surrending to this happy logic, I got up from my chair and gratefully gave it over to my wife. "Good idea," I said. "Good night, Emily Rose. Merry Christmas!"

"Merry Christmas, Daddy!" A hand poked out from under the covers and gave me a wave good bye. I stepped out of the bedroom into the hall, closing the door behind me. I went into the kitchen, poured myself and my wife a glass of wine, and took the drinks into the living room where a small fire burned in the fireplace next to the Christmas tree. A few minutes later, Alex appeared and sank into the sofa next to me. I handed her her wine.

"Thank you," I said. "That bit about storing presents for Santa was brilliant. I wasn't sure what I was going to say."

She poked me playfully. "Thank you. Next year you'll have to do a better job hiding everything!"

I grinned back. "Five years old and she thinks like a twenty-something. She's wicked smart, that one. She'll be a handful when she gets older."

"What do you mean, 'when she gets older'? She's a handful now!" Alex laughed wryly. "When her Dad's a successful children's novelist..."

"And her Mom's a successful lawyer..."

"...she's got a lot of imagination..."

"...and smarts." I poked her back, making her giggle and almost spilling her wine. I smiled to myself. I was very proud of my two women.

We sat for awhile in silence, just appreciating the fire in the fireplace and the glow of the Christmas tree nearby. Finally, I looked at the clock on the wall. "You figure she's asleep?" I asked.

"I would say so. She went off pretty quickly after you left."

"So, it's safe to bring out Santa's stash?"

She got up. "Let's do it!"

We went out to the garage, removed the tarp and gathered up the presents to bring indoors. It took us a couple of trips. Then I disappeared into my study to get the gifts I had for Alex, knowing that she was bringing out what she'd stashed away in a little-used hamper in the laundry room (I'd done some snooping around myself).

When we were done, and the presents were all arranged around the tree, I said, "It's still early. How about a movie?"

"*Miracle on 34th Street,*" she responded immediately. I'd been hoping to watch an old Cary Grant film, *The Bishop's Wife,* but I knew she liked the trial scenes in the Maureen O'Hara movie and I had to admit that Edmund Gwenn made a perfect Santa. *It's only an hour and a half long,* I thought. *Maybe we'll watch both.*

Alex went off to make some popcorn, and I got the movie ready in the DVD player. Then I got out some chocolate truffles I'd saved for just this moment. I went into the kitchen to help my wife with the popcorn, then refilled our wine glasses. A moment later, we were on the couch, ready to go.

"Wait!" said my wife, pushing herself away from me and getting up. "We've forgotten Hermann!"

Hermann was an heirloom passed down from mother to daughter through Alexandra's family ever since they had emigrated to the United States from Switzerland at the start of the Second World War and long before then, apparently. It was a carved wooden figure about a foot in height. It was a thin, old man with a long beard wearing a hooded robe and holding a staff taller than himself in one hand. Attached to a belt at his side was a lantern, and on his back was a pack. On the statue's base was carved the word *Wallfahrer*, which meant *Pilgrim* in German.

Alex ran off into the bedroom and brought out the box in which Hermann was carefully packed. As she was unwrapping the bubble wrap around him, I asked, "Tell me again why he's called Hermann?"

She shrugged. "I don't know. He's always been called Hermann. My grandmother said her grandmother called him Hermann. Maybe that was the name of the person who carved him, or maybe it was the name of the man who was the inspiration for the figure. No way to know now."

I watched as my wife picked up the figure and put him on the mantle next to the glass of milk and the plate of cookies. This was her family tradition. On Christmas Eve, Herman was placed on the mantle of the fireplace, or if there were no fireplace, on a table near the Christmas Tree. My wife thought it was because he was an early version of Father Christmas, but to me, the figure was more reminescent of the image on *The Hermit* card in the Rider-Waite Tarot deck.

Whoever he was, the family tradition was that if Hermann was on the mantle at Christmas Eve, he would come alive and bless the house with good fortune for the year to come. He would stand on the mantle throughout Christmas Day and then be packed away until the following December. Again, there was no reason why this was so. It was just the way it was done, and I had to admit, it added to the mystery and magic of the figure. And I couldn't deny the fact that since I'd married Alex seven years earlier and Hermann had become part of my Christmas celebration, I really had had good fortune in my life, including several best-selling novels for children and teenagers.

Herman now in his proper place and Alexandra back on the couch beside me, we turned off the lights and turned on the movie. Whether it was the warmth from the fire, the effects of the wine, or the comfort of snuggling up close together after a very busy day, before the final credits rolled on the movie, we were both asleep. And so we remained as the minute hand moved inexorably towards midnight.

The soft chiming of the grandfather clock woke me up. The room was in shadow. The television was dark, the dvd player having shut itself off when the movie ended. The fire was only a few red embers in the fireplace. Most of the light came from the Christmas tree.

I saw something moving in the shadows on the mantle over the fireplace. *What is that,* I wondered sleepily. With a thrill of alarm, I came more awake as I had my next thought. *Is it a mouse...or a rat?*

My sudden movement woke Alexandra. "We..we sure conked out," she said sleepily, starting to stretch, but I laid an arm across her and whispered, "Shhh. I think there's a mouse on the mantle. Probably going after the cookies. If we frighten it, I won't be able to catch it."

She sat up, too, and peered into the shadows. "Michael," she said, "that's no mouse. It's Hermann!"

I looked more closely. As I did so, the movement and shadows resolved themselves into the figure of the old man who, impossibly, was in fact now moving slowly, as if stretching and waking himself up. *Earthquake?* I thought. *Could a tremor just shake the mantle?*

As the two of us watched dumbfounded, the figure reached down with one hand and unhooked the lantern at its belt. As he raised it up, it began to glow until it gave off a piercing white light. He held it above his head, looking more than ever like the Hermit figure in the Tarot.

"Omigod!" said Alex, whispering excitedly and gripping my arm. "It's true! The legend is true!"

"That's impossible!" I whispered back, unable to shift my gaze away from the figure. Except in my stories, wooden carved figures simply didn't come alive and move around. *We must still be asleep. This is a dream.*

She ignored me. "My grandmother told me that twice she'd seen Hermann come alive on Christmas Eve. It was part of the legend around him, that he was a magical figure, but you know, I never believed her. I thought it was just an old woman's fancy or a Christmas story she was making up for me."

"Alex, she *must* have been making it up. This is just a dream. It's not really happening." I started to get up, figuring this would wake me up.

Alexandra pushed me back. "No, no, Michael. Be still. It's not a dream. It's magic!" Her face seemed transported in the glow of the Christmas tree and the light of the Pilgrim's lantern. She looked happy!

Hearing my very rational, very logical, very no-nonsense wife talk about magic and look the way she did disturbed me. Magic was my territory, not hers. Yet here she was accepting with no hesitation what I found difficult to accept, that some carved statue was coming to life and moving about. *It has to be a dream!* I thought. *We'll laugh about it in the morning.*

I thought I'd play along, though, with the logic of the dream. "If Hermann does this every year," I whispered to her, "how come we haven't seen this before?"

"I don't know. My mother never saw it happen, either. But my grandmother said she'd seen it twice. I just never believed her. But it's true!"

At this point, Hermann began to swing the lantern back and forth, the light reflecting off the plate of cookies and the glass of milk. He looked for all the world like a conductor on a train, signalling the engineer that he could start up. He was absolutely silent, but there was no question he was signaling.

Signaling to what?

I began to feel a chill up and down my backbone. If this wasn't a dream, if, in fact, this was some manifestation of an ancient European magic, then who knew what might come next? Before the presence of the unknown and the mysterious, I snuggled closer to my wife who, to my chagrin, was handling all this much better than I was. "My God, Alex, you're believing in this!"

"Of course! It's right before our eyes! Come on, Michael, you're seeing it, too. Now hush!"

There flashed through my mind Marley's question to Scrooge when he'd appeared before the old miser in Dickens' *A Christmas Carol*. "Why do you doubt your senses?" And Scrooge had said, ""Because a little thing affects them. A slight disorder of the stomach makes them cheats. You may be an undigested bit of beef, a blot of mustard, a crumb of cheese, a fragment of an underdone potato. There's more of gravy than of grave about you, whatever you are!" That was OK for Scrooge to say, but I felt fine. I doubted Hermann was a crumb of popcorn or an underdone piece of chocolate truffle.

As the old pilgrim continued to swing his lantern, all around us, the room began to glow. At first it was so faint I wasn't sure it was happening. But then, as the radiance gradually increased, I realized that everything in the room—the walls, the ceiling, the furniture, the rug on the floor, everything—was radiating a soft, silvery-blue light. It was as if the room and all within it, including the couch on which we sat, was bursting into a cold fire. Yet, though it scared me, I could feel no discomfort from it.

Glancing at my wife's face, I could see her expression transfixed with joy and wonder as she looked about. It was, I knew, her childhood fantasy come to life. She was at last having the experience her grandmother had had and who knew how many great-grandmothers before her. She certainly wasn't afraid of what was happening, so I knew I had to master my own fear.

As if she knew what was going on in my mind, she squeezed my hand and said, "It's OK, Michael. There's nothing to fear here."

"Easy for you to say," I whispered back, but I felt better. Indeed, as the shock began to pass, my storyteller's curiosity and my own sense of wonder began coming to the fore.

My resolve, though, was tested by what came next. For out of the light something began to emerge. It started as a rippling with no detail within it. Then I could see what looked like dozens and dozens of threads—*no*, I thought, *worms*—wriggling out of the light. These worm-like threads were themselves glowing with the same silvery light and as they moved, they began to turn into tiny figures, most almost humanoid, some not. I could even see some of them up close as they emerged from the couch on which Alex and I were sitting. They indeed looked like miniature people with very sharp features and pointed ears.

"House fairies," breathed Alex."

"Your grandmother told you about them, too, I guess," I whispered back.

"Yes! Isn't it wonderful?" I could hardly believe the enraptured woman sitting next to me was the same Alexandra who was such a fierce and logical litigant in a courtroom.

Watching these tiny beings literally pour out of the woodwork, as well as out of the furniture and other things in the room, what came to my mind was the scene in the first *Lord of the Rings* movie when the Fellowship is in the Mines of Moria and hordes of goblins are crawling down the columns and rocky walls, all converging on Frodo and the others. In this case, all these little beings seemed to be converging on the Christmas tree where they stopped, forming a circle around its base. The space these beings occupied seemed very fuzzy for although there were scores of them, they also seemed to blend together in ways that allowed them to crowd together and occupy a small space.

I remembered that in the *Lord of the Rings*, when the goblins had all surrounded the Fellowship, the demonic Balrog had appeared. I wondered what would appear here.

I felt a pressure on my shoulder between Alex and myself. Looking, I saw one of the silvery beings sitting there. He was definitely humanoid and male, and his head was right next to our ears. "Cute old geezer, isn't he, swinging his lantern like that. Calling us out when the time's come. We don't really need it anymore. Never did, comes to that, but don't let him know. We humor him along. Makes him feel important, and what's the harm?"

I gawked at the being. "Alex....there's a thing on my shoulder...it's speaking!"

The little being looked at me, his eyes widening. "You're seeing us, aren't you? Mortals don't usually see us," he said in a high-pitched voice.

"Omigod!" I whispered. "Are you really *talking*? To *us*?"

"Do you see any other mortals around?"

Great, I thought. *A house fairy with lip.*

"Oh, I'm so grateful," Alex whispered to the little being. "My grandmother told me about your people, but I never expected to see you!"

The little being bowed from his waist. "My pleasure, m'am, I'm sure."

"So why *are* we seeing you?" I asked.

The little being shrugged in a very human way. "Who knows? Maybe *he* did it." He pointed to Hermann standing on the mantle. "He's very magical in his way. Someone with knowledge of the fae carved him. for something of our essence is in him. He might have opened your eyes."

The house fairy shook his head. "This is supposed to be a secret, but he forgets now and then. Getting old, you know." He paused, his face screwed up in thought. "Then again, perhaps She willed it." I could hear the capital "S" in the tone of his voice.

"She?" Alex asked.

"The One who is coming," the being replied. *Ah*, I thought, *a female Balrog.*

"But where have you all come from," I asked.

The being made a sweeping gesture that took in the room and probably the house beyond. "From all this. We come from the things you have made and built, the things you use."

"You mean, you live in the furniture?"

"And the floors, and the walls, and in everything."

"Everything. You mean, all this...everything in the house, even the house is alive?"

"Not alive. Filled with life. Yes."

"Filled with life...with beings like you." I was having a hard time wrapping my mind around the implications of this.

He looked at me askance, then turned to Alex's ear. I could hear him whisper, "He's slow, this one, isn't he?"

"Hey, wait a minute," I said, but Alex just grinned. "Not all the time," she said. "He's just shocked. He'll get over it. He's got a good imagination."

"Humph," said the little being. "If anyone should be shocked, it's me. Mortals ignore us all the time. I never thought I'd be seen by one—well, two—of you, much less talk with you."

I was going to make some smart remark in return when both Alex and the little house fairy elbowed me, one in the ribs, the other in my ear. "Hush," they both said. Looking around, I became aware that something was indeed coming. I could feel it. It was like the room was becoming more full.

Then I saw a change coming over the Christmas tree. Although its lights burned as brightly as ever, it was as if they were obscured by a mist that was flowing out from between the branches. As I watched, this mist coalesced into the form of a woman—a very beautiful and very human looking woman. She was covered with a silvery blue light, and her hair was pure silver flowing down the side of her face and over her gown, if gown is what it was. I heard Alex's indrawn breath as she saw this radiant being standing in front of our tree, and I felt more than heard a gasp and a shiver of pleasure from the little being on my shoulder. "It's Her," he squeaked with obvious pleasure.

"Who?" I whispered, not daring—or willing, I must admit—to take my eyes off the figure before me.

"The House Angel," said our little companion reverently.

The woman—or angel—opened her arms and hands out to the circle of little beings clustered before her around the tree, and I felt a collective sigh pass through them. Then as if it were moving down from the top of the tree, a silvery light flowed into her and out from her, gathering us all in its embrace. I felt a deep calm and sense of gratitude come over me. I felt blessed, and I knew that all the little beings gathered in the room were feelng this blessing as well. It united Alex and me in a loving communion with all the life that filled our house.

As this happened, I saw all the little beings begin to glow just a little bit brighter as if they had been given new life and energy, which, I'm sure, is exactly what happened.

"You can do this for us, too, you know," said the little being perched on my shoulder. "Just love us now and then and give us appreciation. It's not easy living in your things. We spend most of our time being ignored and forgotten…and when you humans get angry with each other, oh my, we feel it. Yes, indeed we do, and it's not pleasant!" He scowled at me. "If it weren't for the Lady—the angel of the house—I doubt few of us would stay among you."

"But why do you stay here? I mean, why are you living in our things?"

He looked at me as if I were daft. "We have to live somewhere! And you need the life we bring. You don't want to live surrounded by lifeless things, let me tell you!" He shivered at the thought.

"Honey," said Alex, touching me on the leg. "Look…something else is happening."

At first, I couldn't see anything beyond the light radiated by the house angel standing just in front of the tree. Then I noticed she was turning to her right, towards the hearth. Looking in that direction, I saw a swirl of color spinning in the air. It grew larger and larger, and suddenly it coalesced and he was there.

Santa Claus.

I could feel my eyes widening. Furniture fairies. House angels.

Now Santa Claus?

I closed my eyes, then opened them and looked again. No doubt. The red-and-white suited figure with the black boots and black sash was all too familiar. I suddenly wished Emily was awake to see this. It would make her a believer in Santa forever...or at least for another couple of years!

"It's Santa!" whispered Alex.

"You're surprised to see him?" said the little being sitting between us. "Weren't you expecting him?"

"Honestly?" I said. "No. I mean, Santa's just a myth."

The furniture fairy hooted with laughter. "A myth! Why, mortal, to us, you're more of a myth than he is!" He hooted again.

All the little beings who had clustered around the tree now moved over to surround Santa. We saw figures jumping up and down with joy. The life in the house was celebrating Christmas! As we watched, Santa brought his large sack down from his shoulder and laid it carefully on the floor. He then started to open it.

"Omigod," I breathed. "Is he leaving presents?"

"Presents? What's this about presents? He's bringing replacements!"

"Replacements?" asked Alex, her eyes glued to Santa.

"Well, you don't expect us to stay in your houses forever, do you? Like I said, it's not an easy job! It tires us out. So once a year, Santa comes and takes a lot of us home to recover, leaving the next shift to take our places." He frowned, kicking at the air and hitting my shoulder instead. "Unfortunately, I've still got two years to go on my contract.... No North Pole for me this trip."

By now, Santa had his bag open, and out from it came trooping a number of little beings. They looked around, blinked, bowed to the house angel, then began streaming off in all directions, disappearing into the walls, the floor, the chairs, tables, sofas...into everything. They were joined by a few others who had been standing in the cluster on the floor. I assumed those were those who also hadn't finished their contracts or who wished to stay. But the majority of them clustered around Santa were obviously leaving, and from what I could see, they couldn't wait to leave. They laughed and cavorted and turned somersaults as they all disappeared into Santa's bag. I wondered what it said about the kind of house Alex and I created.

I turned to the little being between us. "That's what Santa does? He's a bus driver delivering and picking up fairies?"

"A bus driver?" said the little being said indignantly. "What bus driver? Santa's a Heart. He circulates life throughout your mortal world. He brings fresh life in and takes tired life away to be renewed. Like I say, he's a Heart!"

"A Heart..." I repeated, and I could hear even myself capitalizing the word.

"Yes. Listen, mortal, Santa's been doing this for as long as you humans have been making houses and things for us to live in. He's in charge of bringing life into your things and keeping it fresh. Not an easy job, let me tell you, especially since you stopped believing in us." He laughed with amazement. "You think Santa started with your Christmas?" He hooted again. "Far from it! Of course, he doesn't always look like that," he added, indicating the red-garbed figure. "You moderns gave him that form to work with."

By then, all the house fairies that were leaving had snuggled into Santa's bag. He closed it up, swung it up on his back, and bowed to the house angel. She reached out and touched him on his head, and I could see a stream of starry light flowing out from her to him. Then he began to swirl, turning into a whirlpool of color in the middle of the air which quickly disappeared.

Standing in the place where Santa had been was one of the new fairies. It was looking around, as if it didn't know where to go or what to do. The angel bent down, and the two of them conversed. Then she pointed to a large teddy bear lying under the tree, largely obscured by a couple of boxes that had slid on top of it. The stuffed bear was one of the presents we'd gotten for Emily. The little being brightened and gave a little hop. Then it scurried over and disappeared into the bear's furry tummy.

"Looks like he was a teddy bear fairy," the little being said. "How nice! They have the cushy job cause children automatically love them. At least at first. Then it can get nasty..." He turned and frowned at me. "I hope your daughter treats him right. No pulling out the stuffing when she gets tired of him."

"Oh...oh," I stammered. "I..I'll see to it." I could see my world view was going to need some readjusting.

"Yes, we'll make sure she treats him well," said my wife more affirmingly. "And we'll be sure to love all of you, now that we know you're there."

Suddenly the light brightened about us. We'd been looking at the little being between us, but looking up, we saw the house angel bending over us, a sweet smile on her face. Her hands reached out and touched both of us on the head. I could feel the shimmering energy flowing into me.

"Oh!" said Alex. "Oh!" I'm sure I said something equally meaningful, but I don't remember.

Then the angel stepped back into the tree and disappeared.

The little being hopped down from my shoulder and landed on the back of the sofa. "Well, I guess that's that for this year. Glad to meet your acquaintance, mortals. Don't forget us! Remember, it's not just Santa. You can be Hearts, too!"

With that, he vanished into the upholstery.

I don't know how long Alex and I sat there. We were both loath to disturb the magical feeling in the room. At one point, I glanced up and saw that Hermann was once again his wooden self.

Finally, knowing that Emily would be up before the crack of dawn, we headed off to bed. On the way, I drank some of the milk and took a bite of cookie. Santa may be real, I thought, but I still needed to keep up the appearances in this world.

As we expected, Emily was up early, and the next couple of hours were spent opening presents and going through all the rituals of Christmas morning. With this difference: as I walked about through the house, I found myself touching things in a loving way and saying things like, "Good morning! Merry Christmas! I...I love you. Thank you for being in our house." And I'm sure it wasn't my imagination that I began to feel a response. I felt love and appreciation flowing back to me. Imagination or not, it felt good!

The world had become a magical, living place, and with a little bit of love, we could keep that magic alive. *Next year*, I thought, *there won't be so many fairies anxious to leave this house! We'll be the best Hearts on the block!*

Later, after all the presents were opened and breakfast had been had, Alex and I were seated on the sofa admiring the tree. Sitting on the floor, Emily was holding her new teddy bear. "Oh," she said, "I love you, Wendy Bear!" And she gave it a hug.

"Like I said, a cushy job," came a high-pitched voice. Looking down, I saw a little head sticking up from the sofa cushion looking over in Emily's direction.

"Don't worry, " I said, reaching down and stroking the cushion and sending all the love I could to the beings within it. "We'll love you, too, Sofa Bear."

A little hand gave me a high five and disappeared.

THE END

The Spirit Of Christmas

Martin Goodman loved Christmas. What was there not to love? There were bright and colorful lights on houses, turning neighborhoods into fairylands. There were festooned Christmas Trees and happy songs. There were good things to eat. There was merrymaking. There was goodwill.

And stores had sales. Yes, shopping could get a little frenetic and crazy, he admitted to friends, but what other time of the year were people so obsessed with a spirit of giving?

Mostly, though, what Goodman loved was Santa Claus.

He filled his house with Santa figures. He put a giant inflatable balloon of Santa and his reindeer on the roof of his house and little cutout figures of Santa's elves on his lawn. He made Santa-shaped cookies with red and white frosting and a touch of chocolate for the black boots and gave them to neighbors and friends. He read *The Night Before Christmas* at least once a week and watched the movies *The Miracle of 34th Street* and *The Life and Adventures of Santa Claus* at least twice each in the month before December the 25th. And the strains of *Santa Claus Is Coming To Town* could often be heard coming from his house.

If you gave him a chance, Goodman could regale you with a history of Santa Claus from his beginnings in the figure of the Norse god Odin who hung upon a Yule tree through the adventures of St. Nicolas, the Bishop of Myra in what is now Turkey, who would throw gifts of gold coins down chimneys for the poor in his parish, to Father Christmas, Kris Kringle, Sinterklaas, and the modern depiction of Santa Claus in the writings of Clement Moore and the drawings of Thomas Nast.

On a corner of his mantle, there was a small nativity scene with the expected cast of characters: shepherds, sheep, wise men, Joseph, Mary, and of course, the baby Jesus. Christmas was, after all, a birthday. It was overshadowed, though, by a large snow globe showing Santa starting to climb down a chimney, his sack of toys on his back. And everywhere else in Goodman's house, Santa was the man of the hour. He was the jolly old elf, the spirit of giving, the master toymaker, the bringer of joy on Christmas mornings.

Many might have said, if they thought about such things at all, that Goodman was a pagan at heart, and while he saw himself as a good Christian, in the depths of his soul, he would not have protested overmuch. For him, Santa Claus was Christmas and Christmas was Santa Claus and all his magic.

So it was that on Christmas Eve, Martin Goodman sat in his favorite easy chair by his fireplace watching Tim Allen transform from a toy company executive into Santa Claus in what was his number one Christmas movie, *The Santa Clause*. As he did every year, he found himself wishing that some magic would strike him, too, and turn him into a magical being like Old Saint Nick. "Ho Ho Ho," he whispered to himself as he dozed off in the chair.

He woke up to the sound of the Santa clock on the fireplace mantle softly chiming the midnight hour. The fire had burned down to a few embers, the DVD had turned itself off so that the television screen was dark, and only the lights of the Christmas tree kept the room from being in total darkness.

"I like him, too."

The voice was rich and full, yet soft. It was a graceful voice, one that immediately inspired trust. But it also carried a hint of sadness.

Martin Goodman jerked up in his chair. "Who's that?" he demanded, looking about.

Shadows moved on his couch and resolved themselves into a figure sitting there, the dying light of the fire playing upon him. He seemed an ordinary man, but he was dressed in a brown robe that had a rope sash around the waist. He had dark hair that had a hint of curliness to it as it fell to just above his shoulders and a short, well-trimmed black beard. His eyes were dark as well, black perhaps, though Goodman really couldn't tell in the dimness of the light. The figure smiled, and the smile was warm and friendly. He'd been afraid, waking up to a stranger in his house, but the smile unaccountably put him at ease.

"Who are you?" Goodman asked.

"Don't you recognize me?"

Goodman thought. He certainly wasn't one of his neighbors. Besides, he was sure none of them would dress up in a robe and sneak into his house on Christmas Eve. He shook his head.

The figure sighed and gestured to the nativity scene tucked away almost out of sight on the mantelpiece behind the snow globe. Goodman looked. "You're a shepherd?" he asked, incredulously.

The man shook his head. "Well, there are those who call me such, but no. I'm not one of the shepherds."

"Then who....Oh!" Goodman's eyes grew round with surprise and awe. "You're not...not..."

"Is it such a shock, then? After all, you *are* celebrating my birthday."

"Omigod!" Goodman exclaimed, then said, "Oh, no, wait, I mean, O, you're God! You're the Lord?" He wondered if he should spring to his feet and then prostrate himself before the man on his sofa.

The figure laughed, and it was a pleasant sound that immediately made Goodman feel more at ease. "No more God than you," he said. "And in spite of what's been written, I'm no one's Lord. Though I would like to be everyone's friend."

"But you...you're the Christ! You're divine!"

"Again I say, no more than you. Can you believe this?"

Goodman hadn't ever thought about it. Theology wasn't his strong suit. But he wasn't about to argue with the Son of God. So he blurted out, "If you say so."

The figure nodded. "Well, we'll leave that for now. But please, call me Jesus. Most people do these days, though in my time in my country I was known as Yeshua."

"O...OK, er, Jesus." Goodman squirmed in his chair. "But why, Lor...I mean, Jesus...why are you here? Why have you come to me? If it's about my church attendance..."

Jesus laughed again. He seemed to laugh easily and often as if the world filled him with delight. "No, Martin. I'm not here about your church attendance. I'm here about your soul."

Goodman gulped. "My...my soul? Omigod! Am I going to hell?" He glanced wildly around the room, his gaze taking in all the Santa figures. Why didn't he have more statues of the Christ? How could he have overlooked him? He really *must* be a pagan, and now Jesus was here about his soul.

"Martin, calm down. No, you're not going to hell." Jesus gestured at all the Santas in various poses. "I told you, I like him, too. You've done nothing wrong. But..."

Goodman gulped again. *Here it comes,* he thought. The *"but...."*

"But I think I deserve equal time, don't you? After all, I, too, am the Christmas Spirit."

He felt like leaping from his chair and kneeling before the figure on his sofa in abject penance. "Oh, yes, oh yes, Jesus. You certainly are! Yes, forgive me! You *are* the Christmas Spirit."

"And so is Santa. And so," Jesus thrust out an arm and pointed right at Goodman, "are you."

"Me?" he squeaked. "Oh, well, yes, I do try to embody what...what Christmas is about."

"A moment ago, you were dreaming about being Santa, weren't you?"

"What? Oh, no! I mean, well, maybe. Is that wrong?"

Jesus laughed again. "Of course not. If more people really embodied Santa's joy and giving nature, the world would be a better place. But let me ask you a question. You watched a movie about a man turning into Santa Claus. But have you ever seen a movie about someone turning into me?"

Goodman thought, *Is this a trick question?* "No," he answered, "but how could they? I mean, you're the Savior. You're the Christ. People don't turn into *you!*"

Jesus sighed. "Yes, that's the problem, isn't it? Why is it easier to imagine becoming a magical being than to imagine becoming Christ?"

"I don't understand what you mean."

"No, you don't." He looked around the room at all the Santas. "Martin, you asked why I was here. I've come to give you a gift. See, I can be Santa, too!"

"A gift?"

"Yes, a Christmas gift. That's what people do on my birthday, isn't it?" He stood up. "As I said, I have a gift for your soul. Here, touch my robe."

Goodman stood up from his chair and reached out, gingerly touching the sleeve of Jesus' robe. There was a flash of light which made him close his eyes. When he opened them, he could see they were no longer in his living room. But where were they?

He looked around and saw they were in a room filled with babies in cribs. One wall was a window looking out at a corridor, and he could see several male faces looking in. Near them, a nurse was picking up one of the babies to show to one of the men.

They were in a hospital nursery.

"Don't be alarmed," Jesus said. "They can neither see us nor hear us." He swept his hand out in a gesture that took in the whole room and all the infants in it. "These are children born on Christmas Day."

"Christmas Day? But...but a moment ago it was Christmas night."

Jesus gave him a mock frown. "Do you think I'm limited by a little thing like time and space?"

"Oh...oh, no!"

"Pay attention, then, or you'll miss the point. All these children share my birthday. But the important thing is that they're born on *their* day, not Christ's Day."

"But you just said..."

"Look at these babies, Martin? Do they know what Christmas Day is? No. What they do know is that this is their first day on earth. For each of them, it's their day, not mine. The beginning of their great adventure on earth, their journey into mortality. For each of them, this is a holy day not because it's Christmas but because this is the day he or she came as a gift for the earth."

"A gift?"

"Yes, Martin. A gift. This really isn't complicated. What does it say in your scripture about me? 'For God so loved the world that he *gave* his only begotten son...' You see, I was a gift." He pointed to the children. "So are they." He then poked Goodman in the chest with his finger. "And so are you."

"I'm a gift?"

"Yes, Martin, just like me. God so loves the world that he sends each of us to be here, to bless it and to be blessed. Or, more precisely, each of us has a sacred part of ourselves—call it the soul—that loves the world and makes it possible for us to be here."

Goodman was struggling with this concept. He had never thought of himself as a gift to the world, much less that anyone had sent him. "But, Lor...I mean, Jesus. You were God's gift to save the world." He struggled to find words. "What kind of gift can I be? I'm sure I can't do what you did!"

"Why are you sure? Didn't I say explicitly—and it's right there in what was written down about me—that you all can and will do greater things than I did? Was I just talking to myself? Making it up?" This time Jesus was frowning for real.

"No, no, I'm sure you weren't....making it up, I mean. But how? You're the Son of God, for Christ's...I mean, for Your Sake! How can we do what you did?"

"Do you think you're not a child of God as well? What am I, a unique species all unto myself? I came out of my mother's womb the same as you. I took my first breath in the world and cried the same as you. I wore a body the same as you. We are the same, Martin."

"But..."

Jesus sighed. "It's the world savior thing, isn't it? That's what's bothering you."

"Well...."

"Take my sleeve again."

He did so, and again there was a blinding flash of light. When he could see, he found himself in the middle of smoke and flames as all around him a building burned.

"Ahh!" he screamed and pressed close to Jesus.

"Don't worry, Martin," Jesus said. "We can't be seen or heard and neither can we be harmed. But pay attention. Look over there..."

Goodman looked and saw a figure huddled in a corner of the burning room. It was a little girl. He pulled on Jesus's arm. "She'll burn. Save her!"

"Shhh. Wait a moment."

Out of a burning corridor, another figure came, looking at first like a hulking demon from hell, its face a mass of flames. Then Goodman saw it was a fireman, an oxygen tank on his back, with the fire reflecting in the mask of his protective helmet. The fireman made his way over to the little girl and picked her up. "I have you," he said to the child. "You're safe now."

Carefully, he made his way back down the corridor as other firemen directed streams of water into the flames around him. He'd no sooner gotten her to safety than the roof collapsed into the room where she had been curled up, causing an explosion of sparks and flames. Goodman involuntarily threw up his arms over his head and let out a panicked squeal.

There was a flash of light again, and they were standing on a street corner, watching the building burn and the firemen trying to control it. He could see the little girl lying on a gurney being lifted into an ambulance.

"She will be all right," Jesus said. "But let me ask you? Who was the savior here?"

"The fireman?"

"Yes. Remember, he is just a man, like you. He has a wife and three children. He likes Wendy's hamburgers. He roots for the Seattle Seahawks. Perfectly ordinary, you'd say. And everyday he puts his life on the line to save others. Is he not doing what I did?"

"Yes, but...but he didn't save the world!" Goodman insisted.

"He saved her world. For her, what other world is there? And in that moment, wasn't he saving both their worlds? He could have died in that fire with her."

"Yes, I understand what you're saying, but..."

"But you don't agree. My, but you are stubborn! All right, take my sleeve."

This time, they popped into one scene after another, staying just long enough for Goodman to see what was happening and then moving on. He saw a policeman disarming a man with a gun, he saw a teacher in a classroom, he saw a doctor doing surgery, he saw a nurse tending a patient, he saw a teenage girl giving a scarf and blanket to a homeless person, and a mother holding a child that had skinned her knee. Each time, Jesus said simply, "There's a world being saved."

When they stopped, they were standing on a hill overlooking Seattle where he lived. "There," said Jesus. "Do you see?"

Goodman nodded. "I get the point, yes. But still, these people are just doing their jobs."

"And what did you think I was doing? Humanity is our job, Martin. The World is our job. Maybe I made it more explicit in what I said and did, but all I was doing was living my life. I was meeting each moment and seeing how I could fill it with love. That's really all there is to it. Isn't that what these people were doing in their own way? Isn't this what you try to do?"

Goodman sighed. "When I remember to. I'm afraid I forget a lot."

"But you *do* remember. And in those moments when you do, love walks the earth. Christ walks the earth. Isn't that what Christmas is about? Helping you all to remember?" Jesus held out his sleeve, and Goodman took it. After the flash, he found himself back in his living room, surrounded with all his Santas.

Jesus looked about. "I do love these, too," he said. He picked up one of the Santa figures from an end table next to the sofa. A small deer was nestled against the bearded, white-garbed figure of Father Christmas while a rabbit sat in perfect safety at his feet and a red bird perched on his shoulder. "Isn't this cute? Who wouldn't want to be a Santa Claus like this with all the animals loving him?" He put the figure back on the mantle. "*I* wouldn't mind being Santa Claus!"

"But Jesus....you're...."

"I know. Don't say it."

Goodman grinned sheepishly. "Well, you *are* different! But then, I guess we all are, and that's the point, isn't it? We each bring God to the world in a unique way."

Jesus smiled. "See, the evening hasn't been a loss, after all! You can learn new things!" He swept out his arm to indicate all the Santas. "There's nothing wrong with this, Martin. Have as many Santas as you wish. But don't ignore me. Don't forget about me."

"Because it's your birthday."

"No. Because if you forget about me, you forget about who you are, too. If you ignore me, you ignore your true nature. This is the gift I bring you, for you to remember who and what you are. It's the gift I brought everyone." He grinned. "I tell you, Martin, a time will come when to call an individual a *person* will be the same as to call him or her a *Christ*, for the truth of the sacredness and love at the core of all your beings will be recognized."

Goodman thought of the news broadcast he'd seen the night before. "I'm afraid that day is a long way off."

Jesus shrugged. "Maybe. Maybe not. The important thing is that we keep taking steps towards it. I took my step. It created a holiday, but that wasn't my doing! Now it's time for you to take your step, Martin, and to help others to take theirs. And if you do it right, it will seem normal. There won't be a need to celebrate *your* birthday because all birthdays will become special." Jesus laughed. "Remember, I'm not asking you to do *what* I did. I'm asking you to do *as* I did, but to do it in your way."

"To greet each moment with love."

"Got it in one, Martin. Got it in one."

He felt a rush of love that was almost overpowering. "Oh, Jesus, I will do it. I will! I will keep your Christmas spirit in my heart all the year!"

Jesus smiled. "I know you will. Just remember. It's your spirit, too!" He leaned over and kissed Goodman on his forehead. "Blessings, my brother! And Merry Christmas!"

Jesus looked at the fireplace, laughed, yelled "Ho Ho Ho!" and vanished in a stream of light that went up the chimney.

Goodman sat down in his chair, his mind reeling from what he'd experienced, but almost immediately he fell into a deep sleep. When he woke up in the morning, feeling better than he had in years, he immediately got up to move the nativity scene into the middle of the fireplace mantle. But as he was picking up the figures, he saw that something had been changed. The baby Jesus wasn't in his crib anymore. Instead, he was being carried in the arms of Santa Claus.

THE END

A Christmas Tale by David Spangler
Cover illustration by Josh McDonald

Peter lay in bed, covers pulled up to his chin, luxuriating in the delightful feeling of tired muscles melting into warm sheets. It had been a long day, but he was at last completely moved in to his new house and more than ready to enjoy his first night's sleep in a new bed and a new bedroom. *Actually*, he thought, *a very old bedroom*. The house had been built at the turn of the last century, just over a hundred years earlier.

Lying there, he couldn't help but feel how lucky he had been. It was not for the first time. His life had taken such a turn for the better the past few months. The computer game his company had developed had been the number one seller for most of the year and had topped the charts throughout the Christmas shopping season now nearly ended. He'd decided to buy a house with some of his profits. With the economic downturn, he'd expected to find some bargains on the housing market, but this house had been a steal. Why some family had not snatched it up, he didn't know. The house had apparently sat on the market for several months after the previous owner's death, much to the realtor's puzzlement. *It was just waiting for me*, he thought smugly, closing his eyes...

And he immediately opened them again as he felt a weight on the bed pressing against his legs. "What the...." he started to say, but his voice caught in his throat as he saw a dark shadow sitting on the end of the bed. Reflexively, he pulled his legs up and tried to scoot back against the headboard behind him. *Omigosh,* he thought. *There's an animal in the house and it's on my bed.*

"Whoa, ther', Boyo," came a rough voice from the dark. "Nothin' t' be afraid of, ya know."

Peter yelped and drew himself back even further against the headboard.

"A l'il light would help. Everythin's scarier in the dark."

He heard the snap of fingers. Suddenly a little man appeared sitting on the end of his bed, his body softly glowing, illuminating the room. A red and white Santa's hat sat askew on his head, and under a bulbous nose, an unlit cigar was clamped between grimacing teeth. Large teeth. The man's body was clad in green tights that barely held a bulging stomach in place, while red pointed boots adorned his feet.

"Omigod, omigod, omigod..." was all Peter could get out between lips that seemed to tremble with a life of their own.

"Ah, hey, there's no need to call on the Big Lady," the apparition said. "Likes I said, I'm harmless."

"Ha..ha..harmless...?"

"That's what I said. Say, is something wrong with ya?"

"Wrong with....!" Peter tried to pull the covers up to cover his chest, but the weight of the little man kept them firmly in place. Putting indignation in his voice, he said, "Who the hell are you? What are you doing in my bedroom?"

"Why, I'm checkin' out the N.E.W. kid on the block."

"Listen, whoever you are, just because I just moved in doesn't give you any right to invade my bedroom in the middle of the night."

The little man chuckled, and Peter suddenly noticed that his eyes were gleaming green as if little emerald fires burned within them. "I don't mean "new" like "recent." I mean N.E.W. as in Neighborhood Elf Watch. And I'm yer supervisor, boyo, so ya'd best be sitting up straight and showin' me some respect."

"Respect..." Peter sputtered. "I'll show you the door, is what I'll show you. Damned dwarf invading my house. I'm calling the police!" Anger had now thoroughly burned away his initial fear, and he swung his feet around to get out of bed. The little man snapped his finger again, and Peter found he couldn't move.

"Dwarf? I ain't no dwarf, ya big lummox. Ya'd best keep a civil tongue in yer head if we're to have a good relationship...and believe me, ya want us to have a good relationship." He smiled broadly, and his teeth seemed even larger than before. Peter gulped, all his anger evaporating as quickly as it had arisen.

"Omigod," he said. "the house is haunted! That's why it wouldn't sell. You're a ghost! I've bought a haunted house. I'm phoning the realtor tomorrow to get my money back..."

"Oh, for Holy Santa's Sake, settle down, kid. I'm no ghostie. I told ya, I'm the N.E.W. elf supervisor for this district, and y'are the new coordinator for this neighborhood."

"You...you're an...an elf?" Peter said incredulously. "An elf...?"

"Say, ya don't listen very well, do ya? Makes me think your Christmas lights are one bulb short. Speaking of which, where *are* yer Christmas lights? Where's yer tree? Yer living room was as bare as a glacier's bottom."

"My tree?" Peter repeated stupidly. "I...I haven't gotten one yet. I just moved in today. It wasn't high on my list of priorities..."

"Hmmm. Yer running late, then. Not a good way to start yer N.E.W. career. Ya'd best get it up first thing in the morning. After all, ya need a place to hang the Orb."

Peter tried again to move, and this time found he was able to swing his feet out of the bed and down onto the floor. He started to stand up, then realized he was naked and ducked back under the covers. "What Orb? What career? What in the devil are you talking about?" he shouted, partly to cover his embarrassment.

The little man took the cigar out of his mouth and put a large finger in front of his lips, his eyes glancing about the room. "Shhh! 'Tis not wise ta be speakin' o' the opposition." Then, putting the soggy end of the cigar back in his mouth, he glared at Peter, the green fires in his eyes seeming to flare up again. "Say, don't ya know anythin'?" He pulled the cigar out of his mouth again and pointed it at Peter. "Would y'be mindin' if I lit this baby up? Regs say no smoking indoors, but if ya said yes..." The little man looked at him hopefully.

Peter held up his hand. "On one condition. You have to explain to me what's going on here."

Now it was his visitor's turn to look incredulous. "Ya really don't know, do ya?" Peter shook his head, hoping that perhaps a negative response would make this creature disappear.

The elf tore off his hat and threw it onto the bed. "By Stars and Moon, someone's screwed up royally here! No one tells poor ol' Shamus that we've got a *really* new boyo on the job, a tyro of the first degree! And here 'tis the night before Christmas Eve Day." He began to jump up and down on the bed. "Whatta they expect of me? Miracles?" He stopped bouncing and looked at Peter, his face an expression of pained misery. "I'm only a supervisor, but of course, I get all the tough jobs! Holy Santa!"

He plopped down on the bed and held out the cigar. "D'ya mind? A good smoke'll calm me down, and I promise ta tell ya what ya need to know. After all, 'tis my job on the line, too, if'n ya don't perform."

Wearily, his sore muscles feeling tighter all the time, Peter waved his hand in acquiescence and leaned back against the headboard of the bed. The elf nodded with a grin and held the cigar up in the air. It immediately began to glow at the tip, and a fragrance of frankincense and myrrh filled the room. Peter recognized it from the Christmas candles his mother had burned when he was a child.

"All right, lis'en good, y'hear, cause I've only got time ta tell this ta ya once. There are other N.E.W. coordinators I have ta see tonight. Why yer father didn't do this, I'll never know. What's happened ta tradition?"

"My father?" Peter thought of his father, a buttoned-down insurance salesman. A loving man to be sure, but not possessed of much imagination. The thought that his father was somehow involved with elves was even more unbelievable than the sight of the cigar-smoking, green-clad little man sitting on the bed before him. "What's my father got to do with..." he waved his arms in a sweeping gesture, "...with whatever you and... and this is?"

The elf blinked. "What's yer father....? Say now, ya wouldn' be puttin' one over on old Shamus, now would ya, cause if y'are, I'll not be takin' kindly ta it, especially not this close ta the Big Night."

"If anyone's putting anything over on anyone, it's not me doing it to you," Peter said primly.

The elf glared, his eyes momentarily brighter than the burning end of the cigar. "Well, as if ya didn't know, for over a hundred years members of yer family in this house have served as N.E.W. coordinators. The office is passed down to from parent to child, and..."

"Wait a minute!" Peter felt a surge of relief. "You said 'the members of your family.' But this isn't my family. That is, I'm not part of this house. I mean, I own the house, but I just bought it. I never knew the family that lived here. The realtor said the guy who owned it before me died in some accident, run over by a bus, I think."

Shamus hopped up and began jumping up and down on the bed again. "Oh, fine! Oh, great!" he shouted, waving his cigar in anger. "A broken lineage and did anyone think to tell ol' Shamus? Oh no! I mean, I'm *only* the supervisor for this district! Great Santa in the North Pole! This is one steaming pile of reindeer sh..." He stopped and looked hopefully at Peter. "You're not related ta the deceased at all, a distant cousin or somethin'?"

"Nope. Does this mean you have to go and leave me alone now?"

Shamus gave him a shrewd look. "Afraid not, boyo. If'n you're in this house and ownin' it, then it means the Powers That Be have chosen ya and ya're the N.E.W coordinator. Sorry." He sat down again.

Peter's shoulders slumped. *This has got to be a dream*, he thought. *No, a nightmare. I strained something carrying all those boxes today. I don't know how but my brain's come loose.*

"See," the elf went on, "this house sits on an IMP..."

"An imp?"

"Interdimensional Matrix Position." He thrust the cigar at Peter, who found himself enveloped in a cloud of Christmas aromas. "And if ya're gonna keep interruptin' me, we're never gonna get this sorted out and we'll have a worse disaster than we've got now. And boyo, if that happens, I wouldn' want ta be in your shoes, let me tell you."

Peter gulped. "Why?"

"Why, you'd be on Big Red's naughty list, and believe me, he *does* check it twice!"

"You mean..."

The elf nodded. "Coal in the stockin's and nothin' under the tree. Take a lot of milk and cookies ta make up fer it....But hey, now *I'm* digressin'. This whole thing's got me all snookered." He reached down to the bed and picked up his hat where it lay, putting it back on his head. "See, all these lines of magical power concentrate right here where this house is. Creates a doorway through which we can come into your world, prepare the way for Santa. This is the major entry point for this neighborhood. The man who built this house in the first place knew that. By buildin' here, he accepted the post of bein' the Neighborhood Elf Watch coordinator. And that job gits passed down through the family line of whoever lives in the house."

"And now that I'm here, that means me."

"Bingo."

"But what do I do?"

"Well, the first thing ya have to do is hang the Orb on yer Christmas tree." He held up his hand. "I know, I know, ya've no idea what it is. Well, it stands for Orthogonal Resonance Broadcaster. Big mouthful, eh? But 'tis simple. When placed on a Christmas tree, it sends a signal at right angles 'cross the dimensions from yer world to mine. It's like a key. It opens a door and helpers come through."

"Helpers?"

"Never mind. Ya'll see tomorrow night."

"But...I don't have any ortho...goner..whatever...I have no Orb ."

"Ah, now that's easy ta fix. Darn things break down, so what kind of supervisor would I be if I didn't carry a spare." He lifted a hand and seemed to reach into something that Peter couldn't see. The hand disappeared for a moment, but when it reappeared, it was holding a sphere whose surface was covered with coruscating rainbow colors. "Here," he said, handing it to Peter, who took it very gingerly. It was warm to the touch.

"Looks like a Christmas tree ornament. Will it hurt me?"

"Nah. Well, long's ya don't drop it. Last fellow that did that, scattered him through all the dimensions. We're still finding pieces of him."

Peter thrust the Orb back at the elf. "I don't want it!"

The little man grinned, the cigar bobbing up and down between his teeth. "Just kiddin'. Elf humor." He took the Orb and suddenly hurled it across the room. It struck the far wall then came flying back. A sound like a gong echoed through the room, making Peter clap his hands to his ears. Shamus caught the sphere effortlessly and handed it back to him. "See. Practically indestructible. But just don't try heating it in a microwave."

"I...I won't." In spite of the demonstration, Peter clutched the Orb carefully to his naked chest as if it were made of the most delicate China.

"All right, so first thing is ya've got to have a tree. And it's got ta be decorated real nice and pretty. Don't forget the tinsel. Otherwise, the proper resonances won't be set up and the Orb won't work. Ya don't want that."

"The naughty list...?"

Shamus nodded his head approvingly. "See? You're catchin' on."

"OK. So I get a tree and decorate it and I hang the Orb. Then what? Is that all I do? Sounds pretty simple. I think I can handle that."

"Well..." The elf cleared his throat. "Nah, it's not all ya do. But," he added quickly, "don't fret about it now. I'll have to fix something up for ya, ya bein' a newbie and all." His eyes closed for a moment. Then he looked at Peter and pointed his cigar at him. "Tomorrow night ya will be visited..."

Peter sighed. "Let me guess," he interrupted. "I think I know this part. I'll be visited by three spirits, right?"

The elf blinked. "Nah. Not enough money in the budget to send three guys here to help ya. Besides, he won't be a spirit, though truth be told he doesn't mind having them around, if ya know what I mean. Say," a look of concern crossed the elf's face. "Speaking of spirits, where do ya keep your booze?"

"Booze? Um...I don't have any here yet. Like I said, I just moved in and…"

"Good. Good." Shamus said, relief in his voice. "Take my advice and don't get any either, least not till Shaun's been here and gone."

"Shaun? Hey, are you guys elves or leprechauns?"

"Lepre…" He glared at Peter and blew a cloud of smoke in his direction. "What did I tell you about not bein' insulting? Conniving little creatures…."

"Sorry. It's just that your names sound so…"

"So what? It's a nickname. His real name is Shaunerglasendel. A good Elven name, just like my own, Shamuselderel. But I figgered ya wouldn't want to say that all the time, what with being a human and all. Ya're always abbreviatin' everything. Livin' yer lives too fast, if'n ya ask me. Course, when those lives are as short as yers are," he smirked at Peter, "reckon I can unnerstand." He stood up. "Anyway, Shaun will see ya tomorrow night when the bell tolls ten. "

"What bell?"

"How the Dickens would I know? Ya're the one who brought up the three spirits. Sheesh!" The elf grinned, waved his cigar and disappeared in a poof of frankincense and myrrh, plunging the room back into darkness.

Amazingly, in spite of what had happened, Peter did eventually fall asleep. Tired muscles are tired muscles whether one has been visited by a cigar-smoking elf or not; the body will have its rest even when the mind is spinning in circles. The sun was well up in the morning sky when he finally opened his eyes.

As he lay in bed, slowly coming to, a faint odor tickled his nose. Smells like my mother's Christmas candles, he thought lazily. And then he remembered.

He sat bolt upright, looking wildly around. *Right there on my bed*, he thought. *He'd been right there. A cigar-smoking elf named Shamusel..erel.. um..Shamus.*

But now there was no elf, nor any sign there had ever been any. *Wow!* he thought, rubbing his eyes. *What a dream! What had he called it? The Neighborhood Elf Watch…Ha! I must have been more tired than I thought 'cause boy, did my subconscious take over! Hey, maybe there's a game in it…*

He threw back the covers, swung his legs over the side to get up, and stopped. Lying on his nightstand was a shiny sphere sparkling with rainbow colors. *Omigod,* he thought. *The Orb! It's all true!*

He reached out a hand to tentatively touch the sphere. As his fingers touched its warm surface, a familiar Elven voice rang out. "Remember, N.E.W coordinator! Get a tree, decorate it, an' hang the Orb!" He jumped back, half expecting Shamus and his cigar to appear before him. But nothing else happened, and when he touched the Orb again, it remained silent. He sighed and got up. A half hour later he was in his car, heading out to find the nearest Christmas tree lot.

He had not intended to have a tree this year, but since the need for one had now been thrust upon him in a most unreal way, he was determined to do it right and be discriminating. This meant going to several tree lots before he found just what he wanted. The same was true for the decorations as he combed the stores for lights, ornaments and, of course, tinsel. All of the bargain stores were pretty picked over forcing him to search in the specialty Christmas stores. But with Christmas Eve sales bringing the prices down ridiculously low, he had ended up with a hoard of unique hand-made decorations he might normally never have purchased. Finally, by early afternoon he had found everything he wanted, and he headed home.

The sun had set when he finished decorating his tree, and he had to admit, if nothing else happened , it added a wonderful feeling to his house, and this tree was more magnificent than any he had had in the past. In fact, the more he decorated, the better he felt, as if the house itself were watching him and giving its approval. "That's really nuts," he said out loud. "Houses aren't alive." But the feeling persisted and grew, and by the end he felt as if he and the house had become good friends. *After all*, he thought, *a living house is no more difficult to believe, I suppose, than cigar-smoking elves and Santa Claus.*

When the tree was decorated to his satisfaction, Peter went upstairs to his bedroom and got the Orb from where he had left it laying on the nightstand by his bed. But when he brought it back downstairs, he stood before the tree and hesitated. "Do I really want to do this?" he asked out loud. "Do I want to open a door to some other world?" For a moment, his imagination pictured hordes of elves and who-knew what other kinds of beings all packing automatic rifles and bandanas of ammunition pouring through some interdimensional rift to invade the earth. SANTA'S ARMIES CONQUER EARTH, CNN would say on the six o'clock news. "NOW WILL YOU BELIEVE IN ME?" SANTA DEMANDS AS ELVEN COMMANDOS SEPARATE THE NAUGHTY FROM THE NICE.

He snorted. The problem with being a successful game designer was that your imagination could picture anything. But in spite of a wave of assurance that swept over him that he was about to do the Right Thing, he still hesitated.

As he stood in front of the tree, his stomach growled. He realized that he hadn't eaten anything all day. *Well, whatever happens, I should face it on a full stomach,* he thought. He put the Orb down on a chair and grabbed his coat. *No food in the house yet, so it's off to that Chinese restaurant I saw nearby.*

An hour later he was finishing the last of his Szechwan shrimp, vegetable chow mein and fried rice. His hunger sated, he felt he could think more reasonably. *Come on, Peter,* he told himself. *Think this through. There's a reasonable explanation for all of this. I stopped believing in Santa Claus years ago, and elves....Ha! I mean some of the guys at work could have snuck into the house and set up a virtual reality projector, or hired a little person to wear a costume and jump up and down on my bed. You can do amazing things with special effects these days. And hey, I was exhausted. I was in no shape to tell fantasy from reality.*

In fact, the more he thought about it, the more he was sure he was the victim of some elaborate practical joke. It was just the kind of thing some of the people on his staff would do, and they had the technical expertise to pull it off, too. He laughed. He'd go into the office in a couple of days, and they'd all have a good laugh. Hell, maybe he'd even give some of them a bonus for their creativity. After all, no harm had been done, and on the plus side, he now had a beautiful Christmas tree to go home to.

Sighing with relief, he drank the last of his tea and reached for the fortune cookie the waiter had brought with his bill. Cracking it open, he was startled by a whiff of frankincense and myrrh and by the little slip of paper that exploded out of the cookie, unfolding and expanding itself into a small piece of parchment. "THIS IS NO PRANK," it said in a bold hand. "GO HOME AND HANG THE ORB. NOW! P.S. REMEMBER THE NAUGHTY LIST...."

Ten minutes later his car pulled into his driveway with a squeal of tires and slammed to a stop. With trembling fingers, he unlocked the front door and dashed into the living room. Grabbing the Orb, he carried it over to the tree. "All right, all right," he muttered. "I'm hanging the Orb, OK?" But then he realized he didn't know how to hang it. The sphere was completely smooth with no place to attach a hook. But as he held it near the tree, it suddenly lifted out of his fingers and attached itself to the nearest branch.

"Wow…" he breathed. He reached in and gave the Orb a careful tug. It didn't budge. It might as well have been part of the tree itself. "Wow!" he said again.

He stepped back and looked around the room. "OK," he said out loud. "I've hung the damn Orb. Now what?" He waited for something to happen, lights, sounds, anything. The room was still. He looked at his watch. The digital numbers read 8:15. He remembered that Shaun-what's-his-name was not due until 10:00. Had he hung the Orb too early?

But even as he thought this, a wave of comfort came over him as if the house itself were reassuring him. He sighed and sat down in his favorite easy chair. *This is beyond crazy*, he thought, *but I've done my bit. I've hung the Orb. The rest is up to…whatever.*

Sitting in the chair, looking at the tree with its lights twinkling and the Orb glowing, he felt his eyelids grow heavy. It had been a very busy couple of days, he thought. He closed his eyes…

The next thing he knew a bell was ringing off in the distance. He blinked blearily, then remembered what Shamus had said. He looked down at his watch. 9:45. *Wait a minute*, he thought. *He said when the bell tolls ten.*

There was a soft sound like a sigh of wind. Peter looked up and found himself staring at what looked like a young man in his early twenties dressed head to foot in a dark-green, one-piece jumpsuit. He had a Santa's cap on his head as well, from beneath which golden hair flowed down to his shoulders. His face was movie-star handsome, and like Shamus, his eyes glowed with a green fire.

"Um…let me guess," Peter said, trying to affect a humorous nonchalance in the face of weirdness. "The Ghost of Christmas Present, right?"

The elf's eyes widened and he quickly looked around. "A ghost? Are there ghosts here? Shamus didn't say the house was haunted."

"No, no," Peter said, "I meant…oh, never mind. You're Shaun, right? And you're early. You weren't supposed to come till ten o'clock."

"Sorry. No watches over there, just a bunch of bells. Not worth a damn for telling time." The elf looked at him, concern still on his face. "Um, are you sure there're no ghosts about? I really don't like ghosts!"

This is my helper? Peter thought. But aloud he said, "No, far as I know, there aren't any ghosts here. But they wouldn't be any stranger than you are, you know."

The elf pulled himself up to his full height, which, Peter guessed, was a hair under five feet. "There is nothing strange about me! I'm a perfectly normal handsome elf." And he thrust out his chest, as if daring Peter to say otherwise.

Trying to save face, Peter thought. *Maybe I should tell him there are ghosts in the house and mess with his mind a bit. These elves are certainly messing with mine!* Instead he said, "Well, you certainly look—and sound—different from Shamus."

The elf leaned in close and said in a whisper, "Shamus is a good supervisor but lately he's been letting himself go. Sartorially speaking, of course. And his accent comes from the Old Country."

"Ireland?"

"Atlantis."

Peter gaped at the elf. "Atlantis. Ah….of course..." He swallowed, then nodded sagely. "Why didn't I spot that right off?" He shook his head. "Wow! OK, then. So…what do we do now?"

Shaun leaned back and gestured at the tree. "Well, you've hung the Orb. That's good, that's good. Shamus told you it's a key? Yes? OK, then now you have to use it to open the door. Only a human can do that because you have to invite us into your world and all. We can't open it from our end."

"But I didn't invite you and Shamus."

"Oh, well, that's different, you see. He has a special license being a supervisor and all, and I do, too, being an N.E.W. troubleshooter. We don't need doors. We climb through the window, so to speak. Ha, ha!" Shaun looked smug.

"You sound like burglars. Are there many of these 'windows' around," he asked.

"Only where there are IMPs," came the reply.

"Oh, yes, the IMPs." Peter sighed. "All right, can we get on with this? How do I turn this…key?"

"Oh, that's easy," Shaun said. "Just go and put your hand on the Orb and recite what I say."

Peter got up from his chair and went over to the tree. Reaching out, he put his hand on the Orb. It was as warm as ever.

Shaun came up and stood beside him. "Now say," and he deepened his voice, "In brightest day, in blackest night, No evil shall escape my sight; Let those who worship evil's might, beware my power..."

"Wait a minute!" said Peter, letting go of the Orb and stepping back. He glared at the elf. "I know this! That's the Green Lantern oath from the comic books. You're using the Green Lantern oath?"

The elf blushed, which made his green eyes stand out even more. "Er...well...I didn't think you'd recognize it..."

"Hey, I'm a game designer! I design games with superheroes in them. Of course I recognize the Green Lantern oath. What gives?"

The elf blushed even more furiously. "I...I...like human comics. And elves are partial to green, you know. I just thought it sounded... well...impressive and all."

"And the Green Lantern oath is what it takes to use the Orb?"

"Actually, no. You can say anything as long as you have an intent to activate it. I just thought...."

Peter seized the Orb again and said simply, "Open!"

Immediately Peter felt a wave of...well...something pass through him and into the room beyond, as if he'd been standing in a lake and had dropped a large stone in the water beside him.

"Very good," said Shaun. "Not particularly eloquent, but it got the job done."

Around the tree, little beings began to materialize. They ranged in size from a few inches to about three feet in height. Otherwise, they looked identical, all dressed in green overalls, a red bandana around their heads, and heavy work boots on their feet. In their hands they each carried a long handled broom and dustpan. They looked up expectantly at Peter, who in turn looked at Shaun.

"Omigosh! A bunch of elvish streetsweepers?"

"Helpers. And the correct word is *elven*. Elvish is one of your singers. Rather good one, if I remember..."

"But they've got brooms."

"Of course! We go forth to battle the forces of darkness!" All the little helpers raised their voices in a cheer and knocked their booms and dustpans together enthusiastically.

"Or they will as soon as you give them permission," Shaun said pointedly. The elves all looked intently at Peter.

"Um..." Peter wondered if he was supposed to say something

inspirational, but settled for "Go for it, guys!"

Immediately the throng of elves turned and ran off in all directions, brandishing their brooms and dustpans and cheering as they passed through the walls of the house and vanished.

Peter's felt his mind whirling. "Where did they go?"

"Why, into your neighborhood, of course. Remember, we're the *Neighborhood* Elf Watch. And now it's time for you to follow them."

"What?"

"You're the coordinator, remember." Shaun reached into nothingness and pulled out a green tunic and a pair of tights. "Your uniform."

Peter backed away. "Oh no! You're not getting me into tights!"

Shaun shrugged. "If you insist." The tights disappeared and were replaced in his hands with green coveralls. "These should do then, though they're not as elegant." He gestured at Peter who felt a pressure all over his body. Looking down he saw that he was now dressed in the overalls. "Oh, I guess they're not too bad," the elf said condescendingly. "They're functional, at least." Then he reached into nothingness again and pulled out a larger, human-sized version of the streetsweeper's broom and dustpan. He handed them to Peter. "Here, take these."

Peter took them. "You mean, I'm going to be a *janitor*?"

"Well, I'd hardly put it so crudely....here, put this on." He passed over to Peter a whistle on a chain. "Just in case."

Peter took it warily and slipped it over his head. "I'm getting a bad feeling about this. In case of what?"

"Oh, not to worry. Probably nothing at all. But if we run into trouble, this will call the police."

"The police? There are elvish..I mean, elven police?"

"Of course. Didn't Shamus tell you? As long as you're on the scene, the helpers will do their work, but occasionally they flush something out that doesn't want to be swept up. If that happens, it will come for you. If it takes you out, then all the helpers have to go home."

"Take me out!" Peter could hear his voice rising. "What the hell do you mean, 'take me out?'"

"Come, come, Peter. We can't just stand here talking. We have to be seen on the scene. We have to get to work. Big Red will be through here in, oh, I don't know, a bell or two. By midnight anyway. So let's go!" He reached over and grabbed Peter by the arm.

"But...but...waaaaiiit...!" Peter howled as he found himself levitating off the floor and rushing towards the wall of the house as the elf pulled him along. He closed his eyes, waiting for the impact that would certainly knock him out if not kill him.

There was a moment of coolness like passing through a thin spray of water, then nothing. Peter opened his eyes. He and Shaun were outside, floating above the trees and houses in his neighborhood. Looking down he marveled that he could not only see the houses but in some strange sense he could see into them as well, or at least sense what the myriad of helpers were doing. And they were all busy, sweeping, sweeping, sweeping, up and down streets, around the trees, and throughout the houses. Where they swept, Peter could see little black clouds being churned up and sucked into the dustpans.

He looked over at Shaun who was viewing the scene below with evident pleasure, his green eyes glowing. At that moment, Peter wholly surrendered to what was happening. It was crazy. It was awesome. It was magical. And as a game designer, he knew all about creating magic. He'd just never thought it was *real*.

"What are they sweeping up?" he asked Shaun.

"Old, stale emotions and thoughts, mostly. Things you humans put out during the day and then forget. "

"You mean, like psychic dandruff?"

The elf gazed at one of the houses down below where a great many helpers were industriously sweeping great clouds of dark stuff into their dustpans. "Yes, exactly. And few humans even think about cleaning up after themselves, so the old thoughts and feelings just lie around. Usually they dissolve and disappear, but sometimes they accumulate, especially if they're heavy, like fear or worry or sadness."

"I get it. You need to clean all this stuff up so Santa doesn't see it and get himself dirty with our negativity."

Shaun turned and looked at him. "Oh, no, Peter. You have it wrong. This stuff can't hurt Santa. We're not cleaning up to help him; we clean up to help *you!*" He paused, obviously trying to find words for his thoughts. "Christmas is a time of joy and love. That's what Santa spreads throughout the world; as a Lord of Light, it's his gift to all humans everywhere. And if the world can absorb it, this joy will last throughout the year, seeing you through the hard times that life can bring and inspiring you to make good times for each other. But if there's lots of 'psychic dandruff' as you call it lying around, then what Santa brings won't stick. There's a moment of sparkle, then it fades. We clean so that when Santa comes his blessing will stay."

"Gee," Peter said thoughtfully. "I never knew. Humanity, the psychic litterbug of the earth…"

Shaun reached over and patted his arm, which made Peter bob up and down a bit in the air. "It's not as bad as all that. There are humans who know how to keep the realms of thought and feeling clean and clear, and more of you will learn as time goes by. And in the meantime, there's the Neighborhood Elf Watch!" He grinned.

Peter looked at his broom and dustpan. "So shouldn't I be down there sweeping, too?"

Shaun shook his head. "Nah, your job is to be up here where everyone can see you and remember who invited them. The broom and pan are just for solidarity so the workers feel you're one of them."

Suddenly a shrill whistle pierced the air behind them. All Peter had to do was think of turning, and his body swirled around. Below him, outside a modest ranch-style house, a group of elves were confronting and corralling a large, shadowy shape. Before he could ask Shaun what it was, there was a burst of light and two new beings appeared.

Peter could tell even at a distance that both were tall, maybe his height or a little taller. And one of them was easily the most beautiful woman he had ever seen. Even garbed in what appeared to be silver armor, she gave off a glow of sensuality and femininity that he had not experienced before.

"Omigod! Who is that?"

"That's a Sidhe."

"I'd say that's pretty obvious, even from here. And what a she!" Peter gave a low whistle. He noticed her companion, a man who was every bit as masculine and handsome as the woman was womanly. "And who's that?"

"Another Sidhe."

Peter looked incredulously at Shaun, who was gazing admiringly at the two figures below. "You've got to be kidding me. If that's a woman, I'll eat this broom."

"What?" Shaun looked at him puzzled. Then his face cleared. "Oh. No, no, I said 'Sidhe,' not 'she.' I know they sound the same, but I meant their race. They're the High Elves, the Sidhe."

Peter felt foolish. Of course he knew who the Sidhe were, the fabled rulers of all Elfdom. He'd just been distracted by..well..by the she Sidhe below. "What are they doing here?"

"Why, they're the police. Watch!"

Below them the dark figure was swelling in size and taking on shape. It was a fearsome monster, all glowing red eyes and large fangs in a mouth that could easily swallow several of the smaller elves in one gulp. It roared its defiance. But the female Sidhe stepped up to it, drew a long, narrow sword and skewered it. The roar became a little squeal, and the monster collapsed in on itself, becoming a small, humanoid figure no more than two feet in height. "Ah," said Shaun, "stabbed him with the Sword of Truth. They're great illusionists, you know. But the Sword of Truth shows what they really are all the time."

"I'll bite. What is it?"

"A boggart, left over from Halloween, no doubt. Probably got drunk and found itself trapped when the sun came up. Trouble is, they can't be swept up into the dustpans cause it's one of ours, not one of yours. Needs the police to get rid of it."

Peter looked at the two Sidhe bundling the boggart into a sack between them. "Hmmm. So, Shaun, if I blew this whistle around my neck, this she...I mean, Sidhe...would show up?"

"Oh yes, but you don't want to do that unless you really need to. The police get angry if you summon them unnecessarily."

Peter nodded wistfully. "Just like in my world," he said.

The elf grabbed his arm. "Come on, we need to fly around a bit, make sure you're seen throughout the neighborhood, and observe what's happening. That's your job, you know."

Following Shaun, Peter began to fly over the houses and treetops, enjoying it more and more. *Now this was real magic*, he thought. *Wait till my staff hear about this!* But then he thought, *like they're going to believe me?*

For the first time, Peter got a real look at the neighborhood he had just moved into. He realized he liked it very much. It was an old neighborhood, lots of old houses, though few as old as his, and lots of trees and grassy areas. And on the whole, it didn't seem as if the elves were stirring up very many dark clouds.

"Pretty clean neighborhood, actually," Shaun said, as if reading Peter's mind. "That's because there are so many trees. Trees are great for keeping energies flowing and things clean. We'll get this finished in plenty of time before Santa comes. Not like the last job I had in the city.

We hardly made it. Had to call in extra help from other Watches. That was....arrgh!" The elf stopped with a strangled cry.

Peter had only half been paying attention, his mind mainly taking in the view below as they flew over what appeared to be a park filled with old trees. He could see a line of light rising up nearby and knew somehow that that marked the limits of his neighborhood. On the other side of that line, another N.E.W. was at work doing it's job of cleaning and preparing the land for Santa.

When he heard Shaun cry out, he stopped and looked back. To his horror, the elf was encircled by a black tentacle rising up from a place deep within the shadows of the parkland. It was dragging him down, and though he could see Shaun struggling to be free, the tentacle was winning. Around this area he could see dozens of small elven helpers, sweeping madly with their brooms and brandishing their dustpans, but unable to get close to the shadowy thing that was rising from the woods.

"Ca...call the police!" Shaun cried out. "Use your whistle...gak..." Another tentacle reached out from the seething, black mass and wrapped around his throat. Suddenly, Shaun disappeared.

Stunned, Peter was frozen into immobility, even as the whirling mass rose up in his direction. *It's eaten Shaun! Get out of here or it'll eat you, too!* his mind yammered at him. But he couldn't do anything except watch in horrid fascination as doom climbed towards him.

But then the thing stopped. It began to shift and flow, and as he watched, it took on a shape. An awful shape. A horrific shape. A shape filled with fangs and tentacles, a bulbous, slimy body, and baleful eyes.

A shape he recognized.

"Cthulu?" he said in wonder. Then, the game designer in him took over and he laughed. "Give me a break! Is that the best you can do?" It obviously was another boggart, this time taking on the appearance of one of the evil Elder Gods born from the imagination of the horror writer, H. P. Lovecraft. Peter had played too many games—and even designed a couple—where Cthulu was the "boss" you had to defeat to win. And defeat him he had. "I don't need the police to take care of you!"

He advanced towards the entity, lifting his broom and dustpan. "Back off, buddy, or I'll smite you!" He was conscious of all the elven helpers watching him from below, and he determined to put on his best show for them. "I am the N.E.W, coordinator. I may be new with N.E.W. but I've got what it takes to do the job."

With that he swung his broom at the entity. It passed through the body of the thing and when it emerged from the other side, most of it was gone. Dissolved. Vanished. *Hmmm, I don't think that's what's supposed to happen,* he thought.

Then two tentacles shot out and gripped him, and he could feel their pressure through his overalls. An awful stench rose up in his nostrils. Then he knew. This was no Boggart. No illusion. It wasn't Cthulu, he knew, but whatever it was, it was dangerous and out to get him.

In that moment he remembered something his realtor had said. She'd pointed out the park to him, and he remembered that earlier in the year, someone had been savagely murdered in it. The murderer had been caught, but the psychic residue of the act—all the pain and fear and fury—had remained. And it had grown, drawing to itself all the negativity from the surrounding homes and neighborhoods, gathering strength, becoming this…whatever it was.

He could feel the pressure increasing around him as the tentacles held him. His arms were pinned so he couldn't reach the whistle around his neck. Then it opened a slavering mouth and began drawing him to it. He felt more than heard a collective gasp from the helpers down below.

Staring into the gleaming eyes and the fangs dripping with reddish ichor, a thought hit him: *This is way too over the top; no game designer would ever foist something like this on kids today. They'd laugh it out of the marketplace.* And with that he laughed.

The tentacles lessened their pressure.

He laughed all the more. The tentacles weakened even more. *Of course,* he thought. *It feeds on fear. It can't handle laughter.*

Suddenly he was free. He knew he could call the Sidhe police, and probably should. But this thing was infecting *his* neighborhood, a neighborhood where good people tried to make a better world, where kids lived and played, and where one day any kids he might have would live and grow. This could not be allowed. It was spreading evil on *his* watch. No way was he going to back down. No way was he calling for help. This thing was going down, right now, and he was the one to do it!

"In brightest day, in blackest night, no evil will survive my might!" he intoned! "For I am a Game Designer! And you have no place in my neighborhood!" And with that, he swung the dustpan which struck the creature and opened wide, wider, and wider still, fired by Peter's anger and steely intent. The Cthulu-shape totally dissolved, and the whole seething mass was sucked into the now-giant dustpan and disappeared.

A cheer rose up from below and, belatedly, the sound of many little whistles being blown. *Thanks, guys,* he thought. *And why didn't you blow those things before?* And then he realized that elves, like everyone else, love a good show. Why stop it before the hero wins?

The two shining figures he had seen before appeared near him, and between them was a chagrined but thoroughly healthy Shaun. "Shaun!" Peter exclaimed. "I thought you'd been eaten!"

"No, just kicked out of your dimension into a very dark place. But I blew my whistle and fortunately, the Sidhe found me and brought me back." He looked around. "I guess you didn't need any help."

"Well," said Peter, grinning broadly, "I AM the N.E.W. coordinator, after all."

At that, the female Sidhe smiled, and as the two figures disappeared, he was sure he saw her wink at him. *Hmmm,* he thought, *there may be more compensations to this job than I'd thought.*

But before he could follow that lovely and intriguing thought any further, Shaun touched his arm and pointed up to the sky. "Look. Santa Claus is coming to town!"

At first Peter looked to see the familiar flying sleigh pulled by eight reindeer. But instead he saw a giant figure so large as to cover the horizon. Like a great, jolly red and white cloud, Santa rolled in over the earth, his joyful laughter ringing in Peter's heart like thunder. This was no single elf that hopped in and out of chimneys but a Lord of Light indeed, a being so vast that Peter had a hard time grasping all of him.

As Santa passed over the neighborhood, Peter could see everything becoming a little brighter, a little lighter, a little happier. It was as if this great being left "Santa-dew" behind, which soaked into everything, into sleeping children and parents, into the Christmas trees and the presents beneath them, into the houses, into the streets, into the trees and bushes and lawns.

And as he was engulfed in Santa, Peter heard a voice saying, "God Bless Us, Everyone!" and he felt Santa entering into him.

After awhile, the pull of Shaun's hand on his arm brought him back from whatever place of bliss and joy he had gone to. "It's over now, Peter. Time to call it a night."

Peter whispered to the elf. "A Being with that much love can't really have a naughty list, can he?"

"Nah. That's just Shamus's way of instilling a little fear in N.E.W. coordinators! Especially new ones." He winked. Then he looked slyly at Peter. "By the way, you wouldn't have a wee drink or two at your house would you?"

"No, but with a little magic, we might find a bar still open on Christmas Eve night."

Green eyes twinkled in the darkness. "Aye, we might at that..."

And together they drifted back towards his house as the hundreds of elven helpers slowly winked out like stars fading in the coming of dawn.

A year later, Peter stood before his Christmas tree, ready to touch the Orb and open the portal that would bring all his helpers into his world. But before he did, he glanced over at a poster on the wall. It showed a handsome, muscular man in green overalls brandishing a glowing broom and dustpan in the face of a slavering, black many-tentacled monster while to one side a ravishingly beautiful woman in silver armor with long black hair and a sword looked on admiringly. Above the picture were fiery letters that spelled N.E.W.

It had been the top selling computer game this Christmas season. And he was...the Game Designer.

THE END

The World Tree

Webster Graham was awakened to the sound of sirens. Opening his eyes, he saw yellow shadows flickering on the walls of his bedroom. *What's happening?* he thought, and then almost immediately the thought came, *Fire!*

He sprang up from his bed, his stomach tightening with panic. As his feet hit the floor, though, he realized the fire—or whatever it was—wasn't in his house but outside. He ran to the window and pulled back the curtain to look out.

It was a scene of chaos. Bright flames were licking out of an upstairs window in the house across the street, dancing and flaring in the wind. Fire engines were pulling up, and firemen were jumping off their trucks and deploying hoses, yelling orders to each other. And on top of it all, heavy snow was falling, whipped about into little eddies as the wind blew down the street, carrying gray clouds of smoke with it. And of course, in spite of the weather, a crowd of neighbors was gathering, men and women and even children, heavy coats thrown over their pajamas and robes.

It's Quirky's house, he thought. Crazy old woman. *I bet one of her candles caught fire. She keeps more of them burning than in a church.* Then as the full import of what he was seeing struck home, he was sorry for his thought. Crazy or not, Mrs. Quercus was losing her house and maybe even her life.

He turned and grabbed his robe from where it lay on the floor at the foot of his bed. Throwing it on, he quickly thrust his feet into sneakers and ran out of his room, almost colliding with his younger sister, Amanda.

"What's happening?" she said sleepily.

"Quirky's house is on fire," he said, passing her and running down the stairs. As he headed for the front door, he heard his father shout from the living room where he and his mother were looking out the big picture window at the drama outside, "Webster, if you go out, stay on the porch. The firemen don't need more people getting in their way."

"And put your coat on. You, too, Mandy. It's cold out there!"his mother added.

Webster opened the closet by the front door and pulled out his heavy coat. Shrugging into it, he opened the door and stepped onto the porch. He immediately felt the bite of the cold wind as it whistled around the house, driving the snow sideways into his face. But at the same time, he could feel the heat from the fire just a few yards away across the street.

Behind him, he heard his sister and his parents coming out as well. "Oh, that poor woman!" his mother exclaimed. "I hope she's all right!"

"What about all her animals and birds?" Amanda asked, her voice trembling. Mrs. Quercus's house was notorious in the neighborhood for being practically a wildlife sanctuary, a fact that had brought complaints from some of her neighbors. Cats, dogs, ferrets, mice, injured birds of various kinds—if there were a stray animal anywhere around, Webster thought, it seemed to find its way to Quirky's house.

"I don't know, dear," his mother replied. Then she said, "Oh! There's Emily!" Without another word, she drew her coat about her and stepped off the porch, heading into the crowd gathered around the fire engines.

"Where's Mom going?" Amanda asked.

"I think she saw Mrs. Quercus," her father replied. "She probably wants to find out if she's all right....hey! Where are you going?" he yelled as Webster leapt off the porch after his mom.

"I'm going with Mom," he said, racing through the snow to catch up with his mother before his Dad could call him back. But instead his father called after him, "Just stay out of the way."

Webster grinned to himself. He wasn't that interested in seeing Quirky, though he felt sorry for her; he just saw an excuse to get closer to the fire and the fire engines. Apparently his dad understood.

Moving through a crowd of friends and neighbors, he saw his mom stop by one of the firemen and say something, pointing to an older woman standing beside one of the fire trucks, wrapped in a blanket and watching her house burn. The fireman took his mom by the elbow to help her over the hoses now lining the street and together they started toward the woman.

"Hey, Mom! Wait up!" Webster yelled, rushing forward and nearly slipping on a bit of ice. His mother looked back and held out her hand to him. The fireman waited. "Hurry up, Webster," his mother said. "And take my hand." Although he felt a momentary pang of embarrassment at holding his mother's hand in public—after all, he was almost thirteen—he reached out and grabbed her fingers.

Together the three of them made their way over to where Emily Quercus was standing. "The paramedics are on their way," he heard the fireman say to his mother. "They'll want to check her over."

"Well, they can do it in the warmth of our living room instead of out here in the snow," his mother said in a tone that Webster knew all too well brooked no argument from anyone.

The fireman smiled. "Yes, Ma'am. They certainly can. It's very kind of you."

"Nonsense, she's our neighbor." With that, she stepped forward and put her arms around Mrs. Quercus. "Oh, Emily," she said. "I'm so sorry." Webster watched for a moment, then turned his attention to the fire, which was far more interesting. By now the flames had spread throughout the house in spite of the efforts of three teams of firemen directing streams of water into the blaze. As he watched, the central part of the roof collapsed in an explosion of sparks and flames. The firemen backed up quickly. He heard one of them say, "What's in that house, anyway? It's burning like a torch!"

As if on cue, a fireball lifted up from the hole where the roof had fallen in. For one incredulous moment, it seemed to Webster as if it had a face, its eyes black pits framed by swirls of smoke. *And it's staring right at me,* he thought. But he no sooner thought that then something in him seemed to say, *No, not at me. At Quirky.*

As the fireball dissolved in the wind into sparks and flames, he turned to where his mother was still comforting Mrs. Quercus. The older woman seemed to have been looking up at the fireball, too, a scowl on her face. His mother looked at him, and said, "Come, Webster, we need to take Mrs. Quercus back to our house and get out of the way of these firemen."

"What?" he murmured, his mind still swirling with the image of the fiery face.

"I said, help Mrs. Quercus so she doesn't stumble over these hoses. We're taking her back to our house." His mother gestured that he should take Quirky's arm, which was under the blanket. The woman herself was still gazing at the fire, mumbling something.

The thought of touching the odd woman he and his friends all called Quirky momentarily unnerved him more than had the face he'd imagined he'd seen In the fire, but his mother said in her no-nonsense voice, "Hurry, Webster. She's in shock, and we need to help her until the paramedics arrive." So he reached forward and grabbed what felt like her arm while his mother held the woman close against her and moved her forward away from the fire. Her head bowed, Mrs. Quercus seemed to close her eyes, allowing herself to be led and trusting in Webster and his mother. As their neighbors parted before them, a couple of other women coming forward to help, Webster could almost hear what the woman was muttering. She seemed to be saying, "Fire cleanses the forest, fire cleanses the forest," over and over. *What's she talking about?* he wondered. What forest? *It's her house that's burning down, not a bunch of trees.* He mentally shook his head as he stepped back and let another neighbor come forward to help in his place. It was like he and his friends always said. Ol' Quirky was crazy.

And as if to confirm his judgment, she suddenly opened her eyes and smiled, her whole face lit up with joy, as if the destruction of her home was the happiest thing that had ever happened to her.

With the neighbors' help, they got Mrs. Quercus to their home, where Webster's father came down the porch to help her up the steps. From there it was only a matter of minutes until she was sitting in an easy chair in the living room, wrapped in blankets, being checked over by the paramedics who had arrived. On her lap lay a plain square wooden box, apparently the only thing she had rescued from the fire. She gripped it as if it might escape at any minute.

Webster decided more exciting things were happening outside. He knew his parents wouldn't let him run back over to the fire, so he went upstairs to his room to watch from his chair by his window. By this time, the house had almost wholly collapsed and the firemen were concentrating on protecting the adjoining houses from catching fire as well. But fortunately the wind and snow seemed to be dying down, so their work was easier.

After awhile, in spite of the activity outside, Webster felt his eyelids growing heavy. A glance at his bedside clock told him it wasn't even three am yet. *Leave it to old Quirky to do something crazy that gets us all up in the middle of the night,* he thought. He figured he should go back to bed. The fire was now under control and he doubted there'd be much more to see. *Certainly not any more fiery faces,* he thought wryly. Funny what your imagination could do.

"Still up?" came a voice from his doorway. He turned in his chair and saw his father come in. "You should get to bed, Webster. I think the excitement's over for the night."

"Yeah, I was just thinking that." He got up and was surprised when his father gave him a hug. "Everything OK, Dad?"

His father released him. "A-OK, Sport. But when something like this happens, it makes me feel...well, you know...glad that you kids are all right."

"I'm fine, Dad," he said, climbing into bed. "Um, how's Quir...I mean, Mrs. Quercus? Is she all right?"

"Yes, she seems to be. Mom and the paramedics are having a talk downstairs right now. But it's a tragedy nonetheless. The poor lady seems to have lost everything she had in the world."

""That's too bad," Webster said sleepily. And with that, it was as if his eyelids said, "time to close up," and he fell into a deep sleep.

But not a dreamless one. He found himself sitting on the branches of a great tree, a tree so tall he couldn't see the ground below him or the top of the tree above him. When he was six years old, he'd climbed a tree and fallen out. It had seemed a frighteningly long way down, and he'd broken his arm. Ever since, he'd been afraid of heights. But in his dream, he felt perfectly safe, as if the tree itself were holding him and would let nothing harm him.

Around him he could hear creatures moving in the branches, but he couldn't see anything. Intrigued, he thought he'd climb around and explore. But as he began to maneuver among the branches, a large bird suddenly appeared before him. At first he thought it was an owl, and then it looked like a hawk, and then he wasn't sure what it was. It clung to a branch just opposite him so that its eyes looked directly into his. Then, it spoke to him. "Home," it said.

"What?" he said.

"Home!"

The bird's face changed, its beak and feathers rearranging themselves. He was looking instead into the face of Mrs. Quercus. The Quercus bird took a step towards him, and, startled, he tried to back up. But his foot slipped and there was no branch behind him or under him. As he had six years earlier, he felt himself starting to fall, then he was falling, even as the bird with Quirky's face came toward him, shrieking, "Home! Home!"

He fell, and it seemed to him he fell forever until a fiery face appeared under him, its eyes black as dirty smoke, and its mouth opening to swallow him down a gullet of flame and sparks. He could feel the heat of it, feel his skin burning.

"Fire cleanses the forest," a voice said.

He screamed.

And opened his eyes, his heart racing. "Uh..." he said, gasping for breath, looking around, the sensation of falling still in his body, heat on his face from the sunlight pouring in from the window. He grabbed for his bed and waited a moment for everything to settle down and his head to stop spinning. *Wow!* He thought. *What a freaking nightmare! And with Quirky in it, too…*

Then he remembered the fire during the night. Springing out of bed, he went to his window and looked out. Across the street were the charred remains of a house surrounded by a circle of slush where the heat had melted the snow. The ground around was churned up where the fire engines had been and where the firemen had dragged their hoses. Puddles of ice were here and there, reflecting the light of the morning sun. *Poor Quirky,* he thought. For a moment he wondered where she was and how she was. Then he shrugged mentally. *And why should I care?*

He turned and looked at his clock. Eight o' clock. But that didn't matter. He was on vacation. And even better, he remembered, today was Christmas Eve day, which meant it was Tree Day. Today was when they would go out to the forest and cut down a tree and bring it home and decorate it.

Excited, he threw on his clothes and raced out into the hallway from his bedroom, thoughts of the day's adventure ahead already banishing memories of the past night's tragedy. But as he passed his sister's room, he was stopped by the sound of soft crying within.

"Mandy…?" he asked, opening the door to the bedroom. "What's wrong…" And then he stopped, nonplussed. For sitting on the bed, looking at him with eyes watery with tears, was Mrs. Quercus. And for a moment, he was back in his dream, seeing her there not as a person but as a strange bird crying "Home! Home!"

Startled, he stepped back. "Oh," he said, "I…I'm sorry…." He closed the door and turned and ran down the stairs. He could hear voices in the kitchen, and when he ran in, he saw his mother and sister at the table having breakfast and his father cooking pancakes at the stove.

"Hey, it's the sleepyhead," his father said. "I was wondering if I should come up and roust you. We have a tree to cut this morning."

"Mrs. Quercus is in Amanda's room crying," Webster blurted out, looking at his mom.

"I know, Dear," his mother replied. "She's staying with us."

"I slept in Mom and Dad's room," Amanda interrupted. "Why is she crying?"

Webster slid into a chair at the table and looked at his sister. "Like maybe because her house burned down last night?"

"I know that!" she replied. "I'm not stupid. But Quirky said it was all right this morning when I went in to get some things. She wasn't crying then."

"Please don't call her Quirky. Her name is Emily Quercus, Mrs. Quercus to you two," their mother said in her no-nonsense voice.

"OK, Mom," Webster replied, "but what did you mean, she said it was all right her house burned down?" he asked his sister. "That's crazy!"

"That's what she said this morning. And she seemed happy, that's all I know."

"That's crazy!" Webster repeated.

"Well, I'd better go find out if I can help," their mother said, getting up from the table. "She's probably having a quite understandable reaction. And," she added, fixing Webster with a glare, "when people are in shock, they say and do strange things, but that does not mean they're crazy. So lay off the remarks, OK?"

"OK. But why's she in Mandy's bedroom? Doesn't she have someplace to go?"

Webster's father placed a plate of pancakes in front of him as his mother left the kitchen to go upstairs. "Apparently not," his dad said. "She's a widow with no children and no relatives, according to what she told us last night. The paramedics wanted to take her to the hospital, but as there was nothing wrong with her, your mother insisted she spend the night here instead. There may be things she can salvage today from what's left of her house, though," he added, glancing in the direction of the front door, "I can't imagine there'd be much. That place went up like a tinder box. One of the firemen told me he'd never seen anything like it. I gather they want to question her some more to find out what she had in there, but Mom insisted they wait until after Christmas." He smiled.

Webster chuckled. "Yeah, *no one* argues with Mom...say, what do you mean, 'until after Christmas'?"

"Mrs. Quercus," and Amanda emphasized the name to show she was saying it the way Mom had wanted, "is staying with us through Christmas."

"What! You're kidding me, right?"

Amanda smirked. "Mom was going to give her your room, but she said mine was neater!"

"*My* room?" Webster looked at his father. "Dad, she's not serious, is she? Quirky's going to be here for *Christmas?*"

His Dad shrugged as he sat down with a plate of pancakes for himself. "You have a problem with helping out a neighbor who's just lost everything in the world?"

"Well...no...but...aren't there places for people whose houses have burned down? Shelters or something...?"

"Yes, they're called 'friends' homes.' What's the matter, Webster? Why are you so pushed out about this?"

Webster thought. Why was he feeling so upset? What did it matter to him if old Mrs. Quirky stayed with them for a day or so? Normally, it wouldn't matter to him at all. But...but this was Quirky! Whatever Mom said, she was a crazy lady, and he didn't want a crazy lady staying with them. And what would his friends say when they found out Quirky was staying in his house? Besides, it was Christmas, and Christmas was for families, and.....

And he realized he was making excuses. The fact was, he didn't know why it bothered him so much. Quirky had always bothered him, and he didn't really know why. She was just too...different.

As if his father had read all these thoughts going through his mind, he said, "Webster, I know Mrs. Quercus is different. Your grandfather would probably have called her a hippie. And I know she's had some problems in the neighborhood with all her animals. But she's a loving, friendly lady, and as long as I've known her, she's only ever tried to help people out. You wouldn't remember, as you were only a year and half old then, but when Mom was in the hospital with Amanda and there were some complications, it was Emily who came and stayed with you and later helped out with meals and things until I could arrange matters at work to be home till Mom was better."

"She *baby-sat* me while Mom was in the hospital?"

Yep, and you survived just fine. Now I figure it's time to be there for her, and I'd appreciate your cooperation."

"Yes, sir," Webster said, admitting that his Dad could put on a pretty good no-nonsense voice as well when he wanted to.

"My friends all say she's a witch," Amanda piped up. "Her kitchen's filled with bottles and bottles of potions. That's what Lacey saw when she and her mother were visiting Qur—I mean, Mrs. Quercus."

This time a warning note came into their dad's voice. "I think we've had enough talk about witches and crazy people. The fact is, Emily is a fine herbalist and for your information, it was her so-called potions that got Mom back on her feet after you were born and kept you from getting pneumonia three winters ago. So cool it, you two, or there'll be two less people on our Christmas tree outing. OK?"

"Yes, father," they both said in unison.

"Great. Now that that's settled, what say you finish your breakfast so we can get going to the tree farm? The day's not getting any younger!"

Thirty minutes later, breakfast finished and the kitchen cleaned up, Webster, Amanda and their father stood at the front door putting on their coats. "Is Mom coming, too?" Amanda asked.

"I don't really know," her father said. "I haven't talked to her since she went up to be with Emily. I'll go find out."

But at that moment, their attention was drawn to voices on the floor above, and a minute later, Webster's mom and Emily Quercus started down the stairs. She was dressed in clothes that Webster recognized as her mother's and was momentarily surprised that they fit. He had never seen Quirky in anything other than layers of voluminous gowns and sweaters and shawls, in variations of greens and yellows. He realized he had unconsciously thought of her as fat, but in fact, he could now see she was thinner than his mother.

Reaching the bottom of the stairs, the older woman, seeing the children, hurried forward and took one of each of their hands. Webster did his best not to cringe.

"Oh, Amanda and Webster," she said, her voice soft, "I'm so sorry to intrude on your Christmas plans, but thank you so much for taking me in."

I had nothing to do with it, Webster thought, but out loud he said, "Oh, it's ok. I'm sorry about your house, Mrs. Quercus. That's a tough break, and just before Christmas."

She squeezed his hand. "Thank you, Webster."

Amanda shyly put her arms around the older woman. "I'm sorry, too. What about all your animals and birds? Did they all die?"

Mrs. Quercus smiled. "No, Amanda. I had taken them away earlier."

"Wow, that was lucky," Webster said. "Why did you do that?"

"Webster," his mother said, "Mrs. Quercus doesn't need to explain everything to us. Let's just be thankful no lives were lost."

"It's all right," Mrs. Quercus said. "I don't mind Webster's questions or Amanda's concern."

"That may be, but right now's not the time to discuss it. We'll have plenty of opportunities later. Right now, we have to find a tree." Webster's mother opened the closet door and pulled out her winter coat. "I was going to stay home with Emily, but she says she wants to take a nap and insists I come with you."

"That's right. I don't want to be a bother. And I really need some time to rest and think things through. But I know you'll bring back a fine tree. It's out there waiting for you right now."

"Really? That's wonderful!" Amanda said.

"Right! That's what I say, too," said their father. "So let's not keep our tree waiting." He opened the front door. "Make yourself at home, Emily, and have a good rest."

"And don't worry," added his mother. "We'll get everything sorted out for you, you'll see."

"Thank you, Jane and Paul. And thank you again, Amanda and Webster. Now go find your tree."

Where they got their tree every year was from a patch of forest owned by one of their father's uncles. Only the family came here, and over the years as people moved away or bought their trees from a commercial lot, fewer and fewer family members came to cut down a tree. The uncle himself had moved to Florida, and one of their cousins looked after the property now, though from the sorry state of the road leading into it, he wasn't doing such a terrific job. Fortunately, their family van was a four-wheel drive, so they made it in to the clearing that served as a parking lot in spite of the snow on the ground. As they piled out of the van, the snow was beginning to fall again and the wind was rising.

"I'm afraid we may not have much time," Paul Graham said. "We don't want to be caught up here if the snow really picks up. So let's look quickly."

They all began to walk between the trees, checking out possible candidates. The going was hard, not only because of the snow but because there was more underbrush than Webster remembered. His father's uncle had kept part of the land cleared to make it easier to get to the trees, but obviously his son wasn't continuing that tradition.

A flash of movement and color off to his left made Webster turn to look. Off among the trees, he saw someone in bright green and yellow clothing moving. Was one of his cousins up here getting a tree as well? But there'd been no other car in the clearing. So who might it be?

Intrigued, Webster headed off in that direction, and as he walked, he noticed the underbrush became less dense. He pushed through some branches into a small clearing. There, standing in the snow, pointing to a tree, was Mrs. Quercus, dressed in the flowing green and yellow gown and shawl she usually wore. She looked at him, smiled, and then pointed at the tree.

"Mrs. Quercus," he yelled in surprise. "How did you get here?" He started forward, tripped on a root hidden in the snow, and fell on his face. He picked himself up, unhurt but embarrassed. As he wiped the snow from his eyes, he looked again, but Quirky was nowhere to be seen. He looked all around him. *No way could she have run far in those clothes in this snow*, he thought. But wherever he looked, there was no sign of her. He approached the tree at which she had been pointing. There were no footprints. The snow lay undisturbed all around the tree.

What's going on here, he thought. *I've got Quirky on the brain! I knew she'd be trouble!*

Then he looked at the tree. It was beautiful, just what they were looking for. It was about eight feet tall and perfectly formed. He turned around to where the others were a little further away. "Hey, everyone! Come look at this!"

His mother and father and sister made their way over to the clearing where he stood, pushing aside undergrowth and branches. Amanda got stuck and had to be lifted over a particular dense spot by her father. But when they all gathered around the tree, the "ooos" and "ahhhs" made it pretty unanimous that they had found their tree.

"Well done, son," said Webster's father. "How did you spot it way over here?"

"Well, I..." What could he tell him? That he'd had some kind of hallucination starring ol' Quirky herself? "Just dumb luck, I guess."

"Mrs. Quercus said our tree would be waiting for us!" Amanda said happily. "She was right, wasn't she, Webby?"

"Um...yes, I guess so..." he stammered, all the while thinking, *maybe Mrs. Q and I need to have a talk when I get home. Something really weird's going on, and I want to find out what.*

But when the Grahams returned home, Mrs. Quercus wasn't there. "I know she hasn't left," said Webster's mother, after going upstairs and looking about while her husband and children wrestled the tree into the living room. "Her box is still in Amanda's room, and the way she was clutching it last night, I'm sure she wouldn't have gone and left it behind."

"Maybe she's out for a walk," Amanda said.

"In this weather? Get real!" Webster replied.

"So, what? I go walking in the snow. Just because you like to stay indoors...."

"Never mind," said their father. "Come on, let's get the decorations from the attic. I'm sure Mrs. Q will turn up soon.

But an hour later, with the tree half-decorated, Webster began to feel uneasy. *No, no, no,* he thought to himself, *I'm not going to start worrying about Quirky. But worry he did. And as he was picking up an ornament to hang on the* tree, he suddenly knew where she was as certainly as if it were written on the wall of the living room.

He went to the closet and took out his coat. Everyone else was busy decorating, and he didn't want to tell them where he was going. If he was wrong, he didn't want to make a fool of himself. Though why he was so concerned about Quirky, he didn't know.

Slipping out of the door, he headed across the street. It was still snowing but not as much. The clouds above were a pearl grey, and the afternoon had a soft luminescence about it. In the midst of all the whiteness, the burned rubble of the house stood out like the mouth of an ancient volcano.

Part of the front wall was still standing, and the wall with the fireplace and chimney. Everything else was in a huge pile. If it weren't Christmas Eve Day, he bet there would already be workers here clearing the rubble... or did Quirky have to hire them? He had no idea.

The front door had fallen down. Carefully, he picked his way across the threshold and into what had been a living room. But now it was simply a pile of debris from which wisps of smoke still trailed. A part of the ceiling extended a couple of feet over his head and then disappeared, the whole having collapsed into the center of the house.

He looked over to his left, and there he could see a dark shape huddled in the afternoon shadows against an intact corner of the room. He called out to her, but there was no response. Sighing, he realized he would have to make his way across the debris to get to her.

Careful how he placed his feet, especially in the shadows cast by the remaining wall, he began picking his way across to where Mrs. Quercus was sitting. But still, something shifted under his feet and he stumbled, only catching himself by putting his hand out against the wall. But then he saw, under some of the rubble, something glowing. At first he thought it was an ember from the fire, but then he realized it wasn't that kind of light. And he felt no heat coming from whatever it was. Getting down on his knees, he shifted some burned wood to one side to get to the glowing object. Was it a jewel of some kind? It was a sphere a little larger than a marble, but it glowed like a miniature Christmas tree light.

Stretching out his hand, he could just reach it without climbing onto more of the rubble out in the room, something he was afraid to do. Gingerly, his fingers closed around it. It was neither hot nor cold, just pleasantly warm. Drawing it out to look at it more closely, he was disappointed when the glow disappeared. It was hard to make out what it was in the shadows, but his fingers could trace lines of carving on it.

Well, whatever it is, it can wait until I get home to examine it, he thought, putting it in his pocket and getting up. *Right now I have to see what Quirky's doing.*

He carefully made his way over to the woman. She sat with her shoulders hunched down and inwards, closed in on herself, looking dejected. And in that moment, he didn't see Quirky, the strange woman with the outlandish clothes and all the animals that all the neighborhood kids thought was crazy…or worse. He simply saw an older woman who had lost everything in a terrible fire. In his nearly thirteen years, he had never seen someone in the throes of loss or misery. His mother had been very sick for a time after Amanda was born, but he had only been a year and a half old then and didn't remember what that had been like. And Quirky…I mean, Mrs. Quercus took care of me then. Now, as his dad had said, it was time to take care of her.

He came up to where the woman sat, wrapped in a blanket but seemingly oblivious to the cold and snow. The little bit of roof remaining above her sheltered her. She sat unmoving with her eyes closed, and for a moment, Webster thought she was dead. Hesitatingly, he put a hand out to touch her. Quick as a flash, a hand darted out from beneath the blanket, seizing his wrist in a surprisingly strong grip. Her head turned towards him, and she opened her eyes.

Webster thought he was going to faint. Her eyes were green lights, like fire seen through emeralds. And through them he thought he could see…what? A forest? It was as if for a moment he was looking not at her but through her, beyond her, seeing a vast world that was nothing but trees, nothing but forest.

Then the moment passed and he was looking into the soft brown eyes of Mrs. Quercus. "Oh," she said, letting go of his wrist. "You startled me!"

Webster swallowed down a desire to turn and run. "You startled me, too, Qurik…I mean, Mrs. Quercus. Are you all right? You should come back to the house now. It's cold out here."

"Is it? Why, yes, I think you're right. I'm sorry I startled you, Webster. I was…looking for something."

"Sitting here in this ruined corner?"

"Yes." She got to her feet and brushed off the blanket. "There are many ways of looking."

"And…and did you find what you were looking for?"

A look of such sadness came over her face that Webster thought his heart might stop. But then she smiled, and the sadness vanished, though he was sure it was still there beneath the surface. But what did he expect? She had just lost everything she owned in a fire.

"No," she said. "No, I couldn't find it. I'm afraid the…the fire burned away all traces. That's what it was supposed to do, you see, so I can't fault it. Fire cleanses. That's its job. But still, this one time, I wish….I wish it had been less thorough. And it came before I expected it…"

"Before you expected it? Um…don't go all crazy on me now, Mrs. Quercus. You've had a shock here, losing your house and all, but I don't think fires work to schedules."

She looked at him and laughed, and while Webster didn't really know what the laugh of a crazy person would sound like, Mrs. Quercus's laugh sounded normal to him. "Oh, Webster. I've alarmed you." She patted his hand and smiled again. "Don't worry. I'm not crazy. I'm just different. Isn't that why you and your friends call me Quirky?"

Webster felt a flush of embarrassment start up his neck and into his cheeks. "Oh, Mrs. Quercus, I don't…I mean…"

She laughed again. "It's quite all right. I don't mind. You see, I am quirky. It's who I am. But I'm sorry if I've frightened you and your friends."

"Oh no, Mrs. Quercus…"

"And you can call me Quirky if you like. In fact, I wish you would.

I like it! I think it's funny!"

"Um..OK, Mrs...er...Quirky." Then Webster smiled and laughed. "I think it's funny, too!"

"And now, Webster, you came out here to rescue me, I think, so we should be heading back to the hospitality of your house." She started to walk across the rubble to where her front door had stood, one hand holding the remains of her living room wall to her right. Then she stopped and turned to Webster, who was scrambling to keep up beside her. "How did you know I was here?"

"I don't know. We were decorating the tree and...and I felt worried, and then I just knew. Somehow I knew you'd come over here."

She bent down and looked him in the eyes, and for a moment he thought he saw the flash of emerald green deep inside the brown of her irises. "Interesting," she said. "Most interesting." Then she headed on, reaching the door frame and stepping out into the slush-filled yard. She stopped and looked back, giving Webster a hand out. "I loved this house, you know," she said. "I'll miss it."

"Ah, you'll build another one, Quirky. The insurance money will cover it, I bet."

"But I have no insurance, Webster," she said, walking across the lawn towards his house.

"No insurance? But...that's..."

"Crazy?" she laughed again. "I told you I was different."

"I didn't know you meant that different," he muttered as they reached his porch.

They went inside, where they found the rest of the family wondering where he'd gone to as well. "We were beginning to think we were being visited by aliens," his father joked. When that prompted a blank stare from Mrs. Quercus, he added, "You know, abductions and all..."

"I'm sorry you were all worried," the older woman said. "I was looking for something in my house, and lost track of time. Thankfully, Webster came and got me."

"Oh my," said his mother, coming over. "That could have been dangerous."

His father looked at him. "How did you know where she was?"

Webster shrugged. "I don't know. I just guessed, I guess. I thought, if Quirky's not here, maybe she's over at her house."

His father frowned at him. "That's fine, Webster, but you know what

I said about names..."

Mrs. Quercus laughed. "It's all right, Paul. I told him to go ahead and call me Quirky. I know the kids all call me that, but I don't mind. I rather like it. You can use it too!"

He smiled, "Thank you, but I think I'll stick to Emily."

"And did you find what you were looking for, Emily?" asked Webster's mother.

"No, I'm afraid not."

"Well, then, tomorrow we'll all look, if we can. In the meantime, I think a cup of tea would be in order. Amanda, would you please go and put the hot water on for tea." Turning back to her guest, she said, "There's still a little decorating to be done on the tree as well, if you'd like to join us."

Mrs. Emily 'Quirky' Quercus bowed her head, then looked up and smiled a radiant smile. "I would enjoy that," she said.

Later that evening, with the tree all decorated, Christmas carols sung, stockings hung by the fireplace, and milk and cookies put out for a possibly hungry and thirsty Santa, Webster sat in his room in his pajamas, listening to the wind howl outside as a fresh storm blew in with more snow, and thought about what had happened during the day. He no longer thought Quirky was a crazy old lady, but whatever she was, she was definitely strange. At least strange things seemed to happen around her. Like, how did she appear to him in the woods and point out their tree? Or had he really been imagining things? And how had he known where she was?

Well, he thought, she had said to call her Quirky. Maybe she'd be willing to answer some of his questions.

He went across the hall from his bedroom. Downstairs he could hear his parents talking. He knocked on Amanda's door. He heard stirring inside, and then a soft voice said, "Come in."

He opened the door and let himself in. Quirky was sitting up in bed, pillows propped up behind her, wearing a pair of his mother's pajamas and his father's robe. The box that she had carried out of the fire sitting closed upon her lap.

"Hello, Webster. Shouldn't you be in bed? Santa won't come if you're up, you know."

"If you believe in Santa," he said, sitting down in his sister's chair. "Do you?"

She smiled. "I believe in me, so I can believe in Santa."

Webster thought about that for a moment. It didn't make any sense, but then that seemed to be the way of things with Quirky, so he let it pass. "Quirky, did I see you this afternoon when we were out getting our tree? Were you there somehow?"

"This afternoon? No, Webster, I was here, and then I went over to my house."

"But I saw you! I saw you as plain as I see you now. You were dressed in green and yellow, you know, those loose things you usually wear. You were pointing at a tree, the tree that we cut and brought home."

"Are you sure it was me?"

"Why, yes, or if it wasn't, it was your sister."

"My sister…." She paused, looking down at her hands.

"But you don't have any sisters, do you? I mean, Mom said you had no family."

For a moment, Webster saw the shadow of sadness cross over her face again, then disappear as she shrugged. "None that are here. Or anywhere I can get to."

Webster thought. "If you needed an airplane ticket to go where you did have family, I bet Dad would stake you," he said.

Quirky laughed. "I'm sure he would. But I'm afraid there's no plane that could take me where they are." She pointed at the box on her lap. "These were to be my tickets home."

She opened the box and let the lid fall back on the bed. Inside, the box was like an egg carton with seven depressions, five of which were filled with spheres of varying sizes. Most were about the size of the ornaments he'd been hanging on the tree, while the smallest was smaller than a marble. Two of the depressions were empty.

At first, the sphere seemed made of a dark wood, covered with intricate carvings reminding him of the Celtic knots his mother liked to draw. Then, as if a switch had been thrown, they burst into light. Each sphere glowed with shifting colors, reminding him of nothing so much as Christmas lights.

"Oh!" he exclaimed. "They're beautiful!"

"You can see them? You see them alight?" Quirky's voice was filled with wonder and surprise.

"Sure. They're bright! What are they? Christmas decorations?"

"No. They are *hallowime*. They are difficult to explain. They are…

memories carved in wood."

"Memories? Whose memories?" Webster was transfixed watching the colors shift and change in the spheres and between them as well. In fact, the whole room seemed more alive somehow, more spacious. And in the light, Quirky seemed changed, younger, different in ways Webster couldn't quite fathom.

"My memories, Webster. A tree's memories."

"A tree's memories? I don't understand."

Quirky sighed and closed the box lid, cutting off the light. The room seemed not only dimmer to Webster but duller as well. "I'm dying, Webster," she said, now seeming even older than before. "I will not live through the night."

"Have you told my parents? Were you hurt in the fire? We can get you to the hospital…"

She reached out a hand and gripped his arm, and as before, he was amazed at her strength. "Webster, there is nothing they can do, nothing anyone can do. But it would please me for you to stay here and hear my story." She chuckled. "I think when you do you will be sure that I'm crazy. Crazy old Quirky, isn't that what you and your friends all call me? No, no," she put up her other hand to silence his protest, "I've already told you I don't mind."

She reached across the bed and took hold of his free hand. "But Webster, I'm not crazy. I'm different, not what I seem to be. But I think you may understand. You can see the *hallowime*. Not many can do that. You are the first I've met. But I suspected when you were a child that you had deep roots and high branches. So perhaps when I've explained, it will not seem so strange to you. Perhaps if you see the *hallowime*, you can see other things as well. In fact, I'm sure you can. You already have. You saw one of my kind today in the forest. Your mind gave her my form, because I'm familiar to you and some part of you recognized we were two of a kind."

Her kind? Her form? Webster shifted uneasily in the chair. He had no idea what she was talking about. He felt out of his depth and wanted nothing more at that moment than to run and tell his parents that Quirky really was crazy and had said she was dying. But the woman's grip was like warm steel. He wasn't sure he could pull away.

As if reading his mind, she said, "Webster, please, will you stay with me and listen to my story? Your parents can't help me. Going to them will only make what happens more difficult. But you must know I mean you no harm, and if I am crazy as you suspect, then what have you to lose? You will simply hear an old woman's ravings and they will give you and your friends something more to laugh about." She smiled. "But if I am not crazy, then you will have something beautiful, a spark of wonderment, to carry in your heart all your life."

"Quirky. I won't laugh. Honest. Not any more, whatever you tell me, even if you are crazy!"

"Then you'll sit with me and listen?"

Webster sighed. "All right. If there's really nothing we can do to help you."

"There's nothing you can do except listen." She let go of his hands.

She settled back against the pillows she had propped up against the back of the bed and closed her eyes, appearing to collect her thoughts. Outside the wind moaned and whistled. Webster could hear the branches of a maple tree near the house scraping against the roof in the wind, a sound that had more than once sent Amanda scurrying into their parents' bedroom for safety and comfort.

Quirky leaned down and opened the lid of the box on her lap for a moment as if seeking inspiration, and the two of them were bathed again in the coruscating lights of the *hallowime*. She closed the lid again.

"Webster, let me tell you the hardest part first. If you understand this, you will understand everything else." She leaned over so that their faces were at eye level. "Webster, I am a tree."

This was so not what he had been expecting that his first reaction was to laugh. *She really is nuts,* he thought. But as the laugh began to bubble up within him, her eyes changed, and he was struck dumb. He was once again staring into deep pools of emerald fire, and through them he could see....he could see...

He was floating in the air. All around him as far as he could see, a forest stretched. In the distance on the horizon were mountains, their peaks white with snow, but everywhere else there were only trees. Somehow he knew that every kind of tree in the world was in this forest, that every tree that there ever was or ever would be was in this green world before him. It was a planet of trees. It was....

"Home..." said Quirky, pulling back, her eyes normal again. Webster felt like he slammed back into the chair from a long distance.

"Home...." He repeated, and he knew the rightness of it. That forest had felt like home.

"My home," said Quirky. "You saw it didn't you, Webster. You saw the Forest?"

His voice filled with wonder, he said, "Yes. Yes! It was amazing! Trees everywhere, all the trees in the world!"

"Yes. All the trees in the world. That's where I come from, Webster. I really am a tree, or perhaps what you would call the spirit of a tree. Do you believe me?"

Where before there had been a laugh rising up within him, now there was a feeling of certainty. Amazingly, he *did* believe her. There was no doubt in him anywhere. "Yes," he said. "Yes, Quirky, I believe you. But how? You're a human being. How can you be a tree?"

"I'm only human on the outside, Webster, though in the years I've been here I've learned a lot about your kind, so in a way I'm now human, too." She closed her eyes. "It was twenty years ago tomorrow that I came here. This time of year is very magical, you know, and makes many things possible."

"Were you born?"

"Not like you were. I was formed, by thought and magic and with the help of those humans who know of my world and of the spirits of trees and nature."

"Your tree world...is it another planet? Are you an alien from outer space?"

She laughed. "No, I'm as much a part of this world as you are. Maybe even more so. For the Forest is this world as it once was, and still is in a higher dimension. Webster, do you believe in heaven?"

He was taken aback by the question. "I...I guess so. Sure."

"Ah, good, but for you it's just a belief, isn't it. But Webster, in fact there are many heavens, many worlds of spirit. What you saw, the world I come from, think of it as a heaven for trees, a real place from which the essence of all trees come, just as your spirit is part of a place beyond this physical world."

"Then you're an angel?"

She laughed again. "Hardly! But you have the right idea. Angels are emissaries, aren't they, messengers from God?" He nodded. At least that's what Rev. Albon had said once. "I, too, am a kind of emissary, a spirit sent from the Great Forest. There are many of us walking among you."

"Trees that look like people?"

"Yes, trees that look like people."

"But...why?"

"To be teachers."

"Teachers? Are you serious? Trees come to teach school?"

She laughed. "Not the way you're thinking! But we do come to teach people."

"But what do you teach them? How to take care of trees?"

"More than that, Webster. We teach how to take care of everything." She was silent a moment. "Webster, what does 'home' mean to you?"

"Home?" He was puzzled. Heaven, angels, tree spirits, home...what was she talking about? She kept jumping from one idea to another, and he felt confused. "I don't know....it's where I live. Home is a place to live."

"Yes, it is. But for us, it's more. Home is the first act of creation, the heart and love of God made visible. . It's the spirit of taking care of everything." She leaned forward and took his hand, more gently this time. "Think of it, Webster. Home is not only where you live. It's something you are."

She began to cough, and with it, her body began to shake. She gripped his hand harder until he thought he might cry out. "Sor..sorry," she said. "I think...I think I need some water."

"Oh, I'll get it for you," he said, springing to his feet.

As he headed down the stairs, he heard his parents talking in the living room, and he thought of Quirky's strange story and her comment about home. What *did* home mean to him, anyway?

It is this house, he thought. He paused at the entrance to the kitchen. There was the table where he and Amanda had breakfast every day, and over there was the stove where Mom or Dad cooked. And all around were familiar drawers and cabinets, and the broom closet where he used to hide playing hide and seek when he was younger and smaller and could fit into it. *This house is my home,* he thought, getting a glass down from the cupboard. As he filled it with water from the faucet, he thought of his room with all his things in it, and how familiar it was. The very thought of it made him feel relaxed and safe.

As he made his way out of the kitchen and towards the stairs, he glanced into the living room. There he saw his Mom and Dad sitting together snuggled up on the couch, looking at the Christmas tree with its sparkling lights. *A couple of old snuggle-bunnies, Dad would say*, he thought. He paused. It struck him how much they loved each other, and following that thought, he realized how much they loved him and his sister. It was their love that made everything around him possible, the house, his room, the life he enjoyed.

It's not just the house, he thought. *Home is Mom and Dad and how they love Amanda and me and take care of us, and how we love them. It's being part of a family. It really is a spirit, something Mom and Dad and Amanda and I share and make together.*

Excited, he hurried up the stairs into Amanda's bedroom and handed the glass of water to Quirky. "I get it!" he said. "I get what home is. It really is something we make together, isn't it, not just a place to live."

"Ah, you understand. Home can be everywhere, Webster, if we will it so. You have a saying that in the beginning there was the Word. But we trees say, In the beginning, there was Home." Her voice took on a new quality as if she were reciting something she'd learned long ago.

"In the beginning, there was Home.
Its Roots held the Universe together.
Its Trunk gave strength and purpose.
Its Branches gave shelter and protection.
Its Fruits gave nourishment.
And the First Home was Tree."

"And the First home was Tree," Webster whispered, repeating what Quirky had said.

"Yes. You see, we're not so different. We each believe Creation begins with our kind and revolves around us!" She smiled. "But before there were people, there were trees, and trees were homes to countless lives. We were created to be homes. And we are more ancient than you. We are your teachers in being homes to each other." She grinned. "We want you to learn to be like trees."

Webster grinned back. "With roots instead of legs and branches instead of hair? I don't think so!"

"I should have said, we want you to be human trees, with all you legs and arms and hair...but with hearts that encompass all as well, and hands that stretch out to help and hold, and with minds that know how deeply rooted you all are in each other and in the world. We want you to be a Forest for each other for the sake of the world."

There flashed into Webster's mind the image of all the animals and birds that Quirky had had in her home. He could see it now. She had made a home for them. Her house had been like a tree, giving shelter and a place of caring.

"You don't have to do it my way," she said, apparently reading his mind again. "You will find your own way. A person can create the spirit of home and be like a tree in many ways. But you must let your roots go deep and spread your branches wide so that more than just those like you can find a home in the world."

Suddenly, she jerked as a spasm passed through her body. "Oh!" she cried out. "It's starting!"

Webster jumped to his feet, reaching out to hold her shaking body. "Quirky! What's happening? What's starting?"

"My transition! It's how…how I return home, but without all the *hallowime*, the door won't fully open for me. I will be caught between your world and mine….and…."

"…and what? And what, Quirky?"

"And I'll disappear."

"Disappear? You mean, vanish? Forever?"

"Yes. I will be without home, not here, not there, not anywhere."

"No!" Webster said. "We can't let this happen! Why would this happen?"

Quirky pushed back the lid to the box, and once again the light and colors of the *hallowime* filled the room. "I said these were memories. They are more than that. They are the keys to the magic that lets me come into your world in this way. There is always a danger when one of us takes on human form that we may forget who we are. The *hallowime* carry our memories of our true home, the Great Forest. But they also carry the Forest's memories of us. When the time comes to leave this world and make the transition back, we place our *hallowime* beside a tree and the memories merge, opening the portal through which we return home."

"So what's the problem? You've got the *hallowime* here, and there's a Christmas tree downstairs. Does it have to be a special kind of tree?"

"No, any tree will do, but I'm missing two of the *hallowime*. Without them, the portal won't open. It takes all seven."

Webster sat down and looked at the box again. Sure enough, two of the depressions were empty. "Where would they be? Maybe we can find them."

Quirky sighed. "No, I looked. Remember? I was trying to find them when you found me in my house."

"But you were just sitting there with your eyes closed."

"There are many ways of looking, Webster, and not all of them use eyes. Sometimes you have to look with your heart to see what's not visible on the surface. But....I couldn't find anything. I fear they were burned in the fire."

Webster stood. "Wait! I remember!" He dashed out of the bedroom, across the hall and into his room. He snatched his trousers up from the floor and felt around in his pocket. Yes! There it is! He pulled out the small sphere he had found in the rubble of the fire, smiling as it burst into light and color like the one's in Quirky's box. One of the *hallowime*, he thought.

He turned and ran back into her room. "Look, Quirky! I found this underneath a board when I was in your house. It was shining, so I picked it up and put it in my pocket. I just forgot it was there!"

Eagerly, she reached out and took the glowing sphere from him. "Yes! Oh, Webster, this is indeed one of the missing pair." She put it in the box with the others. "But how is it you found it and I could not?"

"I don't know. Just lucky, I guess?"

"No, there's more than luck here. As I said, you have deep roots and high branches. You sense things others do not. But even still, I should have known...."

She grimaced. "The *griwaldin*!"

"What's a *griwaldin*?"

"A fire spirit. I knew my time of transition was coming. The magic of this time of year is especially potent for making the transition between your world and mine. I didn't want to leave my house behind for it was filled with tree magic. I was afraid if a human family lived in it, they would find it unsettling. They would think the house haunted."

"With ghosts?"

"With my energy." She smiled at him. "You should know about that, Webster. You were uneasy around me, weren't you? Many people are, especially if they're sensitive. Because in spirit I'm a tree, I feel different to people and this can make them uncomfortable. Didn't you feel that?"

"Um...yes...I...well, I thought you were creepy."

She laughed. "You see? It's OK. I'm not offended. I'm used to it. But that's what a family might feel in my house, that it was creepy."

"So you decided to *burn* it down?" Webster asked incredulously.

"Fire cleanses a forest and makes way for new growth. I thought...I thought it would be safer this way, cleansing the land for a new home. It's the way a tree thinks, Webster. But as you might imagine, trees and fire have an uneasy relationship. We are allies in some ways, but in others....well, fire cannot always be trusted, especially not a *griwaldin*. But I thought I needed his help anyway. So I asked him to come."

"You summoned a *fire spirit*?"

"Not a summoning, no. A tree cannot control fire, which was my mistake. I asked him as an ally to cleanse my forest...to burn the house. But he came in a way I had not expected, stronger and faster than I'd thought. I thought he would be tamer, but he was true to his nature." She frowned. "I had been warned, but still..."

Webster remembered the face he had seen rising in the fireball out of the house and the comments of the firemen about how fast the house had burned. "That was one heavy dude of a fire spirit!" he said. "He was frightening."

"You saw him? But...of course...if you have the Sight to see me as I am, you could see a *griwaldin*, too."

"I saw him twice. I saw him in a fireball in your house, and then I had a dream in which he swallowed me up."

She frowned. "I'm sorry he frightened you. He was more than I anticipated, and he was more, well, enthusiastic than I'd thought he'd be."

"Is he evil?"

She looked startled. "Evil? Oh my no! Just very young. He's like a puppy."

"A puppy? You're kidding!"

"Well, maybe not exactly like a puppy. But young and excitable. Like a kid. I did not have the power to contact one of the great *Jinns*, the older fire spirits. The *griwaldin* was the best I could do." She sighed and patted the box before her. "I barely got out in time myself, and only had time to grab the box of *hallowime*. That's when two of them must have spilled out. I...I'm sorry. I put all your homes in danger, and I had not planned to do that."

"Hey! It's ok, Quirky. The fire department took names and kicked *griwaldin* butt, so it's all right." But even as he said it, Webster remembered the face in the fireball and thought, *if he's one of the kids, I hope I never meet one of the grown-ups.*

"But it's not all right, Webster. It was an error in judgment on …oh!" She grimaced, her arms and legs suddenly jerking up and down on the bed. The spasm lasted a few seconds, then stopped.

"Quirky!" Webster was on his feet and practically dancing up and down in his alarm. "What's happening?"

"It's the energy in my body. It wants to go home. It's building up a charge, and this body can't handle it. I've little time left."

Webster pulled on her arm. "Come on, then! I found one *hallowime*. The other must still be over there. We can still find it and you can go home."

She allowed herself to be pulled out of the bed. "I don't know. I tried before. The energy of the *griwaldin* is still in the house. It will fade, but not until the house is fully cleared away. For now, that energy blocks my own. I could see nothing with my inner sight when I was over there."

"But I found one of them. Maybe I can find the other one. Come on! We've got to look. We can't just sit around when there's a chance. I'm getting dressed."

He ran out of the bedroom and back into his own room. Hurriedly he put on his clothes, then went back and knocked quietly on the door to Amanda's bedroom. Quirky opened the door. She stood there, still in pajamas and robe, barefoot, holding the box of the *hallowime* as if unwilling to put them down even for a moment. She also looked older than earlier. "Hey, come on! We need to go!"

"Webster, this is not a good idea." She pulled him into the bedroom and closed the door. She might look older, but she was still strong. "It's dark and snowing. It would be dangerous to look through the house even in daylight. At night, and in a storm…no, Webster. I've made one error in judgment. I'll not make another."

"But Quirky, we have to do it! We can't just let you fade away or die or whatever it is that's going to happen to you. I'll take a flashlight, and I'm very good on my feet. I'll be careful. We can do it!"

Quirky was adamant. "No, Webster. Thank you, but I forbid it."

"I'll go on my own…"

"And I'll tell your parents. Would they permit you to do this?"

"Sure.…Um, well, no, probably not…but we can get them to help."

"Webster, would they believe my story? Would they believe enough to go hunting through the rubble of a burned out house in the middle of the night in a snowstorm, not even knowing if what we seek is still there?"

Webster thought. "Yes," he said. "Yes, they would…"

Quirky nodded. "I believe you're right…but only if they believed me. And it would take time to convince them. They would think me a crazy old woman, just as you did. How long would it take to convince them otherwise? I do not have that time, I think…"

"But you're a tree! I mean, you've got magic, otherwise you couldn't be here. Right? So can't you work some magic to make my parent's believe?"

"Webster, I'm a tree. I'm not Merlin. I don't have magical powers the way you think."

"But you summoned a freaking *fire spirit*, Quirky. That's magic!"

"No, Webster, I told you. I didn't summon it. I talked with it. There's a difference. I can't make your parents believe."

"But we *have* to do something!"

She sat down, letting the box fall from her grip onto the bed beside her. She passed her hand over her eyes. When she looked up, Webster could see pain in her expression. "No, Webster. We don't. Everything has a life cycle. We trees know that better than most. When the time comes, you fall to the forest floor, but you are still a home for many other lives. And from you, new trees will be nourished. Death is not to be feared."

"But Quirky, we're not talking about you dying here. We're talking about you disappearing as if you'd never been. Right? You won't be a home for anything…ever. That's not right!"

"I knew the risks when I came here…"

He pulled her up from the bed, ignoring that she winced as he did so. "I'm not giving up. Come on. You've got six *hallowime*. Maybe that will be enough." He grabbed the box and pulled her along into the hallway.

"Webster, this won't work."

"Why not? How do you know? Have you done this before?" He pulled her along to the top of the stairs.

"No, but…"

"Then don't argue, Quirky. Just get downstairs."

Together they made their way downstairs and into the living room. No one was there, but he heard his parents' voices coming from the kitchen. He led Quirky up to the tree where she sank to the floor. "All right," he said, "now what?"

"Webster, this won't..."

"Won't work. I know. You said that. What do I do with these?" He held up the box.

"I...you...you lay them out so they're touching the tree. The tree has to feel them."

"Hey, what are you two doing up?" came his father's voice. Turning around, Webster saw his parents standing at the entrance to the living room.

He held up the box. "Um, Quirky has these...ah...ornaments she wants to put on the tree, Dad. It's an old family tradition. I said I'd help her." He opened the box to show his parents, who came forward to look.

"Oh, my, these are beautiful," said his mother, touching one of the spheres. "Such wonderful carving and design. Wherever did you get them, Emily?"

"They're...they're family heirlooms."

"Well, I'm glad you saved them from the fire."

"Beautiful colors, aren't they?" asked Webster.

"Colors? What colors, Webster?" asked his Dad. "It's beautiful wood, but..."

"I think he means how they reflect the lights from the Christmas tree," Quirky interjected.

"Oh, yes, I see that now," his father replied. But Webster knew neither his Dad nor Mom could see the *hallowime* as they really were, shining and sparkling with light. For them, they were only carved spheres of wood.

He took a deep breath. "Dad, one of them is missing. Mrs. Quercus thinks it might have fallen out over in the house when she was getting out. Could we go look for it? It would mean a lot to her to have all seven on our tree."

His father looked at him incredulously. "You mean, look for it now? In the dark? In a burned out house?" He chuckled. "You're kidding me, right? Maybe we might find it tomorrow, but if it was in that house, chances are it's gone. That was quite a blaze, you know."

Webster thought it had been a forlorn hope, but he'd had to try. "Sure, Dad, I was just kidding."

"Well, let's put the one's you've got, Emily, on the tree. Do they have hooks or something to hang them?"

"No," said the older woman. "We just put them on the branches." So they each reached into the box and took out the *hallowime* one at a time and laid them carefully amidst the branches of the Christmas tree. To Webster's sight, they glowed even more than before, but nothing else happened. He glanced over hopefully at Quirky, but she just shook her head.

"Wow! Look at the time!" his father said. "Time for bed,"

"I would like to sit here with the tree a little longer as well," said Quirky.

"Oh, that's fine, Emily, but there are certain someone's who should be in bed before Santa Claus can come.

Webster knew a signal when he heard one, but he hadn't given up hope that something would happen. "OK, Dad," he said, "but I'd like to stay here just a few more minutes to keep Quirky company."

"Well, all right, but don't stay up too long." He gave him a pointedly significant look.

As his parents left the room and headed up the stairs to their bedroom, Webster leaned over to Quirky who was now sitting slumped. "Anything? Is a door opening?"

She shook her head. "No. It's as I said. Without the seventh *hallowime*, the memories are not all activated." She sat upright. "Oh, Webster, I can feel the energy building in me. I think I had better leave."

"What?"

"I fear I may put you and your family in danger. I don't know what will happen when the magical energies within me find no place to go. I might explode!"

She struggled to get up but didn't have the strength. "Help me up, Webster. I must leave your house."

"But where will you go?"

"To...to my house." Her voice was little more than a whisper. "Can't...do more damage...there."

And then she fell to the floor, her body shaking. He could see a glow beginning to form around her. He looked around wildly, trying to figure out what to do. Should he run over to the wreckage of her house and try to find the missing *hallowime*? Did he even have the time? There was no guarantee he could find it, or that it was even there. It could well have been burned as she thought. And she might be gone when he got back.

What was he to do?

Quirky stopped shaking. But she was now clearly unconscious. And the glow around her body was growing stronger. Her spirit was obviously rising to go home but when it found the door closed, what would happen? Would she really explode?

He laid his hand on her. *Maybe I can push her energy back into her or something,* he thought. He tried to picture a huge hand holding Quirky and keeping her energy from leaking out. As he did so, he leaned back and touched the Christmas tree.

It was as if an electric shock passed from the tree into him. For a moment, he simply couldn't move. He was caught in a current passing between Quirky and the tree. His muscles were starting to tremble but he felt paralyzed. *What's happening,* he thought. *Maybe I'm going to explode, too!*

His mind opened up, and he saw again the great forest stretching endlessly to the horizon. *Quirky's home,* he thought. And then, towering over it all, he saw a tree that seemed to go up and up until its top was lost in the clouds, perhaps even going into space. It was the tree he had seen or felt in his dream the night before.

A peace descended over Webster, and he felt his muscles stop shaking. The current between the Christmas tree and Quirky was still running through him, but now it seemed as if something else had added its presence.

A voice spoke in his mind. *Think of home.*

Who are you, Webster asked.

I am the Tree of the World, it said. *Think of Home.*

Think of home? What did that mean?

But then Webster remembered what Quirky had said about home and Tree as the First Home. He had no idea of the full meaning of that, but he knew what home meant to him. He knew about love and protection and nourishment. He remembered that the *hallowime* were memories, memories of what it meant to be a tree, memories of home and of creating home.

So he thought of home. He thought of Quirky and the home she had created for so many animals and birds. He thought of the way his parents gave of themselves to create a home for Amanda and him. He thought how trees gave of themselves to provide homes for birds and insects and many other creatures of the forest. He thought of what it would mean for a person to create a spirit of hospitality and home in the world so others would feel safe and loved.

He thought of home as the heart of God made visible.

And as he thought, he saw the great Forest spread out before him and the World Tree rising above it, holding the earth in its roots.

After a time, he realized that he no longer felt the current running through him. In its place, he felt spacious and at peace. He looked around. The room was filled with light. Quirky was nowhere to be seen. Instead, his mother's pajamas and his father's robe lay empty and shapeless on the living room floor.

He got up and picked up the garments. What would he tell his parents about Quirky's disappearance? He realized he wouldn't have to tell them anything. He would put the robe and pajamas back in Amanda's room and then pretend to be as dumbfounded as they about their guest's mysterious disappearance.

He got up and turned around. The radiance was coming from the Christmas tree which was blazing as if it had turned into light. Each branch, each needle, each ornament looked crafted from starlight, almost blinding in its intensity. He stepped back, staring wonderingly at the sight before him.

"Isn't it beautiful? It's the light of the World Tree. Every tree has it, but at this time of year, Christmas trees are especially emissaries of the Light."

He turned to see who had spoken and was not surprised to see it was Quirky. But it was a very different Quirky from the old woman who had been lying on the floor earlier. She was garbed in brilliant robes of green and yellow, and she looked very young. And she was glowing, too.

She smiled at him, and in his mind, he could hear her voice. "Thank you, Webster. You became the missing *hallowime*."

"But how…?"

"By remembering home. That's the spirit that links all the worlds and all beings together. Your thoughts of home forged the link between our worlds. They enabled me to return to my forest."

Webster felt his chest and throat tighten. For a moment, he couldn't speak. Then he said, "I'm glad. I knew we could do it!"

"You'd make a good tree, Webster!" And she laughed.

"Will I see you again?" He noticed that she was turning transparent. He could see the living room couch through her.

"Maybe. I don't know why not. Just visit the forest."

"OK. I will."

"Goodbye, Webster. And Merry Christmas!" She waved, now almost entirely faded from his view. He realized the glow from the Christmas tree was disappearing as well as everything returned to normal.

He had a thought. "Wait!" he said. "Who are you? I mean, what kind of tree are you?"

Laughter echoed down from whatever realm Quirky had disappeared into. "Find my name in the dictionary."

And then all about him, it was a silent night.

Webster snorted. *Just like a teacher*, he thought as he turned off the lights and headed upstairs to go to bed. *Always wanting you to look things up.*

THE END

About the Author

David Spangler has been a spiritual teacher since 1964 and the author of over 30 books including *Journey Into Fire, Apprenticed to Spirit, Subtle Worlds: An Explorer's Field Notes,* and *Facing the Future.* However, he is also a storyteller specializing in tales of wonder and magic that allow him to share his spiritual perspectives in humorous and exciting ways. His stories are those of ordinary men and women discovering unsuspected talents and abilities in themselves and new possibilities in the world around them. Most of his stories originated as Christmas tales to share with friends and family, embodying the wonderment of the Holiday Season, but their insights into human potentials and the unseen dimensions of the cosmos make them timeless.

For more information about David's work and his books, both fiction and non-fiction, please go to the Lorian Association bookstore which can be found at www.LorianAssociation.com.

About the Publisher

Starseed Books is a partnership between Aidan Spangler and Jeremy Berg both of whom are authors.

In addition to publishing we offer editing services, book layout and cover design.

Our company specializes in fiction but also publishes biographies, works by JM Greer for *the Ancient Order of Druids in America* and other material.

Contact Us:

jrcyberg@msn.com
teflonaidan@gmail.com
www.Starseedbooks.com

www.ingramcontent.com/pod-product-compliance
Lightning Source LLC
Chambersburg PA
CBHW030255270626
47156CB00022B/2770